A Girl, In Parts

A Girl, In Parts

a novel

Jasmine Paul

COUNTERPOINT
A MEMBER OF THE PERSEUS BOOKS GROUP
NEW YORK

Library of Congress Cataloging-in-Publication Data

Paul, Jasmine, 1972–
A girl, in parts / Jasmine Paul
p.   cm.
ISBN 1-58243-218-X (hc.); ISBN 1-58243-285-6 (pbk.)
1. Girls—Fiction.   2. Martinsburg (W. Va.)—Fiction.
3. Washington (State)—Fiction.   4. Poor families—Fiction.   I. Title.
PS3616.A944 G57 2002
813'.6—dc21   2002006100

Jacket design by Gopa & Ted2
Text design by Jeffrey P. Williams

Printed in the United States of America on acid-free paper that
meets the American National Standards Institute
Z39-48 standard

COUNTERPOINT
387 Park Avenue South
New York, N.Y. 10016-8810

Counterpoint is a member of the Perseus Books Group

10   9   8   7   6   5   4   3   2   1

For Lenville O'Donnell,
without whose friendship and hard work
this book would not have been possible

9 Years Old

Dorothy, Extraterrestrial

≈ *Fire*

I have one hundred and seven stuffed animals and they're all in garbage bags because of the fire.

The fire hasn't happened yet, but it will. I know it will. I'm very scared of fire lately. It's hard to sleep because I worry about it all night. Everyone knows fires happen at night and everybody dies. Part of me wants the fire to happen.

The whole horrible house with the peeling paint will burn to the ground. The attic will burn and all the rats will die. The upstairs will burn and all the small, dark rooms will disappear. The living room will burn and so will the brown curtains that have weird fuzzy things on them. The kitchen will burn and all the split-pea soup and all the knucklebones in the fridge will be gone forever. The bathroom will burn away and so will all of Gabe's shitty diapers sitting in the plastic pail by the toilet.

I have planned an escape, but no one else has.

As far as I care, all of Martinsburg, West Virginia, can burn to the ground and I wouldn't miss it one bit. The mean stinky boys at the bottom of the hill, the 7-Eleven where I had to buy Mom's Kotex, the laundromat dryer that burned my banky, the weird skinny woman next door, the paper boy with rotten teeth, and Mom's green Ford Maverick with the door taped on can all burn up completely.

I hate West Virginia more than I hate anything.

I will throw all the garbage bags out my bedroom window when the fire starts. I will jump from my window and onto the bags. I will be safe and not burned at all. I will hitchhike to Cleveland and live with Dad.

He will be sad all of West Virginia is gone, but he will be happy to see me and glad I am there.

We will go to Dairy Queen and eat hot dogs and ice cream and talk about how lucky we are to be safe in Cleveland, where there are no fires, only beer and baseball.

≈ Gabe Loses a Toenail

I'm very hungry, but I don't say anything. I suck my thumb until it's wrinkled and all the goodness is gone from it.

Dinner was split-pea soup with a pig foot in it. I put my grilled cheese sandwich right in the middle of the bowl thinking it would soak up the soup and the soup would disappear. It didn't work and there was yelling and no more grilled cheese to eat.

Lyle said something about how I was ungrateful and Mom said for him to shut up and how would he like it if he were nine and afraid of green soup with a pig's foot in it?

Lyle is supposed to be my stepdad, but I won't let him be one.

Mom is going to work and she says, "Dottie, you're nine and you're smart so keep an eye on your brother while I'm gone for a few hours." I look at her and at Lyle who is drinking beer. I nod at her and she leaves.

I roll a ball to Gabe. He rolls it back. He's very excited that he can roll the ball. We laugh and laugh. I pretend to be a frog and I hop all around him while he giggles and tries to hide behind his hands. I try to teach him to talk. I say, "Girl." And he says, "Grul." We roll the ball some more.

Lyle tries to stand up, but he stumbles. When he tries to steady himself, he hits the heater with his hand and the metal covering flips off and falls. It falls right on top of Gabe's fat little foot. There is blood. We are all very quiet, then Gabe howls. He howls and howls like nothing could stop him. He reaches his fat arms up to Lyle, but Lyle puts on his coat and leaves.

I pick Gabe up and say, "It's okay. It's okay. Shhhh."

I pat him on the back. While Gabe howls, he pats me on the back. We sit on the floor, patting each other on the back.

Mom comes home and takes Gabe away and I am all alone in the house. There aren't any lights.

I see a pack of Mom's cigarettes sitting on the coffee table and I take one and light it. I sit in the living room and smoke the cigarette and stare at the toe blood on the carpet.

I think, pig foot Gabe foot pig foot Gabe foot. I put out the cigarette and suck my thumb instead.

≈ Vampires

Don't move don't move don't move.

I am thinking this and breathing in gasps, short and quiet, with blankets wrapped around my neck. I'm curled into a tight ball with one eye open to the dark room. I am thinking, don't move or you're dead.

I can't sleep because of the Vampires. I know they're waiting in corners, wet and evil and straight from coffins, and they're going to kill me and it will hurt.

I turn the light on in the bathroom but Lyle turns it out. I turn it on again and Lyle yells. So I curl up and wait and wait. I wait for Mom to come home. She is out there, somewhere safe, serving people whiskey. If I had whiskey I wouldn't be afraid. Lyle's not afraid.

The walls are crawling with black and peeling paint. It is a big room, my room. The house is huge and dark and ugly. I hate Lyle because he has taken us here. He snores in the next room. I hope the Vampires will take him first. If they take him first, I will hear the screams and be able to escape. I will take Gabe with me.

There are so many rooms here. Gabe is in one of them. When the Vampires come, they'll want him. He's small and fat and smiling all the time. They'll want me the most because I'm scared and my blood is pumping fast here in this huge bed in this huge room, trying to breathe under all these blankets.

I hear something come up the stairs and the bathroom light goes on. Mom is there and her face is covered in Noxzema and her eyes are red. I see her from my bed and know I won't die. When I go into the bathroom she says, "Dottie, it's three in the morning! Why aren't you sleeping?" I look at her white face and into her red eyes and feel the huge horrible house settle and all the dark crowds me and I throw up. I throw up all over the floor and then run to the toilet where I throw up more and more.

She carries me to bed when I am done and there's Noxzema all over me and she says, "You don't have a fever."

All I can think is, I want my dad.

≈ *Balloon*

The electricity is gone on Friday and so is Lyle. Mom says he's coming back, but I'm not so sure. Gabe thinks he went to find some electricity. We think a lot about what to do without electricity, but we don't think a lot about Lyle.

Gabe wants to hear music, but we tell him there's no electricity for music. He wants to watch television, but we tell him the television won't work either. He sits and sucks his thumb and rubs his face in his old gray bunny. He doesn't understand.

Mom goes into the kitchen and starts digging through drawers. When she comes back, she's holding a red balloon that she blows up.

Mom hits the balloon at me and I hit it back. She hits it to Gabe and he hits it straight to the floor.

Mom picks up the balloon and hits it to Gabe again. Gabe hits the balloon to me. I hit the balloon to Mom.

We start to count how many times we can hit the balloon without it falling to the ground.

One, two, three.

"Mom, Gabe messed up again!"

"Hush, Dottie!"

One, two, three, four, five.

"Mom, stop hitting it to the floor!"

One, two, three, four, five, six, seven. Mom starts laughing.

"Mom!"

One, two, three. I start laughing.

One. Gabe hits himself in the face.

We play Balloon until it gets dark. Mom lights candles far away from the balloon and we keep playing.

On Saturday morning we eat cereal and then play Balloon.

"'Loon, 'loon," says Gabe. "'Loon, 'loon, 'loon!"

One, two, three, four.

"Sorry, Mom."

One, two, three, four, five. Gabe laughs and laughs and laughs.

Sunday morning we eat our cereal and then play Balloon. We laugh so hard all day that we can barely stand it.

On Monday there is electricity and Lyle, but it was just fine without either of them.

≈ Gabe Won't Walk

Mom doesn't know what to do.

Gabe won't learn to walk. He refuses to try and stand up. He cries and cries when anyone tries to stand him up. Mom is beside herself. She says, "I am beside myself."

I think it's very exciting. I like that Gabe refuses to do what they want him to. I like that he smiles whenever he sees me. I like that he hugs me and pats me on the back when I am sad. Mom says it's unusual for a child so young to pat someone on the back. She says he learned it from us, but I think he knew it all along. I am proud of Gabe's patting and his dragging.

Instead of walking or rolling or crawling, Gabe drags himself. He doesn't even use both arms, he just uses one. He lies on his stomach with his left arm at his side, lifts his head, and drags himself with his chubby forearm. It's weird to watch, but interesting too. He moves pretty fast.

Whenever anyone calls, I tell them about my brother who won't walk.

When Nana calls, I tell her how Gabe has a powerful right forearm and how he can drag himself anywhere. Nana says dragging shows perseverance and intelligence and Gabe will probably be a surgeon. Nana puts Pop on the phone and Pop says Gabe will be a powerful oarsman and may row all the way to China one day. I tell Pop I think he's right. They tell Mom not to worry and that Gabe will walk when he wants to.

When Grandma calls, I tell her of Gabe's dragging and his trip to China. I tell her Gabe may never choose to get up off the carpet and that I'm proud of him. Grandma says there's no big deal in not walking. She says Hitler walked and he was no good. She says Stalin walked and he was no good either. She says even Nixon walked, so Mom should be happy Gabe is dragging. Grandpa gets on the phone and says, "Ven I vas a child, ve walked when ve wanted too und no sooner. No big deal."

Mom says, "I don't care. They're all from Europe. I am beside myself."

≈ Missy Visits

She is here again.

I don't really know who she is or where she came from, but she's here now and I hate it more than anything. I hate it more than West Virginia.

"Call Gabe a twat," says Missy.

"No," I say.

I don't know what "twat" means and I don't want to call my brother that because I have a feeling it's very bad.

"Call Gabe a twat and I'll be your best friend," says Missy.

I want Missy to like me. I want her to be nice to me. She is fourteen and smart and mean and scary. When she visits, Lyle smiles and drinks less beer and buys her things. She's his daughter and I envy her because he's nice when she's around.

Mom comes in the room and looks at the three of us. Mom smiles.

"Gabe," I scream, "you're a twat!"

Mom crosses the room in two steps and swats me. I howl. Missy laughs. Gabe cries. Mom screams. I scream. Lyle comes in and screams. We all scream. I run upstairs to suck my thumb and read *Charlotte's Web*.

I have said a terrible thing.

≈ Tuberculosis

The clinic said I had almost TB.

TB is tuberculosis and you can die from it.

I asked Mom what tuberculosis meant. Mom said the clinic found something in my lungs that meant I could get TB. Mom said I don't have TB and I won't ever get it. She promises I will never die from tuberculosis.

I tell her I don't want to die from TB. She says I won't and all I have to do is take pills for a while. The pills make whatever could be TB go away.

I take them three times a day.

I lie in my bed at night and think about the almost TB in my lungs. I wonder how big it is. I wonder what it looks like. I wonder if everyone is really lying to me and how long I have to live.

I read my Wonder Woman comics and dream about the island the Amazons live on. I dream I am running and don't have asthma or TB or anything bad. I run and run and wear white clothes flowing around me.

When I wake up I still have almost TB.

Dad calls and says not to worry. Dad says a lot of people have almost TB and that I will be fine.

"Do you think it's because of West Virginia?" I ask.

"What do you mean?" he asks.

"Do you think I have almost TB because of West Virginia?" I ask.

"No," he says.

I have almost TB and long hair. Those are the only two things that I have. I tell Mom I want to cut my hair.

"I thought you wanted long hair like Wonder Woman," says Mom.

"I did, but now I don't," I say.

Mom has one of her friends cut off all my hair. I watch it fall onto the bathroom floor. My head feels light and I feel amazing.

We go to the clinic and they x-ray my lungs again. They tell Mom there's no sign of almost TB anymore. Mom cries right in front of everyone because she is so happy. She cries so much that Gabe starts crying and pats her on the back.

The clinic says all I needed were the pills.

I know all I needed was to cut my hair because I'm a different kind of Wonder Woman. I'm the kind who survived the almost TB that West Virginia gave me.

≈ The Extraterrestrial

It's summer and Mom sends me to Dad's apartment in Cleveland. When I am done at Dad's, he will drive me to my grandparents' farm in Ohio. When my grandparents are done with me, they will drive me to Nana and Pop's house in Detroit. This is what we do every summer. I always start off in Cleveland.

We see a lot of movies in Cleveland. Dad calls most of them "films" and I don't understand them. After we saw *Repo*

Man, Dad apologized because he said he hadn't realized there was so much bad language in it. It's because of Dad's roommate, George, that I get to see *E.T.*

I can tell George doesn't like it when I stay over. He mutters that kids are annoying and I try to stay out of his way. Dad has to go see his girlfriend, Cecilia. He asks George to watch me for a few hours. George looks at me and I look at George. We both look at Dad. I don't want George to watch me. George doesn't want to watch me. George sighs and his shoulders slump. I stare at the floor. Dad leaves.

I sit on the couch and look at *Mad* magazines. I am very still. George stalks up and down the hall slamming cabinets and randomly hitting keys on his typewriter. George is a journalist. He's also working on a novel. I think it must be very difficult to do all that. George walks up to me and says, "Do you want to go to the park and play catch?" I think about it for a minute, even though I know I should say yes right away. The truth is, I hate George and his sighs and his pacing and his stupid journalism. There's no way in Hell I want to go to the damn stupid park and play catch with him.

The park isn't too crowded when we get there. There's lots of room to play. I'm really nervous and I'm not able to catch as well as usual. Every time I miss, George laughs. He says stuff like, "I thought your dad said you knew what you were doing." I try harder, but he starts throwing the ball really fast. I catch almost all of them because I'm afraid they're going to hit me in the head and crack it open and my brains will spill out. A dog runs by. I watch the dog. I don't watch George. When I turn my head back to George, there's a blinding flash and I fall on the ground. I don't mean to cry but when I realize I'm not dead, I can't help it. Once I start, I can't stop.

Back at the apartment, Dad and George argue. Dad says, "What the hell were you doing? She's nine years old!" George says, "Well, it's not my fault she wasn't paying attention." None of this makes me feel any better. Dad asks me how I'm feeling and I tell him I'm okay and it's not George's fault. I tell him there was a dog. I tell him I was clumsy. He asks me what I want to do and I ask him if we can go see *E.T.* He says we can go see *E.T.* even if it is a Hollywood movie.

George and his girlfriend, Margaret, go with us. Dad brings Cecilia. After we get our tickets, Dad and George disappear. I ask Margaret where they went. She says they will be back. She says they went to do something they think will make the movie better. When Dad comes back, he doesn't talk to me. He just smiles a lot. I know they have been smoking pot because I can smell it. I know what pot is because Lyle smokes it sometimes and it stinks up the house.

I watch the stupid movie and cry because stupid E.T. leaves in his spaceship and it's been a horrible day and I wish I had never played catch with George.

⁓ One More Day

Dad and I spend three weeks together, but then it's over.

Dad drives me to Grandma and Grandpa's farm up north. He stays for a few days. We swim in the lake. Grandma only goes in up to her knees. Afterward we go to Dairy Queen. In the evening we play miniature golf and go to the batting cages.

Dad is leaving tomorrow. I want him to stay one more day. I think if he stays one more day, he'll ask me to live with him. I think if he stays one more day, he'll take me back to

Cleveland with him. I think if Dad stays one more day, he'll realize how much he'll miss me.

He wakes me up early in the morning. He hugs me and the grass is wet and there's fog and it's humid and sleepy looking outside. He tells me he loves me. I feel an ant crawl over my knee.

Grandma cries and wipes her glasses.

Dad leaves.

I stand in the wet grass with something heavy burning in my throat. I clench my hands into fists.

Grandpa's dog, Sherry, runs up to me and barks. I run with her up the hill. I run with her past the barn and into the garden. We run between the rows of tall corn.

I feel rocks and thorns in the bottoms of my feet, but it doesn't hurt.

≈ The Chickens

I don't like to wake up in the morning on Grandma and Grandpa's farm.

Grandma gives me the tin bucket. I go outside and walk toward the barn. I see Grandpa up on the hill, past the apple trees. He's in the garden and his teeth are back in the house. He waves. I wave back.

"Guten morgen!" he yells.

"Hi, Grandpa!" I yell.

I continue to walk to the barn. I swing the bucket. I drop the bucket. I kick it. I pet Sherry, who runs and nips at my feet. I like Sherry. She's like a person. She looks at me. She always looks at me because she knows I hate the walk to the barn. Inside the barn is a special door leading to the chicken coop. Every morning, every summer I go to the farm,

Grandma gives me the bucket because I'm supposed to get the eggs. I have never been able to do it.

I stand in the dark barn and stare at the door. I hear the rustling and the clucking. I can smell the chickens behind that old brown wood door. I hate chickens. My hands sweat and my knees shake while I open the door just a little. I peek in, expecting a chicken to fly right at my eye. I stick my arm in and shake the bucket. I think this will scare any chickens waiting behind the door. I slowly slip into the coop. I inch and slide toward the nests.

There is a wall of boxes. In every box is a chicken. Some of them face out. Some of them sit backward and you can see the V shape of their butt feathers pointing at you. I stare at the chickens. The ones facing out stare at me.

"Hello, chickens," I say.

They squawk a little. They rustle a little. I move a step closer to them. They rustle a little more. Two chickens stand up in their boxes and start to raise their wings.

"Good chickens," I say.

I reach an arm toward a backward-turned chicken. I think I will sneak up on it. I will take her egg and run. All of a sudden it's terrible. Some of the chickens squawk and holler and jump out of their boxes and run around. I open the door and run. I run into Grandpa. He looks into my bucket. It is empty. He's very tall and I look up at him.

"Dorothy, come," he says. "Ve vill take the eggs."

When Grandpa walks through the door, I know no harm will come to me. He looks at the wall of chickens. The chickens look at him. He moves toward them and they coo and coo. They snuggle against him and he pats them and they lift their butts so he can take the eggs. He says, "Gut chickie!" We fill the bucket. I go back to the house.

"So many eggs this morning," says Grandma. "You took all these from the chickens?"

It's a sad thing to ask because she knows I didn't.

"No, Grandpa did it," I say.

"Maybe tomorrow," she says, "you vill take the eggs."

Grandma made me try creamed spinach even though I cried. Grandma makes me go to church, even though I don't like it. Grandma made me wear a pink dress at a picnic. Grandma always makes me take naps. Every morning of every day, every summer I'm there, Grandma points me toward the chickens. She won't give up. She'll never give up.

≈ The Cow

One summer Grandma and Grandpa had a cow and I named her Suzie. I used to watch her while she stood and ate. She would chew and look at me. I would stand barefoot in the long grass with white dust all over my legs and look at her. This is what we used to do. I would stare at her and say, "Suzie," and she would do nothing. It was very quiet and calm. I didn't even mind the chickens on the farm because Suzie was there.

This summer Suzie is gone.

I tell Grandma that dinner is very good. She says dinner is Suzie.

I stop eating. Grandma grumbles at me in her German accent. She says, "Ven I vas a girl, animals vere for food und nicht for fun." I don't know what to say because I just ate my friend and now there are only the chickens that I hate.

I drive with Grandma and Grandpa through Ohio. They are taking me to Nana and Pop's house in Detroit. Along the way Grandma feeds me red and white swirled mints. Through the car window, I watch the farms go by. Brown and white cows graze and I squint my eyes until the cows blur. I think maybe they could be big dogs instead of cows who will eventually be dinner. Grandma gives me mint after mint until my tongue is numb and we get to Detroit.

Nana and Pop take me to Beefcarver, which is my favorite restaurant, but they don't know why I can't eat. Pop smokes his pipe in the restaurant and chuckles. He says, "That old farm life getting to you?" I nod. He smiles. Nana likes the peas. We leave.

At home, Nana makes me tea with cheese and crackers. We have our tea party and she puts pink rollers in my hair. I lie on the floor and watch Carol Burnett. Pop reads the paper and smokes his pipe. He only turns his hearing aid up for *The Muppets*, baseball, or boxing.

"Nana, I don't feel good," I say.

"Do you want a Coca-Cola?" she asks.

I sit up. I stand up. I stand still. I start throwing up. I run in circles. Nana holds her hands up in front of me. She is from England and very tidy. Pop looks over his paper. He sees me in my pink rollers, running in circles, puking all over the carpet while Nana runs behind me with her hands cupped.

"What the hell? What the hell?" he shouts.

Nana puts me to bed with what she thinks is the flu. Pop sits down on the bed and gives me his copy of *The Guinness Book of World Records*. I look at the fat lady and the midgets and the girls born all stuck together. It says the girls had boyfriends before they died. Pop smiles.

"I lived on a farm when I was a boy," he says and then pulls on one of my pink rollers.

I think Pop knows about the cow. I think he knows everything without me having to say a word.

10 Years Old

Dorothy, on the Moon

≈ I'm Marcia's Friend

Marcia and I wear T-shirts. Marcia's is purple and says, "I'M DOTTIE'S FRIEND" in white capital letters. My T-shirt is green and says, "I'M MARCIA'S FRIEND" in white capital letters. The shirts were Marcia's idea.

I don't know how to feel about the shirt because I don't like Marcia much. She's always pushing me around and I hate it. Marcia and I are friends because our moms are friends. Mom says I have to put up with Marcia. Mom says Marcia's mom deserves a life. Marcia's mom is divorced and has started dating. I put up with Marcia because her mom deserves a life. I tell Mom I deserve a life too. Mom tells me to stop being smart.

On Saturday Mom leaves us alone in the house for twenty minutes.

She says, "Your brother is asleep, so be quiet. I'm going to the 7-Eleven for milk and I'll be back in twenty minutes. Don't touch anything. Don't go anywhere. Don't call anyone or answer the phone. Just sit," she says. "Just sit and stare at the wall."

"We're ten, Mom," I say. "We're not babies."

We watch Mom climb into the Maverick and drive away. Marcia starts moving around the house.

"We're not supposed to move," I say.

"We can move, stupid," she says.

I follow her. She goes into the kitchen and opens the refrigerator door. She pulls out a can of chocolate frosting that we're not supposed to touch. She opens the can and spoons a glob of frosting into her fat mouth.

"We're not supposed to eat that," I say.

Marcia pulls at a wedgie because her shorts are too tight and she sticks out her slimy chocolate tongue at me. I decide I want her to get in so much trouble that she gets arrested and I never have to see her again. Maybe I will visit her in prison and stick my tongue out at her and she can hold on to the bars and apologize for being awful.

She climbs the stairs and I climb after her. I think she may want to do something mean to Gabe and that can't happen. I decide I will push her out a window if she dares lay a hand on him. Poor Gabe just sleeps with his banky wrapped around him, not knowing Marcia is loose upstairs.

She goes into Mom and Lyle's room and circles the bed. I feel sick to my stomach. She stares at things and squints, all the time shoving frosting into her face with a tablespoon.

She sits on the radiator by the window and looks outside.

"Here comes the paperboy," she says.

"Big deal," I say.

Marcia makes a face at me and opens the window. I can't imagine what she could do. The paperboy is mean and ugly and has black teeth in the front. He's very old, maybe even fourteen. He's skinny and has acne and greasy hair. She screams out the window.

"Hey you!" she yells.

I sit on the bed and watch him through the window. He looks around.

"Yeah," she hollers. "Hey you, ugly!"

The paperboy looks up at our window and sees her. She has chocolate all around her fat mouth and she's waving the spoon and then she points it at him.

"Penis breath!" she screams.

We are going to die. I don't know what it means to be called penis breath, but I know what a penis is and that's bad enough.

He starts yelling very bad things at Marcia as he walks toward the front porch. The words he uses get worse and worse. The worse they get, the more Marcia smiles and screams, "Penis breath!"

I think maybe I should get Gabe and run out the back door but I'm frozen with fear because it's all happening so fast.

The paperboy is on the front porch and Marcia sticks her dumb head out the window so he can hear her better. I think it's a perfect time to shove her and her chocolate face out the window, but I don't.

He opens the screen door and wrenches it right off its hinges. He fiddles with the knob on the door, but it's locked.

"PENIS BREATH PENIS BREATH PENIS BREATH PENIS BREATH PENIS BREATH PENIS BREATH PENIS BREATH," she screams.

He starts to throw his shoulder into the door. The door creaks and rattles and I swear I can feel the house shake.

The Maverick squeals into the driveway and Mom jumps out so fast that the car's still running and the door is wide open. She grabs Penis Breath by the hair and throws him off the porch.

"What the hell are you doing?" she screams.

He looks up at the window, but we've ducked and are just listening.

"They called me a name!" he hollers.

"Who did?" asks Mom.

"Those girls up there," he says.

"You get your butt out of here," says Mom.

We peek over the ledge and see Penis Breath walking away. Mom picks up the screen door and leans it against the railing.

By the time Mom comes inside, Marcia and I are sitting on the couch and staring at the wall.

"What did you say to him?" she asks.

"Nothing," we say.

"He started it," says Marcia.

I think this is a good tactic and one I never would have thought of. Why not blame it all on Penis Breath anyway? He's not here to defend himself. We're only ten and girls and all alone in a huge house with baby Gabe. Marcia looks at me.

"I was scared," I say.

Marcia starts crying. Mom collapses in the chair with the 7-Eleven bag in her lap.

"I went to get milk," she says. "I just left you alone for a minute."

Marcia's mom picks her up and they leave. Mom looks at me.

"That one has a mouth on her," she says.

I don't say anything.

"What did you girls say to that paperboy?" Mom asks.

"I never said anything, Mom," I say. "I swear."

The next time Marcia comes over to play, she has a black eye and a fat lip. She went to the laundromat with her mom and mouthed off to a boy there. He punched her twice, right in the face.

"What did you do?" I ask. "Call him penis breath?"

"Shut up, Dottie," she says. "Just shut up."

"Make me," I say.

She doesn't do a thing and I smile.

⁓ Charles Thinks I'm Different

Sam Seaver is the best thing about West Virginia.

He is rich and blond and has all the *Star Wars* figures ever made and he never talks to me. I watch him and I dream.

I make things up in my head. I make things up like I am rich and have perfect teeth and leather Nikes and a house with wall-to-wall carpeting. I dream I don't have to get free breakfast or used clothes. I dream I don't have asthma or a house with peeling paint on the walls.

I watch him from my seat in the back of the classroom and smile.

One day he will notice me and love me and think I am wonderful. Until he notices, I talk to his best friend, Charles.

Charles has curly black hair and a way of making people laugh.

Charles is rich too and has all the *Star Wars* figures, but he seems more real than Sam Seaver, who is blond and several rows in front of me.

"Dottie," asks Charles, "can you throw a baseball?"

"Yes," I say.

"That's important, you know," he says.

Charles has dark green eyes and talks about baseball. His father is a doctor and his mom stays home and vacuums a lot. Charles says vacuuming is stupid and doctors are okay. Charles says baseball and *Star Wars* are the two most important things ever.

Charles tells me he likes that I play Four Square. He says it is important to be different.

"I'm not different," I say.

"No other girls play," he says.

"Not here, maybe," I say, "but other places they do."

"What other places?" he asks.

"Detroit," I say.

Charles and I talk, but the whole time I think about talking to Sam. Charles and I laugh, and I think about laughing with Sam. Charles and I eat lunch, and I think about eating lunch with Sam.

One day Marcia tells me Charles wants to be my boyfriend. She tells me Sam told her that.

"You talked to Sam?" I ask.

"So what?" she says.

"What did he say?" I ask.

"He said Charles likes you," she says.

I don't say anything. I think Sam must not like me at all if he can just let his best friend have me. I feel stupid and ugly.

Marcia asks, "Will you be Charles's girlfriend?"

"Okay," I say.

I am Charles's girlfriend for two weeks and during that time we stop talking and having fun. Marcia tells me I'm ruining everything. I tell her I want to break up with Charles.

She tells Charles I want to break up.

Charles and I break up.

Charles and I talk and eat lunch and laugh again. We talk and laugh and I stare at Sam Seaver several rows up.

I stare at Sam and wonder if he thinks I'm different and interesting like Charles does.

≈ *Marcia, the Attic, and Four Radio Dogs*

Marcia says she will guard the door while I go up and look.

I don't want to go up and look.

Marcia says everybody looks at their Christmas presents, everybody. I tell her I never looked because I am too afraid of getting caught and Lyle is mean and I'm scared of him. Marcia says that is the dumbest thing she's ever heard. "Don't you want to know what you got?"

I don't want to know.

Marcia says the presents are in the attic because there's nowhere else for them to be. She opens the creaky wood door. It's painted yellow and when you open it, paint flies into your face. Cold, smelly air hits us in the face and there's dust in it.

"Never mind," I say.

"Do it, Dottie," she says. "Just go and look and stop being dumb."

I hate the attic. Rats can jump on you and eat your eyes out. Mice can run over your feet. There are cobwebs and piles of things in the dark. Anything can happen in the attic and it's all bad.

I decide I will go halfway up the stairs, pretend to look, and run back down. Maybe I will tell her I saw a rat. Yes, I will tell her there was a rat.

I walk up the stairs and sit down. I keep my arms close to my sides. I put my head on my knees and become very small and safe from rats and dusty mice. I hear Marcia talking.

She says, "Dorothy's up there. She's looking at her Christmas presents."

Lyle hollers, "Dorothy!"

I throw up right there on the dirty stairs and all over my sneakers. When I go down, I'm crying and stupid and snotting all over the place. Lyle makes me go to my room. Marcia follows me.

"Geez," she says, "what a baby."

I punch her and she cries.

Christmas morning is bad for a lot of reasons. I didn't throw up on the stairs just because I was afraid. I threw up because I had the flu.

I have never thrown up so much and for so long. I am almost proud of it.

"Do you have to throw up again?" asks Mom.

"Yes," I say.

"But you just threw up," says Mom.

I throw up on Mom and she finally stops asking me if I'm serious and just keeps a bucket by my bed.

When I go downstairs on Christmas morning, my head feels like a huge balloon. I feel light and floaty. I feel like I could fly but I'm too tired to try. Gabe rolls around in wrapping paper and I open things. Mom and Lyle think I've seen all of my presents, so they don't really talk to me. I open my presents, but I don't care about them because I'm very sleepy.

Dad got me a chemistry set because those are the kinds of things he gets me. I am excited to open Grandma and Grandpa's present. Every year they get me the same thing.

Every year I get a radio dog. That's what Mom calls them. It's a stuffed dog with a radio in it and you can listen to music while you hug the dog. The music doesn't come in very well because of all the fur, but I can make out the songs most of the time. I have three radio dogs already. I have four when I open this year's present.

I take my radio dog and go upstairs. I turn the dials on its fuzzy stomach and go to sleep to the scratchy sound of Kenny Rogers singing "The Gambler."

≈ Bertie and the Bottom of the Hill

We all give Bertie our kale.

In the lunchroom, Bertie always has a huge pile of kale on her tray. There's nothing wrong with having a huge pile of kale on your tray when you live in West Virginia. They even let us have seconds and thirds of lunch if we want, but the kale has to be gone first. If you want a second grilled ham-and-cheese sandwich and you hate kale, all you have to do is give it to Bertie.

Bertie lives at the bottom of the hill behind my house. There's a bunch of small wood houses with tires and cinder blocks in their front yards. I never go down into that place because of all the mean boys. The mean boys wait down at the bottom of the hill and yell things like "Assface." They throw rocks at each other for fun. They beat each other up for fun. Bertie never comes to the top of the hill, so I guess she doesn't mind the mean boys. There are probably other girls at the bottom of the hill, but the only ones I've seen are older and they already have babies in carriages. They stand outside smoking cigarettes and rocking their baby carriages with their knees.

They talk to older boys who wear greasy baseball hats and sit in pickup trucks.

I like Bertie. She never says anything even though we're in the same class and see each other every day. We both go to school early to have free breakfast and she still never talks to me. It doesn't make me mad because I think she must be very busy thinking. She looks like she's thinking because she squints a lot and chews on her hair. She has long, white hair and blue eyes with red all around them. Her elbows are pointy and her clothes are worse than mine. I like the way she smells. She smells like smoke from a wood fire, bacon, eggs, and kale.

The hill between me and Bertie is steep and wide. In the summer Marcia and I ride our bikes down it with our arms in the air and our feet off the pedals. We get to the bottom and ride as fast as we can back up to the top. In the winter we stay away from the hill. The hill is solid ice and it's terrifying. Bertie has to walk in the snow on the side of the hill when she goes to the bus stop. She knows one wrong step can send you flying to the bottom. We've never tried to sled it, but we know what could happen. Mom warns me over and over.

She says, "Don't you try and sled that hill, Dorothy. Nothing good can come of it."

Marcia decides we need to sled the hill. Marcia says we might as well sled it because when we do we will be heroes. She says none of the mean boys have ever done it. She says they'll never yell things at us or throw rocks at us again if we show them we can sled the hill. I tell Marcia it's easy for her to talk big, but I live here and why doesn't she just go home? Marcia says there's nothing to do where she lives and her mom has a new boyfriend.

Marcia's plan grows and grows.

She ties Gabe's stroller to a wagon with old shoelaces, and smiles. She tells me all we have to do is sit in the wagon and sit in the stroller and go down the hill. She says we can put the wagon in front and steer with the handle. She says whoever is in the stroller can dig their boots into the ice and snow if we go too fast. She says it's a perfect plan.

I don't want to do it, but I agree anyway because Marcia's a bully and I can always punch her later.

We shouldn't have done it.

I'm supposed to steer the wagon, but I can't. Marcia is supposed to dig her feet into the ice and snow, but she can't. We scream and scream and fly down the icy hill until we roll into a huge snowbank and Marcia gets hurled into the air.

I dig myself out of the snow and stand up. I feel dizzy and my neck hurts. I look for Marcia and I see her sprawled face down on the ice. There are three mean boys gathered around her. I walk over to her. I kneel down and roll her over. There's blood all over her face and she's crying.

"Why didn't you steer?" she screams.

"I tried, stupid," I yell. "Why couldn't you stop us?"

"My face hurts!" she whines.

The mean boys stare at us and smile. There's no way I can get Marcia up the hill. I don't know what to do. They start moving closer and I shut my eyes.

I feel movement all around me and I can smell the snow. It smells sweet and oily at the same time. I feel dizzy and weird and like I'm floating far away. Someone touches my shoulder, but it's not a mean touch. When I look up, I see Bertie and she's just standing there in an old brown coat with a big, furry gray dog next to her. The dog starts licking my face.

"That's Ol' Coyote," she says. "That's my dog."

"Hey," I say.

"Daddy named him that because he looks all like an ol' Coyote," she says.

The mean boys have stepped back from us and they squeeze snowballs in their mittens. I look over at them and I look at Marcia.

"Them's my brothers is all," says Bertie.

"I didn't know that," I say.

Marcia cries some more and says her face hurts. Ol' Coyote licks Marcia's face. She shoos him away and Bertie frowns. I stand up and take Bertie to the side. I whisper in her ear.

"I don't like her, but I think she's hurt bad," I say.

Bertie nods at me. She nods at her brothers and they help pick Marcia up. The three of them drag her up the hill while Bertie and I go and look at the wagon.

"Looks okay," I say.

"Yeah," says Bertie.

We look at the stroller. It doesn't look like a stroller anymore.

"That's no good," I say.

"Yeah," says Bertie.

Bertie and I drag the wagon up the hill in the snow. When we get to the top, the boys dump Marcia into the wagon. We all stand there in the snow staring at each other.

"Thank you," I say.

Bertie says, "C'mon, Ol' Coyote, let's us go."

Ol' Coyote woofs at me and Bertie smiles.

"He likes you," she says.

I pull Marcia up to the back door and leave her in the wagon.

I holler, "Mom?"

"What?" she says.

"Marcia tried to sled down the hill and broke the stroller and her face is bleeding."

"She's bleeding?" screams Mom.

"Yes," I say, "and it's not my fault."

Gabe likes that his stroller is broken because he prefers being dragged around in a wagon instead. He piles his gray bunny, his banky, and his blocks into the wagon and waits for Mom to take him somewhere.

Marcia takes all the blame for everything and never says a word.

Bertie still doesn't talk to me much, but once in a while she'll tell me that Ol' Coyote says, "Hey."

⁓ Gabe Walks

I tell Gabe about the dream I had. I tell him because I think he's very smart and he will be able to figure it out. I tell Gabe the dream because it is important.

I say, "You were riding a big old gray dog. Like the dog Bertie has, you know?"

Gabe says, "Bertie has doggie!"

I say, "In the dream you were riding a dog like Bertie has and you were smiling, but something was wrong."

Gabe makes a sad face.

"Right," I say. "Something was wrong because a boy shouldn't be riding a doggie around."

Gabe nods.

"In the dream I had," I say, "you were riding the doggie and smiling. You rode that dog everywhere. You rode the dog to school. You rode the dog to the 7-Eleven. You rode the dog next to Mom on the way to the library."

"Books," says Gabe.

"Yes," I say. "But it wasn't right. In the dream I had, you knew you shouldn't be riding Bertie's dog. You knew you should be walking on your own instead."

Gabe makes another sad face.

"I know it makes you sad," I say, "but it's not bad walking. I walk, and Mom and Lyle walk. We like to walk places and do things for ourselves. I can walk to the fridge and get milk whenever I want to."

Gabe says, "Milk."

"Yes," I say. "We can all get milk when we learn to walk, but that's not all. In the dream a man came."

"A man?" asks Gabe.

"Yes," I say. "A man came, and he had dark skin and long hair. He rode a white and brown horse. He rode up to you, jumped off his horse, and then kissed you on the cheek. The man smiled and said you were ready to walk."

Gabe shakes his head.

"The man smiled and laughed and he reminded me of Pop," I say.

"Pop?" asks Gabe.

"Pop has the anchor tattoo," I say.

"Pop!" yells Gabe.

"I think you're ready, Gabe," I say. "I think you're ready to walk."

"Okay," says Gabe.

Gabe and I are sitting near the couch. The coffee table is between us. Gabe takes his chubby arm and lifts himself into a standing position. He smiles and walks right into my arms. I hug him and hug him.

"You walked!" I yell.

"Dottie," says Gabe.

≈ *Four Square*

We all go outside for recess.

There are all different kinds of us.

Some people play tetherball. Some stand in line for the swings or slide. The boys who punch each other climb the jungle gym or play football. The girls who kiss boys go play in the tractor tires that are half buried in the ground and painted red, yellow, and blue. They stand in the tires, hiding between the rubber sides, and wait for boys to kiss them. The tires smell like pee. Some people climb on top of the tires to sit while girls get kissed inside them and I think that's gross.

Some of us play Four Square.

Four Square never ends, it just continues from day to day. At the end of recess there's always a winner. The winner can lose the next day or hold the title for weeks.

There is a square painted in yellow on the concrete and inside it are four other squares. Each person stands in a square and you have to hit the ball in the squares between the four of you. You're not allowed to palm the ball. You can't carry the ball either. The ball can't touch the lines and you're not allowed to spike it. Spiking is a tough call, but you know it when you see it.

A line forms to the right of the big square and when someone messes up, the three people remaining shift over and another person comes in. The top left square is the winner's square, and the winner gets to serve.

Eric has been Four Square champion for two weeks. He's very good. He's also very small and mean. He hates girls and I'm the only girl who plays.

He always makes the boys in the squares gang up on me. They hit the ball fast and always in the corners. When three people are trying to get you out, it's impossible to win. The furthest I've ever gotten is to the second square and Eric hated that. He made sure they got me out the next day. I don't let it stop me because I know I am good at Four Square and Eric is a horrible person.

Sam Seaver plays Four Square too. He's good, but I'm better. He's very polite when he plays. He always tries to get the winner out but never messes with anyone else. Even if he's in the second square and trying to get to the third, he'll just work on the winner in the fourth square.

We all stand in line and wait to play. We watch Eric scream and yell and almost spike the ball at people. No one ever yells at him, but I'm about ready to. It's bad enough he thinks he's the best without him yelling at everyone. I have been waiting in line for the past two recesses to play and I am furious at Eric. I have been watching him and waiting for my turn. I have been studying what he does and I think he's a terrible person all around.

I have also spent the last two recesses watching Sam Seaver, who is ahead of me. He is so calm and nice and not like Eric at all.

Sam's turn comes up and I like watching him play. He is beautiful and quiet and smart.

I'm next in line and it's really uncomfortable. It's especially bad because I'm the only girl waiting.

Sam plays well and ends up in the third square. Eric makes a face at me when I take the first square.

"Great," he says, "just great."

I'm in the first square, Sam's in the third square, and

Charles is in the second square. Charles has been standing in front of me for two recesses. He's been winking and smiling at me. He's been making me laugh even though I've been angry at Eric. Charles is a very quick and strategic player, but he isn't mean and nasty enough to beat Eric.

"Are you girls ready?" asks Eric.

I hate Eric.

He serves it fast and right into the corner of my square. I tap it to Sam, who bounces it to Charles, who head fakes and hits the ball into the corner of Eric's square. Eric is caught off guard because he thinks all the boys will be trying to get me out. He hurries and is just able to tap the ball to Sam. Sam taps it to Charles, who whacks it back to Eric. By now Eric has figured Charles out and he almost spikes it right into the corner of Charles's square. Charles tries to get it but he can't. He is out.

Sam is still in the third square and I am in the second. I smile at Charles, who is watching on the side, and he smiles back.

Square one is taken by Jim. Jim is fat and wheezes when he's excited. He has to sneak into Four Square because he has asthma and a doctor's excuse to do nothing. Eric makes fun of him a lot because the playground attendants are always pulling Jim out of line and yelling at him to sit quietly and read.

Jim nods at me. I nod back. We once had a conversation about cats. He said cats made his asthma bad and I said I hated cats. I told him I hated asthma because I had it too, but not as bad as him. We are friends because of cats and asthma.

Eric slams the ball to Jim, who wheezes and taps it to me. I slam it to Eric, who slams it back to me. I tap it to Sam, who hits it to Jim, who hits it to Eric. Eric slams it to me and I tap it to the corner of Eric's square. Eric gets so mad that he tries to whack it to me, but it hits Sam's square instead. Sam misses it. Sam is out.

I move to the third square and Jim moves to second. Jim is so excited he has to suck on his inhaler. Sam stands by Charles and watches.

My heart is pounding so hard I feel like I'm having an asthma attack, but I'm not. I'm just so close to winning that I can't bear it.

A crowd has gathered. Even the girls who kiss boys in the tires are there. Everybody wants to watch Wheezing Jim and the Girl beat Eric. I didn't realize how many people didn't like Eric until this game. I try not to look at the crowd.

Stan is friends with Eric and he takes the first square. They're always on the same football team when they aren't playing Four Square. Eric nods at Stan and Stan looks confused. He looks into the crowd and at big Wheezing Jim. I can tell he's not used to being hated. Stan nods back at Eric.

Eric hits the ball to Stan and Stan hits it hard to Jim. Jim has to leave his square to hit the ball back and when he does, he hits it to me. When the ball bounces in my square I make a decision. Everyone knows Jim would be an easy out because he's off guard. Everyone knows I could get him out before he gets back in his square. I whack the ball into Eric's square instead, right into the corner. Eric whacks it back to me. It almost touches the line.

The crowd makes noise.

I slam the ball back to Eric and it almost hits his feet. It's a perfect slam. He jumps back and swats at the ball. The ball ends up in Stan's square. Stan doesn't want to get Eric out, so he hits it to Jim. Jim taps the ball to me and I slap it back to Eric.

Eric is so mad that when the ball bounces up, he takes both hands and spikes it right into the corner of my square. It bounces so high into the air he thinks he's won.

He jumps up and down, laughing.

I run back into the crowd and hit the ball with my fingertips. We all watch the ball land right in front of Eric while he's jumping up and down. He misses the ball. Everyone is silent.

The bell rings but no one moves.

Jim is wheezing so hard that he has to sit down right in the center of his square. He looks up at Eric.

"You're out," wheezes Jim.

"She spiked it, retard," says Eric.

Everyone breathes quietly and no one says anything. I know I didn't spike it. I know if I say something people will turn on me because I'm a girl. It is better if I'm silent.

"You spiked it, Eric," says Charles.

The crowd makes noise.

"What?" yells Eric.

"You spiked it to Dorothy and she just hit it back to you," says Charles. "You're out."

"You cheated," says Sam.

"You're out," wheezes Jim.

Eric takes the ball and stares at it. He kicks it far into the field.

"You suck," he says to everyone.

The playground lady comes over to us.

"Move inside, children," she says. "Jim, what are you doing on the ground? Where's your book?"

We all move inside. I am Four Square champion.

"I'm gonna kick your ass," says Eric.

I say, "You and what army, loser?"

≈ We're Moving

All of a sudden there's all this noise. I'm sitting on the school bus, but I had forgotten where I was. People are yelling at me and I hear the bus driver saying, "This is your house, girl. I know this is your house!"

I'm sitting there and look out the window and I see this huge, terrible house, sagging and dirty. This is my house. This is the house I live in. Kids are screaming, "Get out, Dottie! Go home!" They're angry because they want to go home and have apple juice and Oreos and watch *Scooby Doo* in color and all sorts of wonderful things. I'm just sitting on the bus with all the yelling and I don't want to get out.

I've been daydreaming about being rich and having a beautiful house. I know every single floor and what color every wall is. I have a dog and a pool and lots of food and it never gets dark.

I have to get off the bus because you can't just stay on a bus when everyone is yelling at you to go away.

The kids on the bus glare at me while I'm standing on the sidewalk. I stare at them. The bus pulls away and I turn and stare at the house. I stand and stand and don't move because I don't want to go inside, but I have to.

When I go inside I see Mom sitting on the couch. She's smoking and looking at the wall.

She says, "Dottie, we're moving."

I say, "To a new house?"

And she says, "We're moving to Washington."

And I ask, "With Lyle?"

She nods and I start crying. I can't stop. I run upstairs to my terrible room. I have to leave my friends and school and Sam Seaver, who I love very much.

We're going to move again and there's nothing I can do to stop it.

≈ *Plastic Wings and a Bag Full of Popcorn*

The last day of school my friends look at me and I look at them. They say what they are going to do all summer and I say, "I'm going to Cleveland." They ask me, "Why are you going to Cleveland instead of playing with us?" I don't answer. They look at me and I look at them and that's how it is.

I don't tell them I'm never coming back. I don't tell them I'm moving to Washington. Sometimes I think it's better to say nothing than to say something so sad.

I keep track of the places I've been, even when it's just a layover. It makes me feel like the world is smaller instead of what it is, which is huge and spinning.

When the plane stops in Philadelphia, I have a sore ear. I always have sore ears. The stewardess takes me by the wrist and slaps some plastic wings on my shoulder. She drags me behind her and I shuffle my feet. I pretend I'm roller-skating. I've had dozens of stupid plastic wings slapped on my shoulder before, and I've never ever cared. Only babies give a crap about the plastic wings.

Every airport is a little different, but the stewardesses are all the same. They all have dried-up-looking faces and flyaway hair. They all wear blue, have long nails, and smell like cigarettes. They all think they're so nice for giving kids plastic wings. The only good thing about a layover is I can now say I've been to Philadelphia.

The stewardess puts me on a big leather couch and says, "Don't move."

I refuse to move. I refuse to look at her. Different women in blue come up to me and pat me. I can tell they're different because of the color of their pantyhose. One of them pins a big white button to my coat. I stare down at the button. It says, "I'm flying alone!" There's an exclamation point at the end of it, like it means I'm really excited to be flying alone. I am angry with the button. I hate the button. I am not excited at all. I hate flying and I hate when people stick things on you without asking. The different pantyhose keep coming at me and shoving plastic wings in my hand. I take the wings and shove them in the cracks between the cushions of the couch. I decide I hate Philadelphia.

I am not moving at all because I want to see how still I can be. I think maybe they will forget about me and leave me alone. Maybe they will think I am dead. I refuse to look around and I become very small. There's a rustling and a sigh and some dragging. I want to look up, but I won't.

"Dorothy?" asks a woman.

I do not look up.

"Dorothy!" yells the woman.

I put my chin to my chest.

"There has been a delay with your flight. I brought you some popcorn," she says.

I hear her walk away, so I look up. There's a black garbage bag on the floor and it's half full of popcorn. I stare and stare. I have never seen that much popcorn before. I look at my Peanuts watch and it's one o'clock. I think the wait will be very very long and there's no way I will eat any of the garbage bag popcorn.

Mom and Lyle and Gabe are still in West Virginia. Dad is in Cleveland. I am in Philadelphia. The thought of this makes me feel strange, like I'm lost. I look down at the button and the exclamation "I'm flying alone!"

≈ The Pigs

Grandma says the Reverend and his wife are coming and for me to hurry and help her. We take all of Grandma's *Enquirer* and *Star* magazines and hide them under the couch cushions.

I ask her why she hides them and she says it's because God thinks the *Enquirer* is evil.

"Does He think the *Star* is evil?" I ask.

"Yah," she says.

"Doesn't He see everything?" I ask.

"Yah, Dorothy, He does," she says. "But the Reverend doesn't need to."

When the Reverend and his family show up, Grandpa and the Reverend drink beer and tell me to marry a man just like them. I tell them I never want to get married. Grandpa reaches for the blackberry schnapps.

I'm supposed to play with the Reverend's kids, but I don't like them. Peter is small and white and looks like he's been drained of something important. There are pink rings around his eyes like he's been throwing up for hours. Mary is big and loud and struts around in gross dresses with lace collars and ruffles. She bosses Peter until he cowers like a scared puppy. She stands in the kitchen with Mrs. Reverend and Grandma.

Mrs. Reverend is really skinny and she puts her paper-thin arm around her big, fat daughter. Her arm looks like the string tied around one of Grandma's roasts. Grandma gives us Faygo Red Pop and Peter spills his all over the floor. Mary barks and stomps like a bull. Grandma throws us out of the kitchen. We walk outside toward the vineyard. Mary starts telling me about Jesus and crap. Peter squishes grapes with his useless fingers and lopes behind us. I want to tell Mary to shove her Jesus up her big, fat ass, but I don't because Grandma would kill me. Mary starts quizzing me on the Flood.

"I bet you don't know what the sign of God's promise to Noah was. I bet you don't know how God showed Noah that there'd never be another flood. I bet you don't know," she says.

"The dove," I say.

"I bet you don't know how many days the flood lasted," she says.

Peter falls into the vines and we have to pull him out. I answer stupid Mary's stupid question. The only reason I know the answers is because I have a comic book on the Flood. Dad bought a bunch of comics at a yard sale for me. Mixed in with the *Mad* magazines was a religious comic. Mary starts to get nervous.

"Well," she says, "it doesn't matter because you don't go to church and that means you're going to Hell."

I know it's not true, but I don't say anything because I hate her and she might sit on me right in the middle of the damn vineyard.

"You're lying," says Peter.

We both turn and stare at him. He's going to get killed. Poor Peter just stands on his two skinny white legs and stares out of his red-rimmed eyes.

"What did you say?" asks Mary.

"You're lying," says Peter. "Dad says people don't go to Hell because they don't go to church. They go to Hell because they sin. Dad says not going to church isn't a real sin like murder."

Mary whips her face in my direction. She glares into my eyes.

"Were you baptized?" she asks.

"No," I say.

"Then you're going to Hell," she hisses.

We both look at Peter. He shuffles his feet.

"It's true," he says.

We all wander out of the vineyard. We are all silent. I am furious because I don't believe them at all, but I can't say anything because Grandma would kill me. We all go up the hill and stare at Grandpa's new pigs. They snort and eat and dig. I am lost in anger. I am hateful. I lean on the fence surrounding the pigs. I forget it's an electric fence. I can't let go of the fence. There is pain everywhere. I feel my lips being pulled into a snarl. Suddenly my hands are loose and I fall on the ground. I hear Mary and Peter screaming. Grandpa comes and picks me up. He carries me to the house. While he carries me, I wonder if a light bulb would light up if I held it.

Later I think about Hell and Mary and Peter. I know they're thinking I was electrocuted because I wasn't baptized. I hate that.

Grandma says to ignore Mary and Peter because they're snobs and don't know what they're talking about. She says God would never send me to Hell because she talks to Him.

Grandpa butchers all the pigs because they electrocuted me. I think about the pigs and feel bad.

≈ *Pop's Garage*

There's a boxing match on the radio.

It's hot outside. It's so hot that Pop sips iced tea while he smokes his pipe. The cherry smoke is in the air while I hula-hoop. He counts.

"One, two, three, four, five, six, seven, eight, nine, ten, eleven, twelve, thirteen, fourteen, fifteen . . ." he says. "Good girl."

It's so hot the squirrels just sit on Pop's shoulders and hold their stale peanuts in their hands. Pop has his fishing hat on, and his white shirt and green pants. I have never seen him in anything else. Pop smells like wood and cherry smoke and stale peanuts and I never want to leave him.

The garage door is open and the smell of wood rolls out.

He makes shelves and bookcases and dressers and all sorts of things.

He smiles at me and I smile at him and hula-hoop until the sun goes down.

Nana calls us inside for pot roast, potatoes, and tea.

Pop takes my hand. His hands are brown and callused. Pop has the longest fingers I've ever seen and my hand disappears in his. We walk toward the house and the heat shimmers around us. I look up at him and he smiles. I feel safe and full of love and like my heart is opening up in the sun.

≈ Waiting

In my dream I'm walking and walking. I walk slowly. It's dark outside and I can't see anything.

I walk with my arms out in front of me because I'm scared I will run into something bad. I'm afraid I'll run into a slimy old tree, spiders, cobwebs, or a pricker bush.

I walk with very small steps. I am afraid I will walk off a cliff and fall into nowhere and die. I am afraid I will walk right into a pit of quicksand and drown.

In my dream I know I need to keep moving, but I am too

scared to get anywhere. I think if I just keep on track, I will be able to see the light of the moon in front of me. I look for the light, but it's never there.

I give up and stop moving. I stand in the dark and close my eyes. I breathe and breathe in all the darkness. I feel something warm on my face and it makes me feel very strong. I feel like I am safe. I feel like I am fast and clever and I could do anything because of this warmth all around me.

I fall to my knees and start to crawl in the dark, but I'm not me anymore. When the eyes of what I am open, I see a big old dog howling on a hill. The moon behind it is huge and yellow and full of light.

I want to run to the big old howling dog. I want to run right up into the moon and jump so high that I fly around it. I want to do these things, but the dog turns to me and says, "Not yet."

The dog looks at me and turns into a beautiful red horse. The horse looks at me and says, "Wait."

The horse turns into a man, but the moon gets so bright I can't see his face. I can't see his face, but I know he's laughing.

≈ We Are on the Moon

"Where is everything?" asks Mom.

"What everything?" asks Lyle.

"Where are the stores? Where's the grocery store? Is there a mall? Is there a movie theater? Where is everything?" asks Mom.

"It's around," says Lyle.

"Jesus and Mary," says Mom, "we're on the Moon."

Lyle has taken us to the Moon.

We drive around in the van and Mom and I look for a 7-Eleven or a Dairy Queen or anything familiar.

"What's that?" asks Mom.

Mom's staring at a huge sand hill in the middle of all the houses in our neighborhood.

"That's a sand hill, honey," says Lyle.

"Why is there a sand hill in the middle of our neighborhood?" Mom asks.

"That sand was left over from when they built the dam," he says. "So they just put it there. It doesn't hurt anyone just being there."

Mom folds her arms across her chest and sighs.

We've already passed the dam and it is huge. Lyle says the dam is three stories tall. We like the way things look, but we're not used to being in the middle of nowhere. We even saw a real Indian man riding a horse on the side of the road. He sat tall and beautiful in the sun. Mom says there's peace here. She says the colors are amazing and the energy is good. I look into the brown hills and squint. It takes a while, but I do see colors. There's red and brown and a little green and yellow. The air is clear and cool and I think I feel the energy. Lyle tells us to wait until we swim in the Columbia River. He says the river is like bath water only bright blue and clear. Lyle says the walleye in the river are as big as Gabe.

Gabe cries because he thinks it's scary to have fish that big. Lyle tells him not to cry because people catch fish and fish can't catch people.

We pull onto our street and it is beautiful. It isn't at all like West Virginia. There are trees and the lawns are green. The houses are new and have aluminum siding instead of brick and chipping paint. Mom sits up and smiles.

Our house is amazing.

The house has a garage and siding and a lawn with sprinklers that turn on automatically. When we go inside, Mom whistles.

There are huge windows in the house and sliding glass doors. There are two huge bedrooms upstairs that Gabe and I get. The paint on the walls is white and fresh and perfect. The wood floors shine in the sun. There are no small, dark rooms or peeling paint and no purple and green walls. It's a real house and it's all ours.

Mom says, "Tell me there's a movie theater."

Lyle says, "There's a theater, I swear."

Gabe says, "Moon!"

I say, "It's not the Moon, Gabe. It's only Washington."

Gabe says, "Ushington!"

Mom and Lyle laugh. I breathe in deep and think wonderful things all to myself. Gabe takes my hand and asks, "Moon?"

I say, "Okay, Gabe. It's the Moon too."

He smiles.

≈ *The Ugliest Girl*

I am new here. I don't know anyone at all. I sit all alone on the bus. I sit and sit and stare out the window at everyone getting on.

Everyone here looks different. They look older and taller and strange. They wear sweatpants pulled up to their knees. They wear laces with the school colors in their sneakers. The boys have long braids and the girls chew tobacco. Lyle says we can all learn a lot from the Indians, but I'm not sure what he means. I haven't really met them yet. So far only white people have said things to me.

I see my breath make a moist cloud on the window. I see the reflection of my teeth and the wide dark spaces between them. In the reflection I look like a rabbit that is wrong. I lean closer to the reflection until I can feel the cold of the glass against my mouth. The closer I get, the worse it is. Mom said I have to go to an orthodontist. I think he will tell me I will be a rabbit that is wrong forever. I pull my face away and think of writing something on the wet glass. People write the year they graduate, their initials, or their boyfriend's name. I don't know what to write. I write an "X," then smear it away.

The green plastic of the seat puckers and rips at the seams. I finger the black tape holding the rips together. In my head, the dull noise of everyone I don't know competes with silence. I look up and into the aisle. An older boy looks at me. His blond hair is short and sticks up. He smiles.

He says, "You're the ugliest girl I've ever seen."

He sits next to me and all I can do is stare out the window at the fog smear of my breath and wonder wonder wonder what to say. I wonder what to say ever again. And he's just there. He's just sitting there, right next to me.

≈ Mom Tries a Garden

"Nothing's going to grow there," says Lyle.

"I'm going to plant tomatoes and herbs and they will all grow," says Mom.

"Nothing's going to grow except maybe weeds and then you'll see," says Lyle.

He storms off into the house while Gabe and I watch Mom. We sit on the grass and watch how she doesn't care about what he said.

She says, "Tomatoes will grow and maybe beans."

I take my pogo stick and practice hopping. Mom gets tools and starts digging up the yard. I hop and Mom digs. Hop hop. Dig dig. Gabe runs back and forth. I can never get past four hops before I fall off. Gabe wants to pogo too, but he's too small so he keeps running back and forth.

Mom keeps digging and digging. Lyle comes out once in a while to shake his head and ask her where things are. Mom keeps saying, "Look in the kitchen! Look in the kitchen! Can't you see I'm planting a garden?"

Mom clears an almost perfect square of dirt. She puts store-bought dirt that's very black on top of our backyard dirt. She waters and waters and begins planting things. Gabe throws crabapples at a bird. I grab my basketball and go to the park.

When I come back, the garden looks wonderful. There are wooden spikes in the black dirt with labels of what will grow there. There's string separating the rows and it's perfect looking. Gabe stands next to the garden. He stares at the dirt. He wants to see something growing.

Lyle says, "I can't believe you spent all that money on nothing."

He ends up being right. Nothing does grow except some very small and very green tomatoes. Mom doesn't care, though.

She says, "Dottie, one day we'll have a beautiful garden and all sorts of flowers and you can help me."

I almost believe her.

≈ I Don't Have a Chin

"Dorothy doesn't have a chin," says Dr. O'Donnell. "She has no chin. It's barely there. This is terrible."

Mom leans in to look at my chin, which is not there. I sit in Dr. O'Donnell's chair under a bright light and I'm leaning back so far that I feel as if I'm standing on my head. I feel the blood rushing into my ears and it muffles their conversation. I know my face is getting red. I'm certain every part of my face is bright red, except for my chin, which is not there.

"I guess I never noticed," says Mom. "I guess we're used to it at home."

"This girl is ten years old and she has no chin and you're telling me you never noticed? Think back," says Dr. O'Donnell. "She must have had a chin once."

He sounds hopeful from his tone, which I can still make out through all the blood in my ears.

"She sucks her thumb," says Mom.

Dr. O'Donnell's face brightens. He clasps his hands together. His eyes get big and he leans his hairy-chinned face into my chinless one.

"Another thumb sucker," he says.

He lets me sit up and when I do I get sort of shaky because of all the blood in my head. I feel it move into my arms and stomach. Eventually all the blood goes back into the rest of me.

Mom and the doctor talk in the other room. I think about how we have to call him Doctor, only he's a dentist. I move my hand up to what I used to think was my chin. It feels knobby like a chin. I look into the mirror above the sink. I think I see a chin below my bottom lip. It's not much of a chin, but it is a chin. I don't like Dr. O'Donnell. He and Mom come back in and find me pinching the knob of what I believe to be my chin. Dr. O'Donnell looks at me. Mom looks at me.

He says, "Dorothy, did I upset you?"

"No," I say as I start to cry.

He walks over and kneels next to me. He seems nicer than when I was upside down.

He says, "Dorothy, I didn't mean to scare you. You certainly do have a chin, my dear. It's that little knob you're pinching. You're right. Now turn to the side and look in the mirror."

He gives me a hand mirror and I can see my sideways reflection with it in the mirror above the sink. In the reflection, I have no chin. My mouth drops open and I look at Dr. O'Donnell.

"Your chin is there, Dorothy. We just need to convince it to come forward a little, okay?"

I nod. I am terrified. What if it doesn't work? All the stories Mom and Pop used to tell me about thumb sucking were coming true. They never said my chin would disappear exactly, but they said my thumb would rot off and my teeth would fall out and all sorts of horrible things would happen. I think if they had only told me my chin was going to disappear, I would have stopped for certain. Dr. O'Donnell sits me down.

He says, "Take a drink of water."

I take a drink of water and I swallow it.

He says, "Do it again."

I take another drink.

He says, "Now this time I want you to take a drink of water and swallow it, but make an angry face so I can see you swallow."

I feel stupid making an angry face at Dr. O'Donnell who believes in my chin, but I do it anyway.

He nods and says, "You have a lazy tongue."

Now I have a lazy tongue and no chin and I feel myself start to cry again. Dr. O'Donnell explains to me that my lazy tongue is pushing my front teeth forward. He explains that when you swallow water you're not supposed to push the back of your front teeth with your tongue. He tells me when I swallow, I need to practice swallowing with my tongue touching the roof of my mouth. I try to do this, but it's awfully hard.

"This is very serious, Dorothy," he says. "We have to convince your chin to come forward and it most certainly won't if your tongue continues to be so lazy."

I swear to him I will stop sucking my thumb and swallow right and all sorts of things.

"I'm going to fit you for a very special retainer. It's called a Bionator and it's the most advanced retainer on the market. It's the best there is and it's made for people just like you," he says.

"What does it do?" I ask.

Dr. O'Donnell clasps his hands together and stares at the ceiling. He smiles and smiles.

"The Bionator," he glows, "is one of the most amazing orthodontic inventions. It is able to both bring the lower jaw forward as well as push back the front teeth. It allows a girl your age to have a chin. Of course," he says, "you'll need a few years of braces after that, but the Bionator is the most important part."

A lot of people come in and out of the room I'm in. They all stare at me and my almost chin. They nod and smile and pat me on the shoulder. Dr. O'Donnell runs back and forth, calling for assistants and instruments. He smiles and smiles and fits me for the Bionator.

A few weeks later Mom drives us all the hours back to Spokane to pick up the Bionator. Dr. O'Donnell is still smiling and smiles even more when the Bionator is in my mouth.

"Perfect," he says.

I don't see what's so perfect because I can't talk at all. The Bionator isn't a normal retainer. It's like two retainers stuck together, one for the top and one for the bottom. There's a plastic piece that fits over the top of my bottom teeth and there's a metal wire going across my front teeth. I can take it out, but I can't talk while it's in. I start to cry. I won't be able to talk for two years because that's how long Dr. O'Donnell says it will take.

"Don't cry, Dorothy. Don't cry," he says.

That's easy for him to say. I hate the Bionator. I don't need a chin. I'll wait. Maybe my chin will come forward on its own. Maybe they can knock me out and break my face and move my chin up. No one needs a chin anyway. I take the huge pink and metal and plastic thing out of my mouth.

"I can't talk," I say. "I can't talk and it hurts awful and it's big and ugly and I don't want it."

"My dear," he says, "you'll learn to talk with it. I've seen it happen every single time. It just takes some getting used to. I promise. You'll have to take it out when you eat or if you're playing sports, but you need to wear it the rest of the time, okay?"

I say okay to Dr. O'Donnell.

In the car on the way home Mom looks at me. She says, "Your father's paying for this, you know. It's expensive and you're very lucky that he's doing it. After all, it's mostly cosmetic."

I can't say anything because the Bionator Dad is paying for stops me.

Eventually, I do learn to talk with it. People think I have gum in my mouth a lot, but I tell them it's only my retainer. I learn to spit it out when I have something important to say that needs to be said quickly. I learn to keep my mouth shut when it's not important. I am more quiet than before and I learn to think before I speak. I develop what Mom calls "caustic wit" and what Lyle calls "smartmouth." When it's hard to talk you have to choose your words carefully in order to make the greatest impact.

I learn to flip the Bionator around in my mouth when I'm bored. I brush it every night. When I leave it on my lunch tray and accidentally throw it away, I learn to dig through the garbage.

Mom keeps harping that it's a three-hundred-and-fifty-dollar retainer and I should be grateful for it. It takes me a while, but I am. Even when Dr. O'Donnell tightens it and I can't eat for days, I'm grateful.

It takes some time to work, but I can already see my chin coming back.

≈ I Ain't an Indian

My face is sore from the Bionator. My mouth feels pulled and stretched in all sorts of ways. I sit in the back of the classroom, hiding behind my hands. I try not to look at anyone and this is easy because they all point away from me. I spit the Bionator into my hand and close my eyes. I pretend I am at a baseball game in Cleveland. I am playing center field.

Someone knocks on the classroom door. The teacher sticks his head out. He sticks his head back inside.

"Dorothy," he says, "there are some people here to see you."

I try to hide the Bionator in my hand as I walk to the door. The metal pushes into my thumb and I am afraid it's going to fly right out into the aisle. I go out into the hall. There are two Indian men standing there. They stare at me. I stare at them. One man is very fat with long black braids and bushy eyebrows. The other man is tall and has his hair tied back into a ponytail. The men look at each other.

"She ain't an Indian," says the fat man.

"She might be an Indian," says the tall man.

"We're from the Bureau of Indian Affairs," says the tall man, "and we're here because they said there may be a new Indian girl. See, there's a few Indians on the Reservation with the same last name as yours."

"Are you an Indian?" asks the fat man.

I think about this question.

I don't know if I'm an Indian or not. Mom said Pop's mom was Iroquois, but we don't know for sure. Pop could be part Indian. He's quiet and smart and tall and has amazing cheekbones that Mom inherited but I didn't.

Am I an Indian?

Mom said her grandmother made flatbread and had long, beautiful dark hair. Mom said it wasn't okay to admit you were part Indian a long time ago. Mom said Pop wouldn't talk about it. Mom said her grandmother had a big old dog who used to follow her around, nip at her heels, and howl when she left the room.

I don't know if I am an Indian.

I have short brown hair and bad teeth and blue eyes. I feel like I could be an Indian. Maybe somewhere, deep inside, there's an Indian part of me. I decide I will tell the men I am an Indian.

They talk before I get a chance to.

"She ain't Indian," says the fat man to the tall man.

"Sorry, honey," says the tall man.

The men leave and I go back to class. I stare at my math book. I stare at the backs of my hands. I stare at my palms and feel something stir in my stomach.

I think I am an Indian, deep inside.

≈ Mom Makes Friends/I Am a Boy

I see the remains when I come home from school.

There are coffee cups with crusted lipstick on the rims and tiny plates sticky with crumbs mashed by too-small forks. When I come home, the house smells like cigarettes and perfume and damp, fat feet in stockings all swollen in their shoes.

When I come home and still don't know anyone, I bring with me the dark cloud that is being ten and horrible looking. When I come home and smell the feet and see the mashed crumbs and the last piece of chocolate cake in its bent box, I get jealous.

Mom has made friends.

I don't know how many there are, but I hear her tell Lyle names like Judy and Vicki. She asks things like, "Lyle, don't you know Vicki's husband Mr. So-and-so?" Lyle says, "He's a rat-bastard piece of dried-up donkey dick." Mom says, "That's what Vicki says." Then she says, "Judy dyed her hair and the dye went and stained the back of her neck and she had to use Windex to get it all off and isn't that so funny ha ha ha ha." Lyle says, "What do I care?"

They've been here, that Vicki and that Judy. They've been here and they've had fun and told stories and puckered up their big fat ugly faces and kissed each other's big fat asses. I hate Vicki and Judy and the cake buying and the too-little forks all lost in their swollen man hands. I throw my books and spill water on the couch and hit Gabe whenever he walks by. That is how angry I am.

I'm angry because Mom has friends and I'm still new. I'm angry she sent me to school on the first day and didn't even go with me and I missed the bus and was late and now I'll never catch up. Everybody knows you can't be late on the first day.

The first day of school, the day I was late and my life was ruined, began very early. I got up and ate my cereal. I put on my best jeans and feathered my hair. I ran and ran and ran all over the house making sure I hadn't lost anything. Gabe toddled after me, carrying his banky and saying, "Go skoo go skoo." He was very excited.

Mom said, "Just walk down the block and down the other block, Dottie, stand in front of the high school, and the bus will pick you up. There will be lots of kids from your school and you can stand with them and surely someone will show you which bus to get on."

I did all that. I walked down the block and down the other block. I stood in front of the high school and waited. I waited and waited, but there was no line and no one my age. I waited and waited and watched some high school boys kick around a ball. They kicked and kicked that ball. I waited and waited.

I decided to walk and stand closer to the road on a big blacktop. Surely the buses would be lining up there soon. I waited and waited. Bells rang. They were ringing and ringing inside the high school. All of a sudden I was on the ground and couldn't breathe. I flopped around on the blacktop trying to breathe. God had struck me down and I was going to die and I hadn't even gotten to school yet.

A woman stuck her face in mine and said, "Breathe, girl. Breathe." I breathed. I wasn't dying. She had an orange face and curlers in her hair. She said, "What are you doing?"

I didn't know.

She said, "Those boys kicked that ball in your stomach and then you fell and started flailing around. Here I am just driving my Impala and there you were, so I stopped and where is it that you are supposed to be?"

I said, "Fifth grade."

"Well," she said, "you're a long way from there. You missed the bus?"

I said, "I'm new."

She said, "Honey, I'll drive you."

The orange-faced lady drove me to school and I was terribly late.

Now, weeks later, Mom's eating cake with strangers and I'm still all alone.

I accidentally met one of Mom's friends. She was late leaving and I came home to find her standing in the living room. I don't know if it was Judy or Vicki, but she was right there. She looked at me and said to Mom, "This must be your son!" And she smiled with her cake-filled mouth. Mom said, "That's my daughter, Dottie."

All I could do was just stand there, wondering what they talked about all day eating their cake and kissing each other's big fat horrible asses.

≈ All of a Sudden, They Were Best Friends

It was weird to watch.

Gabe just stood in the yard with his bowl cut and tiny sweatsuit on. He stared across the lawns to the second house down from ours. He stared and stared and I stared with him.

Standing in the yard of the second house down from ours was a boy the same size as Gabe. He had very short black hair and a plastic rake in his hand.

Gabe started walking to the edge of our lawn. The other boy started to walk over too. They reached the edges of their lawns. They both knew not to go any farther because they're four and not supposed to be walking around all by themselves.

Gabe looked back at me. He wanted to know if he could cross the lawn in the middle. The lawn in the middle belongs to an old couple who take very good care of their yard. They made sure to tell us that when we moved in. It's kind of funny because on either side of them are burnt lawns with cat shit and toys all over.

I nodded at Gabe to go ahead.

I like that he considers me an adult and someone who can tell him what to do. It makes me feel very wise and responsible.

The boy we didn't know looked at Gabe making his way across the rich green lawn. He waved at me. I waved back. He thought I was an adult and someone who could tell him what to do. I waved him on. He toddled toward Gabe.

They met in the middle of the nice lawn and stared at each other. The boy showed Gabe his plastic rake. Gabe took it, looked at it, and then gave it back. They said something to each other.

Gabe walked back to me and the boy walked back home. He took his plastic rake and went into his house. Gabe took my hand.

"That is Zack," he said.

"Oh," I said.

"He is my best friend and we're going to play," said Gabe.

After a while, Mom came out on the lawn and took Gabe's hand. A woman came out holding Zack's hand and the four of them walked into the middle of the nice lawn. The four of them started talking.

Gabe and Zack are now best friends.

It's really weird to watch something like that when you're so much wiser and all alone.

≈ When the Quilts Are Hanging, Just So

The walk home is nothing until the last block.

The final block is when I start to smell the lilac bushes around our house. I wait until the last minute to look into the backyard. There's a clothesline built like a top in our backyard. If the clothesline is spinning in the wind, that means everything is okay.

It's not spinning. The wet weight of Mom's homemade patchwork quilts pulls on it and bends the cheap metal poles. The corners of quilts brush the dirty grass and ants do a slow, desperate crawl onto the weird colors.

When the quilts are hanging just so, I know everyone in the neighborhood knows my shame and I'll be sleeping outside. I know I'll be terrified for days, wondering if it is going to happen to me.

When the quilts hang, just so—just so with the weight of water and poisons—I know my brother has the Worm again.

There's a moment, a silence, the actual stopping of time, where I deny it.

"Goddamnit, Gabriel!"

Lyle storms through the house with his hair sticking straight up, slapping his palms onto the thighs of his Rustler jeans.

"This is it, goddamnit! This is it! That goddamned, fat, filthy bitch next door can ram her cats up her ass!"

Gabriel huddles in a corner with his right hand up his ass, snuffling and sucking his left fingers. I hate it when he has the Worm and there is the howling and the storming around and the stench of what Mom boils and pours all over everything.

I hit him on the head.

"Don't hit your brother! It's enough that he's got the Worm from the filthy cats without you beating him to death!"

Mom boils and pours, pours and boils. She shakes her head at the gracelessness of it. The gracelessness of the Worm. Gabriel lies face down on his sheetless bed, snuffling, crying, "Mom, Mom, my butt itches," until Lyle gets so mad he's forced to go drink at the tavern. And the utmost shame of it, Gabriel with a clear piece of tape sticking out of his bare ass so the doctor can see the Worm for certain and for certain give him the right medicine.

"It's enough," says Mom over the steam of the boil, "that he has the snuffling and the itch and the finger sucking without the shame of the tape in his ass." She pulls it free from him and he howls with the burn. "It itches," he weeps. "It hurts." I hit him on the head. We boil the house in the stench of the poison and check our asses carefully.

Mom has to go next door and tell Zack's mom about the Worm. They both know if one of the boys has the Worm, the other one probably does too.

When Mom comes back into the house, I go into the yard. I can hear the screaming at Zack's house.

The next week Gabriel and Zack have lice.

≈ Night Tracks and the Gum on Gabe's Neck

It's Friday night and the time for *Night Tracks* when ZZ Top and Journey and the Eurythmics come into the basement on the nineteen-inch black-and-white television and I dream about being a rock star.

One time I danced to Stevie Wonder until my pants split and Mom howled as I hissed at her through my retainer, "Don't laugh, don't laugh." I swore one day I would be a rock star and a beautiful dancer like in *Fame*.

I have a plastic cup full of Italian dressing and many many carrots and I dip them into the cup and eat them until the oil from the dressing soaks my chin. In the damp basement, I wait to be famous and beautiful. Gabe follows me and sleeps in his baseball pajamas on the far end of the couch. He smells like outside and pee and sugar and he just wants to be near me.

We snuggle under Mom's homemade quilts and wait.

Mom usually comes home from the Moose Lodge at four A.M. and tells us to go to bed. I'm always angry at four in the morning because I am awake and still in the basement and not a rock star at all and still ugly. Gabe stays awake with me one night. He stays awake until the end. The night Gabe stays awake happens to be the same night he has a wad of bubble gum on the back of his neck. It has been there for weeks and weeks and it is starting to turn gray. It is a very tender spot on the back of his neck and it drives me crazy. I have been trying to convince Mom and Lyle to take care of it.

"Pull it off," I said to Mom.

"It'll hurt him," she said.

"Pull it off," I said to Lyle.

"Leave him alone," he said.

"Gabe, why don't you pull it off?" I asked.

"It hurts it hurts," he said.

I ask him again while he's awake and in love with being up so late. I ask him while he feels cool and smart and famous.

"Gabe, it's three-thirty in the morning and we're watching *Night Tracks* and aren't we just the best of friends?" I ask.

"Yes, we are."

"And how is that gum? That gum on your neck? Is it ugly? It is, isn't it? And is it lousy and terrible in all sorts of ways?" I ask.

"It is," he says.

"So, because we're the best of friends and I love you so and you trust me so, why don't I take it off you?" I ask.

"Oh no," he says. "It'll hurt."

"No, it won't!"

"No?"

"Not at all," I say.

Gabe lays his head into my hands at three-thirty in the morning in front of *Night Tracks* and I rip the gray-pink wad from the back of his neck and there is a second of blissful peace until he howls howls howls. It is a dark dark night this night. Lyle rushes out of his room and Mom comes home and *Night Tracks* is ruined and I'll never be a rock star after all this.

They tell me Gabe is sensitive and I am terrible and that's how it is.

≈ The Cat Lady

I don't want to do it. Mom says she'll give me five dollars to do it and I don't care. Mom says she'll order pizza and I don't care. There is no way I am going into the Cat Lady's house and no way in hell I'll feed those cats for her. I don't care where she went or why. I don't care who died or what was wrong. I don't care why Mom agreed to this or how bad she feels for the Cat Lady.

The cats are a plague like the locusts from thousands of years ago. The cats are like the rats in big cities and those huge flying roaches they had where we lived before. There isn't a day that goes by without someone throwing one of the Cat Lady's cats out of their house, off the porch, or out of their car. The universe and the entire neighborhood are on my side. If those cats starved, no one would care except the Cat Lady and no one likes her anyway.

No one would care except Gabe.

"Dottie! Dottie!" he cries. "The kittens will be hungry! The mommy cats will be hungry! Oh, Dottie! Please feed them!"

Mom sees me weakening. Gabe sees me weakening. He begins to sob for real. He cries and collapses and holds on to my leg and snots all over his chin. I have to go in. I have to feed the cats. I take the keys from Mom's hand and start the walk next door.

There is a tangle of old rose bushes and clumps of dying lilac bushes separating our houses. My skin crawls with the thought of all the cats in those bushes. I swear I hear mewing and scratching and all sorts of evil howling coming from the piles of dead brush.

I face the sidewalk leading to her door. It is littered with shiny cat toys and hardened pieces of shit and there are furballs like tiny tumbleweeds rolling slow in the early evening. I can make out the shadows of kittens through the windows of the house. I can smell them.

"Dottie!"

I am terrified and turn to see Gabe peeking from behind the brush.

"Dottie," he hisses, "take me too! I wanna see all the kittens!"

I say, "Mom said you can't because of the Worm and the pain and shame and burn of it. Mom says she can't stand the howling. Besides, Lyle will kill me."

He says, "I won't touch nothin' inside. Not one kitten. Please?"

I nod because I'm afraid to go in alone. The cats know him. Maybe it'll be okay if he's there. Maybe they won't attack. Maybe they'll just stare and swish their tails and purr.

We stand on the porch and I open the screen door. There is a rustling. Gabe squeezes my hand. I turn the key and the door creaks open. I inhale a mouthful of fur and choke. Gabe stops the furry stream of kittens boiling out the door with his chubby hands. I kick wildly and flip them back inside with my sneaker. I slam the door. Gabe looks up at me and his eyes are huge.

He says, "Kitties."

He says this in a hushed voice and reaches for my hand. I feel nauseated. I kneel down and look at Gabe.

I say, "Gabe, it's just one day. They won't starve. I swear. I swear for real. Not like the time I pulled the gum off your neck and it hurt when I said it wouldn't. Okay? I swear they won't starve."

He looks at me and squints. He looks at the door and then back to me.

He says, "Too many kitties."

He keeps hold of my hand and leads me down the stairs.

≈ A Whole New World

Sometimes you know things without ever having to think too hard about them. Sometimes there's just something you know is right and no one can shake it. This is the way I feel about the saxophone and I think it's driving everyone crazy.

"Please!" I yell.

"What about the flute?" asks Mom.

"A sax, Mom. I need an alto sax," I say.

"A flute is small and quiet and cheap," says Mom.

"Charlie's mom never said that to him. Charlie Parker, Mom! Can you imagine Bird with a flute? Can you? Can you? What about Coltrane?" I ask.

"What about him?" she asks.

"Coltrane on a flute? No way, Mom. No way," I say.

"We'll see what your Uncle Mick can do," she says. "Okay? I'm not promising anything."

"It's your fault anyway," I say. "They were your records I listened to."

"Fine, Dorothy," she says. "Enough already."

Uncle Mick isn't really my uncle. He lives in Detroit and is an old friend of Mom's. Once in a while she'll get a call from him and she'll sit for an hour on the kitchen floor laughing while she talks to him. Uncle Mick is a musician and works in one of Detroit's oldest music stores. He complains the only customers they get are teenaged boys who want to play electric guitar. He's disgusted most of the time.

Mom says, "I just hope I can reach him before he goes Underground."

The last time Mom talked to Uncle Mick he warned her he was taking computer classes and that soon he would have it all figured out. He wants to use his new skills to literally disappear from the face of the earth. He thinks he can do this if he learns about how the system works. Mom asked him what system he was talking about and all he said was, "You know, the System."

I wait and wait for Uncle Mick to come through for me. I know in my heart he will because we both have musician's souls and a love of Charlie Parker. When I call Dad to tell him about the sax he's very excited. He tells me the sax is the coolest instrument in the world and he knows I will be a powerful musician. He also says I shouldn't worry about Uncle Mick coming through for me. He says Uncle Mick has not gone Underground yet and he'll be sure to ship me the finest saxophone they have in Detroit. Mom tells him not to get me worked up because I'm being very difficult.

One day the sax shows up. There's a huge box just sitting in the living room when I come home. When I open the box, there's so much stuffing and padding that the living room gets covered. Gabe giggles and slides through it, then asks me if he can have the big box when I'm done with it. I am feeling generous and I say he can.

I finally unearth the sax case and lay it on the floor. There's a moment where I'm so nervous my hands are shaking and I have to wait for a minute. Gabe tips the big box over and climbs into the back of it. He rattles around in the box and the box shifts with his movement. He reminds me of a cat in a paper bag.

"Play music, Dottie," he says from inside the box. "Play music!"

I open the case. The inside lining is plush and deep red. The sax is gold and shiny. It is the most beautiful saxophone I have ever seen and it's all mine. Mom says I have to send Uncle Mick a thank-you note and I tell her I will.

I know this is the start of something very powerful and the beginning of a whole new world.

≈ Return to Sender

Dear Uncle Mick: I want to thank you for the powerful gold saxophone in the black case with the red velour all around it. It is beautiful.

I want you to know I am not a teenaged boy and all worried with guitars and whiskey drinking and music videos. I want to be like Charlie Parker and maybe sing some Billie Holiday blues songs in a bar, but I will only drink beer and fight if I have to.

I will be the finest saxophone player you have ever heard and if you want to hear me come over any time because our band plays once in a while for the school and Mom will tell you when.

Uncle Mick I want to thank you so much and I hope the government doesn't bother you anymore. I love you.

This is the letter I write to Uncle Mick. Mom says it is a fine letter and very professional.

The letter comes back marked "Return to Sender: Address Unknown." I am upset and discouraged. Mom says Mick must have gone Underground.

"It's still a fine letter, Dorothy," she says. "It's the finest letter I have ever read."

I wonder where Uncle Mick is. I imagine him in a cave, eating bread and playing the bongos.

I fold up the letter and put it in my T-shirt drawer. I save it just in case. You never know when someone will come out from Underground.

11 Years Old

Dorothy, Jazz Musician

≈ Family Trips

Missy turns her underwear inside out when they are dirty, when she's visiting her father, the same man I call Lyle. We watch the ZZ Top "She's Got Legs" video. We sit in the basement and Missy eats Cheez Doodles and sighs with boredom.

Missy says she has perfect hair, with curling-iron sausages on the sides with dark roots at the top. When she has her period, she'll lie down and ask for flat Coca-Cola and *Cosmopolitan* magazines. I swear I will never be that way. I want to laugh at her. I want to make fun of her. She can't catch a baseball and she can't remember what she was told to do. Missy asks me why I look like a boy and I tell her it's because I am one.

Her boyfriend from back home calls her. I write the conversation down. I keep track of what she says, like, "Oh, you don't say" and "If I can sneak out when I get home" and "I won't do what Brandi does 'cause I ain't no slut like her."

I'm always the one who's supposed to put away the laundry and wash dishes because she can't because her pains are here again and it makes me mad. Missy will eventually have to go back to her Aunt Mandy.

When I can't sleep, Missy says I'm completely nuts. She asks me why my father left and says he did it because I'm just crazy and don't I see how that must be true? She says, "It's as plain as the nose on my face." I tell her that she doesn't live with her dad or her mom. I get angry and say she's way worse off than I am. I ask her what was so wrong with her that both her parents left her with Aunt Mandy, who lives far away? She cries and screams and scratches. Mom buys her things when she gets hysterical and I have to put Band-Aids on, go to the park, and shoot foul shots until I calm down.

Mom had her hands up and Lyle had his hands up too. They yelled until Mom screamed and Gabe cowered with me. Missy says these things happen because her dad doesn't like me to be around all the time. Missy reminds me that she's his daughter and just because I live with them doesn't mean anything. She says I better not get any funny ideas.

I tell her she can have her stupid dad because I have my own and he's coming for me as soon as he can. I tell her my dad doesn't drink and swear and come home screaming with his fist in the air. I tell her my dad is rich and kind and loves me so.

She says, "If that's true, why are you all alone?"

I don't have an answer for this, so I run at her yelling and she pounds me into the ground because she's mean and fat and ugly and very old at sixteen. I hate when she visits. They pull out the photo album when she's here. They show pictures of their summer travels in the van.

When I am sent to Cleveland and Detroit for the summer, Missy, Gabe, Mom, and Lyle do things together. They travel and take vacations. There are a lot of pictures with the four of them all smiling together and I am not in a single one.

"This is when we went to Yellowstone," says Lyle.

"Yellowstone!" yells Gabe.

"Dad, do you have that picture of me by Old Faithful?" asks Missy, leering at me.

"Faithful!" says Gabe.

"Dottie, why don't you get us a beer?" says Mom.

"I need an RC," says Missy.

"Juice!" says Gabe.

So I go get the beers for Mom and Lyle and the juice for Gabe, but I don't get the RC. Missy bitches and bitches until Mom takes me into the kitchen to talk.

"Dottie, your sister is visiting. Can't you be nice to her?"

Before I can stop it, it's already out of my mouth.

"Fuck her! She's not my sister!"

This is the first bad word I've ever said in front of Mom and, besides "nigger," Mom considers it the worst word ever. She slaps me across the face.

I run out the door and away from them. I run and run until I'm calm and my chest is heaving. I run to the sand hill and climb it. It's three stories high. I sit on top of the sand hill while my leg muscles burn and twitch and my palms itch for a basketball to hold. I want to throw something or shoot something or hit someone.

I start to cry and I can't stop. I do this until I'm dry-heaving with sand all over my face. Right before I stop crying, I think of Pop and Nana and Grandma and Grandpa. I think about how far away they are and I start crying all over again. The sun sets and I get home in time to hear Lyle saying, "Remember the Grand Tetons?"

Gabe says, "Tetons!"
Mom says, "What do you want for dinner, Missy?"

≈ Uncle Jack

I've never seen Uncle Jack sleep.

I have seen the man who is Uncle Jack once and one time only for almost three entire days. He never slept, never lay down, never closed his eyes even once, rarely sat, and I whispered to Gabe that he never even blinked. Gabe cried over the not blinking because even the cats whose shit he liked to play with had eyes that closed once in a while.

At three in the morning Mom shook me, hissing, "It's Jack! It's Jack, your uncle. Your great-uncle from the East and he's here. So wake up and eat." I thought this Jack must be a great great man to arrive at three in the morning and he must be a wonderful man if he not only woke her but inspired her to cook a spaghetti dinner at such an hour. I went to see my Great-Uncle Jack in my pajamas, following the smell of sausage, tomatoes, and peppers.

Gabe was asleep in his plate, footed pajamas on and spaghetti in his bowl cut.

The blue-flanneled back of Great-Uncle Jack was straight and his body was quaking. His fork cut the air on his left, the knife the air on his right. His thick, red, rolled neck sweated and shivered and I was aware of a booming. A great booming came from Great-Uncle Jack. This was his voice.

I stood rooted to see if the booming would stop, and it didn't. I walked to the fork side of his sweaty quaking and stood behind the sleeping, spaghetti-covered head of my brother. Great-Uncle Jack did not stop his story but swung his eyes at me and pointed the boom of his voice at my face.

I stared into the red, wet face of Great-Uncle Jack and was taken by the huge gray tufts of eyebrow and the wild kindness in his eyes.

Great-Uncle Jack was a trucker.

"A real goddamned Teamster," he said.

"There's two things your Great-Uncle Jack can do," Mom said. "That's eat and tell a story."

Uncle Jack told stories for three days and never slept. He told stories that Gabe and I didn't really understand. He told stories that made Mom howl and slap her leg. Uncle Jack told stories with words like "counterfeit," "blue balls," "forty-five," and "amphetamines" in them.

Then he slipped away in the middle of the night and I could hear his truck barrel down our quiet street.

I was awful jealous of his freedom and his powerful voice.

≈ Perfect Order, Physical Education, Youth, and Exercise (POPEYE)

There are no Indian girls, a lot of whispering, and people keep looking at me funny. I couldn't have done anything wrong yet because tryouts haven't even started. I feel stupid and uncomfortable because I wore the wrong thing. I have on cutoff sweatpants, basketball shoes, and one of Lyle's T-shirts that says, "Don't be a bass-hole! Fish the Columbia River safely!" All the other girls have matching outfits. I didn't realize it was that kind of thing.

Most of the popular girls are here and they smile and flirt with Mr. Stone, our instructor. Mr. Stone is big and blond and his skin is bright red. He talks to the popular girls and when he does, he squeezes their shoulders. They giggle and say, "Oh, Mr. Stone! You're so funny!" I thought this was just a gymnastics team before I showed up. I thought POPEYE would be fun and we'd get to go places and compete. It turned out to be not like that at all.

There's a tall, blond girl in the corner and she keeps staring at me. She's very pretty, but her clothes are as bad as mine. I smile at her because I think she may be able to explain some things to me. She walks over and says her name is Beth. She's in the same grade as me, but we have different homeroom teachers. She tells me this is the third year she's tried out and that she never got in before and she knows she won't this year either. I ask her why she keeps trying out. She tells me she's doing it because once you get in, you're automatically popular. I think she's a complete idiot, but I don't say anything. I feel sort of bad for her regardless. She asks me why I'm trying out and I tell her it's because I try to stay out of my house as much as possible.

Beth tells me she's a Mormon and she'd be in so much trouble if her dad ever caught her trying out. She says she knows he'd let her join if she ever was accepted, but that he wouldn't let her try out. Beth says she's just doing this without his permission because she knows he'd really give her permission if he only understood. I think Beth is very confusing and her dad is an asshole if he thinks turning cartwheels pisses God off, but I don't say anything.

Beth and I stand in line together. I can tell she knows we don't have much in common but that we have come together in the face of something larger. Mr. Stone has set up a long line of blue mats and we are all supposed to have a routine we do. Every girl goes separately and tumbles down the mat. Some of them can't even do a back walkover or even a decent cartwheel. Mr. Stone stands at the end of the long line of blue mats and claps and whistles and squeezes shoulders when they're done. Most of these popular girls are really lousy. It's getting kind of gross when Beth begins to whisper to me.

She says, "Everyone knows Mr. Stone is a pervert. Everyone knows, even the school itself. He's had intercourse with those two girls over there. I've even heard they all three had intercourse together and you know that means they're all going to Hell. When you get accepted into POPEYE your life changes. Everybody loves you and all you have to do is tumble. There's no competition with any other school, Dorothy. I don't know where you got that, but there are shows. Everyone, even boys, comes to the shows. Mr. Stone plays music and all the girls tumble in matching outfits. He makes up the routines and it's beautiful."

I am tempted to run out the door and all the way home, but it's almost my turn. I can't be seen running away or I'll never hear the end of it. Beth goes before me and she's just terrible. She has absolutely no form and no skills at all. When she's done, her face is all red and she gets a squeeze on the shoulder from the pervert at the end of the long line of blue mats.

I start my routine with a cartwheel that leads into a round-off and then into a back walkover. I do really well because I'm not nervous at all. I know when I make the team I'll just quit and show all those stupid, popular girls just what I think of them. When I'm done I give Pervert Stone a tough look and I move away from him so he doesn't dare squeeze my shoulder. Beth pouts when I am done and tells me she'll see me Monday at the bulletin board where Mr. Stone will post the list of who made the team.

Monday comes and Beth and I aren't on the list. This is the third rejection Beth has gotten from Pervert Stone. It is my first and last. I tell her to shrug it off because they're all a bunch of assholes anyway. I tell her there are plenty of sports to try out for. She says she won't have time. I ask her why. She says she's going to be very busy practicing for next year's try-outs.

≈ Cut Time

"Dorothy," says Mr. Smith, "I need you to play this."

"That's okay," I say. "You just go ahead and have someone else do it."

"It's cut time and in B flat," he says. "This should be easy for you."

What no one knows is that I can't read music. I am first-chair saxophone, but I can't read music at all. I feel like the jazz musician part of my soul is all dried up and not paying attention. Mr. Smith thinks he's taught me, but he hasn't. He thinks I am the best saxophone player ever, but that's only because he thinks I can read music. He doesn't know I just listen to everyone else and then play the music. I mean, I can read the notes on the page. I can do that. I just can't read the actual music. I don't know what the notes are supposed to sound like all together.

Mr. Smith looks at me.

"Dorothy," he says, "this is a new piece of music and I think you would be the best person to show the class how to play it. Yes?"

"No, sir," I say.

"Martin," he says, "could you show us how this piece goes?"

Martin is Zack's brother. Zack and Gabe like to watch Martin practice his scales in the backyard. He usually screams at them to leave him alone because he's embarrassed of the flute.

Martin blows on his stupid, stinky flute and we all listen. I get the idea of the piece and feel more comfortable. I know how it is supposed to go. I feel the beat of it and understand how all the notes fit in. When we all play it, Mr. Smith stops us.

"Dorothy," he says, "I want you to play this."

I play the piece and Mr. Smith smiles.

"Very good," he says. "Very, very good."

After class Mr. Smith takes me aside. Everyone is gone and it's just me and him, staring at each other. Mr. Smith smiles and puts a piece of music in front of me.

"I want you to play this," he says.

"I can't," I say. "I'm very late for class."

"It's okay," he says. "I'll write you a pass."

Mr. Smith smiles.

"I really shouldn't be late, sir," I say.

"The piece goes a little like this," he says. "Dum da da dee dum da da dee ba dah ba dee dah dee dah dah dee ba ba."

I play the music and he smiles.

"You can't read the music, can you, Dorothy?" he asks.

"No, sir," I say.

"You're the best player I have," he says.

"Thank you, sir," I say.

"I'm going to make you better," he says.

"Better?" I ask.

"Oh yes," he says, "can you imagine? Just think of it."

"Yes, sir," I say.

"Dorothy?" he asks.

"Yes, sir?" I say.

"Dream big," he says.

I do dream. I stay up late at night thinking of all the dreams that can be. I think of Charlie Parker and John Coltrane and Miles Davis. I think of blue lights and gray smoke and red wine spilling onto the floor. I think of Billie Holiday with that white flower in her hair. I want to be wonderful. I know I will be wonderful. Mr. Smith believes in me and the power and the splendor of the saxophone.

≈ Zack on the Roof, a Bee Sting, and the Runaway Van

I blame Zack for the bee sting. The bee sting happened last that day, after Zack got stuck on the roof and the van was stolen.

Gabe and Zack had a plan, which was to drive Lyle's van. They had this plan between themselves being all of four and boys and dirty from the neighbor lady's cats and all sorts of general trouble.

It all starts when Lyle looks outside and yells, "Where's the van? My van! Where is it, damnit!"

A man comes to the door while Lyle is storming through the house yelling about the missing van.

A man comes and says, "Your van is down the street, so there's no real trouble." He says, "I saw the two of them, the little ones, running from the van and I put it in park." He says, "I watched them run and try to hide."

Lyle storms out with his hair sticking up and sees the van at the end of the block, but then there's a loud howl and we look over toward the howl and there's Zack. Zack's face is beet red and he's clutching the roof of his house.

Mom screams, "Gabriel!"

And Lyle screams, "Gabriel, damnit!"

And I stand there, happy. Gabe comes from around the corner, knees shaking and his hands covering his face.

"Don't look at me! Don't look at me!" he says.

Gabe thinks if he can't see you, you can't see him. Zack keeps screaming until his dad comes out. His dad tries to climb on the roof and gets stuck too. Gabe keeps hiding behind his hands. Lyle goes to the neighbor's house, stares up at Zack's dad, and says, "They drove my van." And Zack's dad says, "I'm stuck on the roof. Do you have a ladder?"

While I'm walking across the lawn to Zack's house to make fun of him, I step on a bee. It is terrible how much it hurts and I look at my foot and the bee is still attached to the stinger. When the bee crawls away from its own ass, its guts come out and I'm staring at this stupid bee and its guts and I start screaming because it's on my foot.

Mom says, "That's what you get for trying to gloat."

The next day Zack comes to play and he's shaved off his eyebrows. When he waggles what used to be his eyebrows, only his brow meat goes up and down. Mom laughs and says, "It must be penance for his sin of driving the van." I think it's only because he's small and dumb. He gets Gabe and they go to play with the filthy cats next door.

I can't do anything at all because my foot is swollen. The boys stay out of my way because whenever they come too close, I swat at them.

⁓ Opium

Mom has bought herself Opium perfume. She holds it up and stares at it. We both stare at it. It is very expensive and very difficult to come by. She unscrews the cap and takes a big sniff. We watch her. She smiles and sighs. This is her favorite perfume.

"No one touch this," she says.

"Oh no," says Gabe.

"No way," I say.

I decide I will be beautiful. I decide someone will fall in love with me. I wear my best Levi's. I blow my hair dry. I draw on my blue eyeliner. I lick my lips until they look shiny. Something is missing. I sneak downstairs and stare at the Opium perfume sitting on Mom's bedside table. Just a little, I think. I'm nervous because what I'm doing is very wrong. My hands shake and I spill the perfume on my pants. I run away. I run to the bathroom and splash water on the stain. I run to my room and look for pants. I run back to the bathroom and splash more water on the stain. I run back to my room. I look at my watch. I will miss the bus. This is my day to be beautiful and I'm about to miss the bus. I look around for different pants. There are none as perfect as the ones I have on. While I walk toward the bus I assure myself the perfume will dry up and disappear.

On the bus someone makes a comment about the smell.

"Smells like a perfume factory," says someone.

I ignore it. I hunch down into my coat. I breathe through my mouth. I make it to homeroom, which is band.

I sit next to Martin. He plays the flute. Every day at band practice I have to smell Martin's stinky flute breath. He blows it right into my face. Mixed with the stink of Martin's flute breath is Mom's Opium perfume. I start to feel nauseated. All around me people are waving their hands in front of their faces. They start talking about the smell. They talk about perfume and how terrible it is. The band teacher, Mr. Smith, asks us what is going on. Someone tells him it stinks like perfume in the flute and saxophone rows and it's making everyone sick.

He says, "Did Mozart stop for stink?"

We say, "No, sir!"

"Then we won't stop," he says.

Martin looks at me. I look at Martin.

"It's you," he whispers.

"No, it's not," I say.

"Mr. Smith," he hollers, "it's Dorothy. Dorothy smells."

"Do you smell like perfume, Dorothy?" asks Mr. Smith.

"I may, sir," I say.

"Sit in the back, Dorothy," says Mr. Smith.

I sit in the back and play my saxophone and wish I were playing blues in an old, smoky club where no one could smell me trying to be beautiful.

⁓ There's a Girl Who Smokes

She's so beautiful.

I see her leaning against the brick of the junior high in her ripped jeans. She's smoking a cigarette and staring at her sneakers. I don't know what to feel. I want to know her. I've heard about her. Beth told me there was a new girl who was older and smoked. Beth said this new girl came from Coeur d'Alene. The name of the town was sweet in my mouth. It felt French. She looked French, or at least how I imagined French girls to look. She looked messy, with her dark brown hair in curls around her face. She looked like she didn't give a shit. I think this must be the new, older girl. She is wonderful.

I stand there just staring at her. I forget I am staring at her. She is that beautiful.

"What the fuck are you looking at?" she says.

I don't know what to say.

"You're going to miss your bus," I say.

"I don't take the bus, stupid," she says.

"Oh," I say.

She says, "You just missed your bus."

I turn to see the buses pulling away. I'm stuck and look like an idiot. Now I have to walk home.

"I'm Shayla," she says.

"Dorothy," I say.

"Dorothy," she says, "have you ever gotten drunk?"

I've never gotten drunk but I don't want to tell her this. I think maybe I should tell her I drink all the time. I think I should tell her I drink as much as Lyle and make myself things like Fuzzy Navels and vodka tonics. I think she will see right through this, being French and all.

"No," I say, "I've never been drunk before."

"Would you like to get drunk with me?" she laughs.

"Okay," I say.

We go to Shayla's apartment and no one's there. I ask where her mom is and she says her mom's probably getting laid. I ask where her dad is and Shayla says she doesn't know.

She pours me a glass of something clear with a lot of ice. I try to sip it, but it hurts to try and swallow. Shayla opens a beer for me. She tells me to sip a little and then to drink some beer. I do and it gets easier to swallow. I start to feel warm.

Shayla's apartment is small and it's a mess. Things are still in boxes and the sink is full of dirty dishes. Shayla doesn't answer any of my questions. She likes to talk about people in school instead. We talk and talk, but I stop drinking. Shayla keeps drinking and we end up in her room. She falls asleep on her bed. I decide to go home because it's a long walk and I have to get started.

I cover her up and she whispers, "I like you, Dottie. I like you."

∼ Someone's Special

Mom's made pizza because it's my favorite, but I can't eat because she keeps smiling at me. I keep looking into my slice and pushing the pepperoni into the cheese. I watch it bounce back up and I push it again. Lyle tells me to stop pushing the pepperoni. I want to tell him to stop drinking beer. He finishes his fourth can and gets up for another. Mom tells him to wait because she has an announcement. She looks at me again. I want to beg her to shut up and to not announce this at the table when Lyle needs a beer. Gabe looks up from his stack of pepperoni. He has piled the pepperoni into a stack because it scares him. He's asked me what pepperoni is before and I had to lie and tell him it came from an Australian cow. He never believed me.

"Dorothy is special!" says Mom.

Gabe claps and smiles because he thinks I'm very special.

"What the hell are you talking about?" asks Lyle.

"She was tested this week and she did so well that they're putting her into a special class." Mom smiles.

"Oh, I thought you meant helmet-and-short-bus special," says Lyle.

He leaves the table for more beer and never comes back.

"I am so proud of you," says Mom.

"Thanks, Mom," I say.

Gabe starts crying, gets up, waddles over to Mom, and sits on her lap.

"What's wrong, honey?" she asks.

"I'm special too," he cries.

"Yes, you are!" she says and tickles him until he starts laughing.

I had to call Dad and tell him I was going to be in the gifted program. He talked and talked and asked me what kind of tests I had to take. I told him and he said it was great I was gifted. He said he always knew it. He and Mom got on the phone and talked for an hour. When she got off the phone she came over and ruffled my hair.

The class I have to take meets once a week and we have to do a lot of work. The class is mostly boys and I don't like a lot of them. Fat Eddie sits at our one computer all day and hogs it. This pisses Robbie off because Robbie is trying to chart some sort of astral graph and he needs the computer. I don't go near the computer at all because it doesn't seem very interesting to me. Robbie says computers are the future, but I don't see how they could be.

I meet Taylor, who seems nice, but he spends most of his time drawing. One day we had to go around and say who our favorite singer was. Stupid Taylor said Barbra Streisand was his favorite and everybody laughed at him. I was smart and lied when I said Mötley Crüe. I tried to talk to Taylor after the Barbra thing, but he ignored me mostly. I did get him to show me his drawings. They were of spaceships, aliens, and clothes. He told me he wanted to be a fashion designer and live in the Big Apple. I told him he should never tell anyone that. He agreed but said he felt he could trust me with the information.

When Mom meets our teacher, Mrs. Modlin, she gets all dressed up and even leaves Gabe at his friend's house. She says Gabe doesn't understand the term "gifted" and that it makes him feel sad because he's not old enough to be gifted yet. Mom and Mrs. Modlin talk for a long time. Mrs. Modlin says it's tough to be gifted in such a poor school with such limited resources. Mom nods. Mrs. Modlin says it's so nice to have another girl in the class. She says it's sad because most girls my age are only interested in boys and clothes and don't work nearly as hard as I do on their minds. Mom nods again.

When we leave Mom asks me what I think of Mrs. Modlin. I tell Mom Mrs. Modlin is really nice and I really like her because she looks like Wonder Woman.

≈ Shayla's House

Shayla's mom has moved in with her boyfriend, Jared. They have a house now. Shayla thinks this is cool.

"Dottie, this is an actual house," she smiles. "It has a yard."

I'm happy for Shayla, but I can't help wondering why she thinks this is so good. I know what it's like when you have a mom with boyfriends. I know what the boyfriends are like. I know what it feels like to have a house and then another house and then another. I look at Shayla and she's so much older than me. I know she isn't, but she acts like she is. I feel like I'm falling in love with her. I want to make her life better for her, but she won't let me.

If she's been drinking, she'll let me be close to her. We'll talk and kiss and hug and she'll even tell me what's bothering her. When she isn't drinking, she yells at me to be more like a girl. She tells me to grow my hair and to wear skirts and eyeliner. We don't ever talk about what we do. I wouldn't know what to say anyway. I know I could say I love her dark brown eyes and her freckles. I know I could say I love her crooked teeth and how she laughs out of the side of her mouth. I could say all of these things, but I know I won't.

I try to be more like a boy.

I wear different clothes and don't talk a lot. I bring her things and buy her lunch. I take her to movies. I never bring up anything that would make her uncomfortable. I talk to her mom and am really nice to Jared. He and I talk about baseball.

The more I'm around, the more Shayla's mean to me. I don't know what to do because there are those times when we lie out under the stars on a quilt and just drink beer and talk.

We're okay in the dark.

≈ Port Townsend

I have to go to Port Townsend. My stupid gifted class got accepted to a stupid competition and we have to drive for six hours. My mom says, "Be respectful and ask for nothing and don't be ashamed of where you come from."

We are staying in the same place where they filmed a Hollywood movie and the curtains are still up. This is what they keep telling us: "Don't pull on the curtains, children! Don't you ever want to be asked back?" And we say, "Oh yes, we do." And we touch the velvet of the curtains when they turn their backs, wondering if we are famous.

I pick up seaweed and run with it because it feels slimy like something from a monster far under the water. Taylor just stands by the water and it makes me think he must be very thoughtful.

It was after dinner and I was cold when Mrs. Modlin said, "Here, take my sweater" and I did because you have to when they tell you to do something. I have been cold for days and so I put on the dark green sweater. Mrs. Modlin says, "Look at how blue her eyes are," and I look for the pretty blue eyes, but they're all looking at me. So I lower my head into my peas while the old women sitting with us exclaim over my eyes. They meant my eyes were pretty and I am embarrassed because a boy shouldn't be pretty. Embarrassed because no one ever said that.

There's no reason for me to be able to sleep any better in Port Townsend than at home. We spend all day answering questions and thinking and being artistic. After dinner and all of it, I am so tired I can't sleep. I can't even lie down. I end up thinking things that make it hard for me to breathe. I think Mom and Lyle have moved without me. I think they've packed up everything and left me a note saying they couldn't wait even one more day.

When I can't sleep, I wake Taylor up. We walk to the water and we talk. Taylor laughs when a wave gets me. We talk about basketball and what happens when the world kills all of the rain forests and we run out of oxygen. That's why we're there, to figure out answers.

I stay up all night and it's very early in the morning when I decide to go back to the water. The mist and fog are everywhere. It falls on me, wraps around me, and I dream and dream and walk and walk until I don't know where I am. Everything is gray and cold and all I can hear is the ocean lapping up onto the brown rocks. I start to panic because I don't know if I'll make it back to find out if we won the competition. They're going to announce it after breakfast and here I am all lost on a peninsula. I run and run and get nowhere.

I see two nuns with their arms around each other's waists and they're laughing. I want to scream to these nuns that I'm lost, but I can't. My voice doesn't work and I'm afraid of nuns all of a sudden. I'm afraid of everything all of a sudden.

I sit in the wet grass and put my stupid face into my stupid hands. I cry because I'm supposed to be gifted, but I'm just lost and stupid and all alone. I'm so angry I'm crying like a baby that I bite my lip to try and stop. My stupid lip starts bleeding and I cry some more. I throw myself back on the grass and stare up into the gray sky and listen to the water. I listen to the rocks. I listen to the fog. Everything is very loud and quiet at the same time. I think about the rain forests and how I can't really care about them right now. I don't care about how to stop all the pollution because it's not my fault anyway. We were supposed to read up on all the rain forest stuff before we came here and then we were supposed to fix the stupid problem, win the dumb contest, and save the world. All I did was just get lost. I lie on my back and stretch out my arms. I want to fly. I just want to fly up into the fog.

Something warm touches my hand and I sit up. There's an old gray and brown dog sitting next to me. The dog stares at me. I stare at the dog. I smile at the old dog and the dog comes closer and licks my face. I start to think I could just stay with the dog in the wet grass until I die and that would be fine. I pet the dog and he gets up and moves away. I watch him walk away, but he stops and looks back at me. He stares and stares at me. I stand up and follow him. I follow him for a while until he starts running toward a pier.

The pier goes far out into the water and the fog rolls over it. At the end of the pier is one of the tallest men I have ever seen. He's so tall that I can tell he's tall from far away. He has long black hair and he's fishing. I think maybe I can call to this man and ask him for directions, but he looks over at me before I can even say anything. I squint and wave at him. He laughs very loudly and it echoes down the pier, into the fog and right into my ear. He points to his right and gestures for me to go over the hill. I point to the hill and he nods and laughs some more. The old dog is next to him. The dog barks. I wave good-bye and climb the hill. Right in front of me is the place where we're staying. I must have gone in a complete circle. I want to thank the man, but I'm late.

We find out that we lost the competition. Mrs. Modlin says we did well, fourth place. She says we're young and not to worry. Mrs. Modlin says we should be thankful for the experience because it was grand and Hollywood was here. Taylor looks at me and I know he's thinking it's my fault we lost. I was supposed to come up with all the original answers. I know he's thinking, Dottie, it was up to you all along to be original.

I wanted to be original and win. I wanted to find the perfect answer for what is the best way to deal with what is called pollution. Mrs. Modlin says the winning team was older and just wait, who knows where we will all be when we are older. When she is finished all I can think is that I want to take a nap for a long long time. Instead we take the ferry to Seattle and eat stew with octopus arms in it and I wish I could have a burger instead. Mrs. Modlin says we are too smart to eat red meat. Robbie says, "Why do we have to eat this ass-food just 'cause we're smart? I wish I was dumb like in fifth grade."

I buy my little brother a top in Chinatown and some incense for Mom because it smells like a faraway place. I don't know what to get Lyle so I get him a small iron dragon that you're supposed to burn incense in. The smoke comes out of the dragon's nose. Mrs. Modlin asks what I'm getting for myself, but I'm out of money that wasn't mine anyway.

When we stop to eat I say I'm not hungry. Taylor looks out the window. I remember the seaweed that doesn't seem like part of a monster anymore. Taylor is the only person I can talk to about the ocean but I don't have anything to say to him in the car. He just seems like every other boy in the world.

When I come back, I go to Shayla. Her Levi's are still perfectly ruined, bleached in just the right ways and cut off at the ankles. Her brown hair is still curly and chin length. She seems different to me somehow. I was the one who went somewhere, but she was the one who changed. She moves into me and I feel her bra under my palm. She feels heavy. Her breath smells like coconut frosting and we don't say anything for a while. She turns on videos and it's Journey's "Separate Ways." She puts on makeup with her index finger. I drink my cream soda. I remember Port Townsend and not knowing the answers.

She says, "You should let your hair grow and wear eyeliner."

She says, "Your eyes are so blue, Dottie."

And I think of her brown eyes and the way the corners of her mouth twitch when she stops herself from saying something.

Shayla says, "I have a boyfriend and he lives on the Reservation and he drinks his father's beer and he touches me on my pussy."

I know it's serious because we've never done anything like that with each other. I don't tell her about the seaweed and Taylor because it's not the same at all and it doesn't matter anyway. I know I am losing Shayla.

I think of that old dog. I think of the tall man at the end of the pier, but I don't know why. Maybe I think of him because he knew how to fish and how to find things and how to just be alone in the fog, laughing.

≈ Taylor Is My Boyfriend

It's not the same after Port Townsend. I'm not the same and the town is different and all the people in it are too. It's smaller now. I'm smaller and Taylor is just a boy I talked to for a while.

Beth tells her friend I like Taylor, but I don't. I thought maybe I did once, but now I'm certain I don't care for him at all. He has a bad haircut and acne and he doesn't say much. All this doesn't matter because stupid Mormon Beth opens her big fat mouth and tells someone who tells someone else and now everyone thinks I'm in love with him.

Taylor tells someone he likes me back and that someone tells someone else and eventually Beth finds out and now he's my boyfriend and I don't even like him.

For a week I see Taylor in the halls and he nods his bad haircut at me and I nod back and this is our relationship. It's not as bad as I thought it would be with the nodding and me just going about my business. Taylor is fine with it too, but it just doesn't seem right this way. We haven't talked since they made us date and now I don't want to. Beth thinks Taylor and I need to have a real date at the movies, but only *Christine* is playing and I already saw that with Shayla.

Beth says, "I don't know what you see in her."

I just keep it to myself.

Beth decides Taylor and I should eat lunch together. This conflicts with watching the cheerleaders practice, but I decide to get it over with.

I stand in the hall holding a chicken-salad sandwich and a Diet Pepsi wondering if a relationship is worth all this when Taylor finally walks up. We go sit on the bleachers and eat our sandwiches without saying a word to each other and when lunch is over he leaves. It wasn't much fun and the chicken salad was dry.

Taylor breaks up with me the next week and I am very upset. I keep thinking how stupid I was not to come up with it first and I hate that now I've been dumped just because I couldn't think of a way out.

Beth says, "It must have been something you said."

Beth turns and quickly walks away from me. From behind, I can see that she's accidentally tucked her skirt into the back of her tights. I don't tell her this, though. Instead I watch everyone point at her butt and laugh.

I don't say a word.

12 Years Old

Dorothy, Utah

≈ Dipping, Suicides, and Making the Team

Some of the girls have long dark hair tied back into braids. Some have short hair and bandannas tied around their foreheads. Some of them have chew in their mouths. They tuck it between their bottom lip and gum and grimace with the sting of shredded tobacco. They call it dipping.

We stand in a semicircle. We all wear big T-shirts and cut-off sweatpants. The coolest thing to do is to wear your dad's or stepdad's T-shirt. A lot of us do and you can tell from what the shirt says. The shirts say things like "Moose Lodge Picnic 1974," "Colville Rec Center, Men's Finals," and "I'm Not as Think as You Drunk I Am."

I try not to stare. I try to be cool and confident, but I'm terrified. There's nothing more important than being on the girls' basketball team. Everyone knows it's the best team in the league. Everyone knows they lose the championship every year to Omak in overtime. Everyone knows this year they'll win. I hear the Indian girls talking about Omak and it excites me. The girls talk about the blood on the court and the screams and the elbows flying.

I want to leave blood on the court and throw my elbows and scream with them. I know I could be powerful at this.

Mom played when she was a girl and she told me it was different then. She said they could only take two steps and then they had to pass the ball. She said they were only allowed to play half-court. I can't imagine any of these girls taking two steps instead of flying down the court with their braids in the air. I can't imagine these girls crowded into half-court and being polite. I begin to think I should start dipping and wearing bandannas.

Coach takes long steps, crosses the room in one second, and gets right in our faces. She shoves a garbage can under Dannie's nose.

"Spit!" she yells.

Dannie doesn't spit.

"I said spit," she screams, "because if you want to play ball this season you better spit out that chew right now, girl!"

Dannie spits.

A lot of the girls spit into the can. I decide not to dip.

Coach is tall with a huge round blond hairdo. She is skinny with a long face and steel-blue eyes. She is terrifying.

"Not everyone is going to make the team," she says. "That's the point of tryouts. I don't care if you made the team last year because it doesn't guarantee you a spot this year. It's a new season, ladies, so get ready for it.

"Drills!"

All the girls run and line up against the wall.

"For those of you who are new," says Coach, "these are called suicides. When I blow the whistle you will run to the free-throw line and touch it. You will run back to the wall.

You will run to the half-court line and touch it. You will run back to the wall."

While she tells us this, she points to the lines with the toe of her sneaker. She tells Willa to show us. Willa is the fastest runner I have ever seen. I thought maybe we would be done at half-court, but we have to go all the way to the free-throw line on the other side as well as to the baseline all the way at the other end.

"Free-throw, baseline, half-court, baseline, free-throw opposite side, baseline, baseline opposite side, baseline," says Coach. "That's one. Now, give me twenty."

I start with the other girls. I try not to panic. I know I can't run like them. I have asthma and I'm slow. I can play a basketball game but I can't run like this. The only thing in my mind as I run is that I can't run.

I want to focus on Willa, but when I'm starting my third suicide, she's on her sixth. All of the Indian girls and some of the white girls are ahead of me. My throat starts to close up and I want to cry, but I don't. I focus on a dark spot inside my head. I let my body move around me, but I stay inside the dark spot.

I don't finish last but very close to last. I am covered in sweat and beet red. Willa isn't even winded. I know this isn't the only drill we will do. I know I can make up for my slow legs with my powerful shoulders. I can do this.

Dannie nods at me and I nod back. Her short black hair is tied back with a bandanna. She is big and tall and very slow. I heard she was one of the best post players they had. I think it is good she nodded at me. Indian girls don't just nod at white girls for no reason. I wonder what she is thinking.

"Shoot around!" yells Coach.

They all go to different baskets and I wait and watch. I don't want to end up under a basket with the white girls. I don't like them. They aren't wearing sweatpants and baggy T-shirts that read, "Head for the Mountains, Head for a Busch." They actually match. I watch them shoot and they are terrible.

"Are you waiting for an invitation?" asks Coach.

"No, ma'am," I say.

"Then move it!" she hollers.

I move it to a basket where Jolina, Willa, Dannie, and Roz are shooting. I can tell they've been playing together for a long time. They all move together, passing the ball and faking each other out. I shoot. Dannie rebounds and passes it back to me. Roz guards me. I fake and dribble and pass it between her legs to Dannie, who banks it. Roz nods. Roz is only half Indian, but you can barely tell. She's the best point guard they have.

We try out for hours and Coach watches us, blowing her whistle a lot. We have passing drills and shooting drills and skill drills and more running. The white girls in matching outfits go limp and whiny. They make mistakes. They take turns sitting on the bleachers when they're tired.

We are not supposed to sit. Everyone knows that. Dannie looks at them and back to me.

"Hey yah," she whispers, "bunch of fuckin' cheerleaders anyway, man."

I nod. Coach blows her whistle.

"Jolina, Willa, Dannie, Roz, Motley, and Dorothy," yells Coach. "Three on three. Dannie and Motley separate teams. I want you to play post. Stay out of the key, Dannie."

"Yes, ma'am," says Dannie.

While Coach talks, she takes us by the elbows and separates us into teams. She's very strong.

"Roz and Willa, separate teams. You're point," she says.

"Yes, ma'am," they say.

"Jolina and Dorothy, separate teams. You're guarding each other," she says. "Got it?"

"Yes, ma'am," we say.

We play three on three and I am too exhausted to be nervous. When we play, we are glorious. Things happen on the court that cannot be explained. I know what Dannie and Willa are thinking. I know what they are going to do before they do it. The three of us work perfectly together.

Roz tries to pass the ball to Jolina, but I steal it. I am very good at stealing. I steal the ball and I fake it to Willa and then pass it to Dannie. I am good at passing. Dannie makes the shot.

We play and play and there is no time and no pain. There is only movement and silence. Things move in slow motion. It's like flying in a dream.

When tryouts are over I grab my stuff and go outside. There are a million stars and the air is cool and fresh. It smells like sage and river water. I watch steam roll off my arms and my wet hair turns to ice on the back of my neck. I breathe and breathe and breathe.

Dannie, Jolina, Willa, and Roz come out and say, "Hey." I say, "Hey" back. They smile and I smile too. I know I've made the team.

I get to do it all again tomorrow.

≈ He Is So Beautiful I Could Just Die

Science shouldn't be like this. It shouldn't be the way it is now with my heart pounding so hard that my face is red. I was never any good at science. I used to forget things, I didn't understand things, and I even cheated on tests. I used to write words on my hand. I used to do this but now I don't. I sit and smile and dream and listen. Mr. Dawson is so beautiful I could just die and it would be a good thing. The Indian girls say he came from Seattle and he could leave us any day. I don't want him to ever leave.

When Mr. Dawson looks at me, I feel like I'm going to melt right into the floor. When he says words like "sedimentary" and "Paleozoic," I think I might cry. When Mr. Dawson looks at me, I know he really sees me. He smiles and smiles and his teeth are straight and white. Behind his glasses, his blue eyes squinch up when he laughs. He tells me I need to pay attention in science class because science made the world and everything in it. I think if science made Mr. Dawson, I will definitely pay attention.

Beth says he's a gigolo. I ask her what that is and she adjusts her bra and says, "Being a gigolo is darn close to being the Devil." I think if Mr. Dawson was the Devil, God wouldn't bother me at all.

Beth asks Mr. Dawson if he believes in God. Mr. Dawson laughs and I want to crawl right up under the floor from the embarrassment there is in such a question. He says it doesn't matter whether or not he believes in God, it only matters whether or not God believes in him. Beth walks away and I stare and stare at Mr. Dawson. I think the Devil must have made Mr. Dawson very powerful to be able to say something like that.

At home, Mom asks me why I'm so interested in science all of a sudden. I bring my book home every night and bother her with questions, so she thinks that I'm very much in love with the subject. I tell her I've taken an interest in science because it is a very important age we all live in. I tell her at any moment the world could explode. She asks me how knowing science will stop the world from exploding. I tell her I don't want to stop it, I only want to understand it. She says, "Oh, I see." She also tells me she met with Mr. Dawson at the parent-teacher conferences and she thinks he's very cute. I tell her Mr. Dawson is not cute at all. I tell her he is a brilliant man who has opened up the world of science to me. I tell her it's rude to be so stupid about these kinds of things. She smiles and says, "Oh, I see."

I just love him so much I can't help it. It doesn't matter whether or not I love him. It only matters whether or not he loves me and I don't know how he couldn't. He must know beyond the retainers and sweatpants that one day I'm going to be a very beautiful and scientific jazz musician.

≈ The Hanging

The Presidential Fitness Awards are coming up. Soon we will be asked to perform physical tasks that will demonstrate our health and well-being. This is what they tell us. The girls' basketball team is under scrutiny because we are popular. Parents come from the Reservation to watch us.

I love the Indian girls because they are all related in some way. Willa told me how Donita was her third cousin and Jolina told me how Willa was her first cousin once removed and Donita never said much because she was tough and dipped snuff and drank beer. I kept thinking maybe, somehow, I was related to Donita and people would have to be nice to me.

"They're all related," says Beth. "That's why you can't trust them." I think, that's why you can trust them. And I do, very much. I like the way they stick together. I like the way they talk, very slow, rhythmic, and low.

I never wanted to eat again because I was practicing for the Presidential Fitness Award. Because I didn't sleep, I had time to hang.

I cleared the clothes out of my closet and hung on the bar. Every night I practiced hanging. I pulled myself up and hung and hung there. I hung until the sun came up and I had to pee and my legs shook and I cried. I hung there until my arms were numb and I wet myself. I actually peed my pants right there in the closet, hoping to win the time for the longest hang. I knew I could win. I knew I could hang there forever. I just had to beat those Indian girls who were all related and who helped each other.

It was time for the hanging and we were all in the gym. All day I had run and jumped and lifted things while thinking about the Indians. They ran and jumped and lifted things too, but all together.

So far I had held my own and placed every time. The girls were watching me. I was the only white girl except Roz, who was half white. Willa was the only Indian and we were hanging.

We hung there and hung there and hung there. Willa finally let go and stared at us. Roz's legs were shaking and her boyfriend watched. Roz hung and shook, hung and shook. I knew I would win. I knew I would win because I had pissed myself in my own closet weeks ago and I knew that after that nothing could stop me. I knew Roz's shaking was leading to a pee and she would never piss herself in front of her famous and important boyfriend, John Garvey.

And I did win.

They all stared at me because they knew I had meant it. We were still friends, but I was closer finally. I was closer to those Indian girls because I had tried so hard. I didn't even have to win, but I did anyway.

≈ Utah and the General Nicknames of White Girls

Beth says you can't trust the Indians because they're dirty and the boys have long hair and the girls dip tobacco. I tell Beth you can't trust Mormons because they're racist assholes and marry too many people. She says, "Dottie, Indians don't even believe in God." I tell Beth their God made the universe and her God just has one state where everybody is inbred and stupid. That shuts her up. You just can't argue with that after all.

I shouldn't have told Jolina what Beth said because Beth doesn't even play basketball, but I did anyway. Jolina tells Willa and Willa tells Donita and Donita tells Dannie and pretty soon everyone knows. That's how I get the nickname Utah.

White girls and half-white girls get nicknames. It's kind of weird how it happens. I mean, all of a sudden everybody knows your nickname. Roz is Roz, Motley is Motley, Bean is Bean, and I'm Utah. There's nothing you can do about it.

At the home games we have cheerleaders. They don't get nicknames because they don't really count. They fight for room on the sideline and cheer their hearts out.

They scream, U-G-L-Y, YOU AIN'T GOT NO ALIBI—YOU'RE UGLY, YAH YAH YOU'RE UGLY.

M-O-M-M-A, WE KNOW HOW YOU GOT THAT WAY—YOUR MOMMA! YAH YAH YOUR MOMMA!

We never pay attention to them really, but it's nice to know they're there.

Dawn is new. She showed up to homeroom in bleached jeans and camouflage high-top sneakers. She has strawberry-blond hair and a tiny scar on her lip. She said she was from Pittsburgh. I don't know Pittsburgh, but I think it must be very exotic and wonderful.

The white boys fall after her. The white girls cluster around her. I sit in the back of the room, watching. She looks like the girls in the music videos and she becomes a cheerleader. The Indian girls don't even notice her, but the Indian boys sneak glances at her. Duncan and Nacho lope behind her like hyenas, but when she sees them they turn to me and make fun. I could like Dawn, but she's causing me more torture just because she's so pretty.

"Hey yah, Utah," says Duncan. "When's your hair growing back, hey?"

I say, "Up yours, fat ass."

Nacho groans and laughs.

I hate Nacho and Duncan and they hate me. I actually nicknamed Nacho. It is the only nickname a white girl ever gave an Indian boy in this school. Nacho's half Indian, so the Indian boys tolerate him even though he's annoying. No one really likes him except Shayla. I actually saw Shayla kissing him one day after school and that was enough for me.

His name was Mom's fault because I told her how he was giving me the business and she asked me what his last name was. I said his last name was Ramirez and she said, "Why don't you call him Nacho?" That was three months ago and it stuck on him for good. In a place where last names are Bigwater and Littlehorn, Ramirez is no big deal. The problem was Nacho let the name bother him.

While Nacho laughs and Duncan holds his stomach, I just stand there in the wake of all the hatefulness. Dawn walks up to me and smiles. Her smile takes all the laughing away and I think she is so perfect.

She says, "Utah, I saw you play."

"Yah?" I say, watching that tiny scar.

"I was cheering for you, hey?" she says.

And that's all it takes for the hyenas to hobble off and for me to fall in love.

I think about my two names.

I think about how it makes sense to have them. I like being Utah better than being Dottie. I like that they named me over.

Beth says it's voodoo and that God will watch over me through all this renaming and spiritual confusion. I think God likes my new name and when I hit those hanging jumpers. I think God likes my new name a lot or He wouldn't have sent me Dawn.

≈ Roz Cuts Her Hair

We never thought she'd do it. Her boyfriend, John Garvey, never thought she'd do it. It is the topic of conversation for an entire week. We watch her. We listen more closely to what she says. We touch her head and wonder about things. The long braid is gone. I never thought it was pretty in the first place, but I don't say this.

A few Indian girls have very short hair, but they're the badasses. A few of the Indian boys have short hair and they're tough as nails. Roz isn't one hundred percent Indian and the fact that she cut her hair makes us all think. Everybody knows white people can do what they want with their hair and it doesn't matter. Indians know better. They know there's more going on and a haircut is never just a haircut.

When Roz comes to practice we all watch to make sure she's still good. We watch her shots, her dribble, and her trademark head fake. Nothing is different. We wonder if John Garvey will leave her. Because he's white, we know there is a chance he will. He does not leave her. Nothing changes, but we all wait and wonder if it will. After a week of this we realize she has not upset the balance of the universe. Near the third week we start to think maybe it's a good thing and this year we'll finally beat Omak and win the championship.

At home I stare into the mirror and contemplate the long hair I always dream about. I think of the silky blond mane I will eventually toss around. I wonder why I haven't started growing my hair. I decide it's time to really make the effort. I go to bed. In the morning there is no change. I know hair grows slowly and I start to do the math. I realize it will take years to accomplish my desired length of hair. This makes me incredibly sad and when I watch the girls in the music video flipping their long hair around, I quietly tug on what I believe will be my bangs.

While I'm working on my hair, Gabe starts realizing there's a difference between boys and girls. We'll be in town somewhere and he'll point and ask, "Dottie, is that a boy or a girl?" I'll tell him and he'll store the information away. Mom says Gabe gets confused because of the Indians and the Filipinos. She says it's hard for him to tell who's what because most of the Indians have long hair. She says Gabe's friend Lily, who is a Filipino girl, has short hair. Gabe just found out Lily wasn't a Colville Indian. He thinks anybody who isn't white is an Indian of some sort.

Gabe isn't upset about any of it or even mean about it. He just asks and we tell him. He seems to be taking it one person at a time. Once, when we were in Spokane, Gabe pointed at a man and said, "Dottie, he's an Indian, right?" I had to tell him the man he was pointing at was black. Gabe didn't know what that was and I told him being black was like being an Indian. I told Gabe white people murdered black people just like they did the Indians. Gabe pointed his bowl cut at me and said he wanted braids.

Lyle makes friends with a Colville man called Jim. They go out drinking together. Because they drink a lot, Jim leaves his seven-year-old, Allie, at our house sometimes. Gabe thinks Allie is the most beautiful person in the world. He follows Allie around and they play and play until Allie has to leave.

He asked me one day after Allie had gone, "Dottie, is Allie a boy or a girl?" I told him Allie was a girl. He nodded at me and wandered away.

I like that Gabe didn't know. I like that it took him a while to ask.

After months of yanking on what I think is going to be my long, beautiful hair, I tell Mom I need a haircut.

≈ Bus Trips and Stick Indians

When you live in the middle of what some people consider nowhere, going places is important. When you go somewhere, you better really want to be where you're going because it's possible you may never come back. Going to a friend's house in Nespelem can take weeks to plan because it's so far away. If you do bother to travel that far to see someone, you stay for days and days. Roz lived with Jolina for a week once. She went to stay the weekend and just kept staying. It was easier than trying to get home. Willa's cousin came to visit her from another part of the Reservation and ended up changing schools and coming to ours. I guess staying here was easier than trying to find someone to pick her up.

When we go to our away basketball games, we all have so much stuff we barely fit on the bus. Every team we play is at least two hours away. The worst teams seem to be even farther. Tonasket, whose team is terrible and embarrassing, is over three hours away. We usually don't get home until two in the morning. We have to bring dinner and snacks for after the game. We bring pillows and blankets, Corn Nuts, Diet Pepsi, coolers with sandwiches and fried chicken, books, and Mad Libs. We have a change of clothes for after, stuff to shower with, and any good-luck charms we see fit to bring. Our uniforms are cleaned and pressed and kept with our socks and shoes in separate bags.

On the way to the games, we're all usually trying to psych ourselves up. We talk strategy. We go over plays and trash the girls on the other team. We discuss our last game with the same team and think about what we could have done better. If someone had a bad day, has cramps, found their dad drunk, got into a fight, or doesn't feel like it's going to be their best game, we talk about how to work around it. We're honest because we know the game is the most important thing. We win nine times out of ten, but we never take it for granted. We know we could lose anytime.

Coach sits up front and talks to the driver. Her blond hair is teased into a huge circle. She's very tall and very strict. She lets us talk and never bothers us. She's the most powerful coach of any team and we all know it.

The rides home are the best because we've usually won, unless it's Omak. The rides home are when we open our coolers and get comfortable in our seats. We share blankets and food and talk about the game. We eat until there's no food left and then the Indian girls start telling their stories. They tell stories about Coyote and Spider Woman. They tell stories about the Great Spirit and the creation of the universe. One time Jolina told the scariest story about the Stick Indians. She said there were little tiny Indians made of sticks. She said the

Stick Indians came to people while they slept and gave them nightmares. She said if you were an evil person, these Stick Indians would visit you and make your life hell. She scared the shit out of Roz. It was so bad that we had to give her Pepsi and Corn Nuts and tell bad jokes to calm her down.

At the end of the trip we always sing to the bus driver. We sing, "Thank you, Mr. Bus Driver! Thanks for the ride!" in rounds.

When we all get off the bus at midnight or one or two o'clock, it's like we've done something great. We know our principal will announce our win over the intercom in the morning. He'll tell the score and give the highlights. We all know we'll be sitting in class and people will pat us on the back and smile because they know we're the best.

When we get off the bus and say good-night, there's a group of tired-looking Colvilles waiting for their daughters and they yell into the night when they find out we've won. We all go our separate ways and they have to drive another half hour back up to Nespelem.

≈ The Football Field When Shayla Lies

It's lunch and we all sit on the football field. Duncan and Nacho are there. They tell dirty jokes. Dawn's there too, just ignoring them. I have a hard time talking in front of her. I get all flustered and I hate that.

Nacho says, "Hey yah, Utah, cat got your tongue?"

Duncan says, "Retainer stuck?"

Shayla sneaks drags on a cigarette while Beth applies neon-pink Bonne Bell lip gloss. She has to hide it in her locker or her Mormon dad will kick her ass. Beth says, "I bet Mr. Dawson's getting married soon, Dottie." I don't say anything.

Dawn says she thinks he's hot. Beth says, "Lots of girls think so."

I hate Beth. I hate Beth's big fat Mormon ass so much. I never told her I was in love with Mr. Dawson, but she has female intuition just because she got her period first and she thinks she's all bad.

Dawn takes my hand and says she can read palms and she tries to read mine. She says, "You were stabbed in a past life, but you won't be stabbed again." She says, "Stuff like that only happens once and then you learn not to let it happen again." Dawn's mom is a Buddhist and that freaks Beth out. Dawn's from Pittsburgh and she's Buddhist. I am in awe.

When Dawn lets go of my hand, I look away because I'm blushing. I see Donita, Willa, and Jolina coming across the field with a few other girls. I think they're coming to talk to me. Shayla lights another cigarette and shifts nervously on the grass.

"Hey yah," say the Indian girls.

We say, "Hey yah."

I start talking to Jolina about the game the other night. I ask her if she's heard how Dannie's ankle is doing. She just stares at me. Willa stares at me. Donita stares at Shayla. There is a lot of staring and the hyena boys start giggling.

Jolina says, "We have to talk to Shayla."

I ask Jolina what's wrong. Dawn pinches my leg and shakes her head.

Willa says, "Shayla knows why we need to talk to her."

"Shayla screwed Manny," blurts Duncan.

Manny is Donita's boyfriend and a really tough, beautiful warrior type. He has scars on his face from lighting a hair spray can and he moves like a ghost. He cut off his braids and that means he's trouble. Shayla wouldn't ever mess with him. She knows better. Donita is just like Manny, only a girl.

"Shayla," I ask, "did you do that?"

She shakes her head.

I say, "Donita, hey, Shayla wouldn't do something like that."

Donita looks at me and I feel terrified, but then her eyes waver. She turns and walks away. The other girls leave with her. Shayla leans back into the grass and closes her eyes.

The next week Shayla shows up to school with a fat lip, a black eye, and her head down. I'm walking with Dawn when I see her. I ask Shayla what happened. She tells me Donita did it. I ask her why. She says, "Because I fucked her boyfriend." Then Shayla walks away. Dawn stands with me.

She says, "Everyone knew about it."

I say, "I didn't believe it."

I am done with Shayla. I am completely through with her.

≈ The Lottery

Beth says our English teacher, Ms. Webber, is a whore. I think Beth is jealous of Ms. Webber. Our English teacher wears tight pants and throws around her long brown hair. She tells us we are special and smart and that we will go places. She says literature is our key out of the Coulee. She says if we can only learn to express ourselves, the world is our oyster. Beth says, "Shows how much she knows."

I agree with Ms. Webber. I think expressing yourself is very important. It's very important to me because it's so hard to talk with my Bionator in. I read all the books she tells us to read and think hard about them. I read Carson McCullers and

Flannery O'Connor. I read John Steinbeck and Roald Dahl. I try to read Ernest Hemingway, but something about his writing makes me mad and confused. Mom says it's because he doesn't understand women.

We read a short story called "The Lottery" and it is very sad. You think it's going to be a happy story because winning the lottery is a good thing. You don't find out until the end that whoever wins the lottery ends up getting stoned to death. Taylor and Beth agree that it is an inspiring story. They say it is an example of irony. I say the story is mean and hateful. I tell Beth and Taylor someone in the town would have saved the person from being stoned to death. Beth and Taylor look at each other.

Taylor says, "What about the Nazis?"

I get mad at Taylor and tell him he can't keep bringing up the Nazis every time he's losing an argument. He brings them up a lot and it's starting to bug me.

Beth says, "What about Stalin?"

"What about him?" I ask.

"No one stopped him," says Beth.

I tell them we're talking about "The Lottery" and not dictators. I tell them if I saw someone being stoned to death I would stop it. I tell them both the Nazis and Stalin were stopped eventually. They get mad and tell me stopping them took a long time and that "The Lottery" is ironic and very good.

I slump in my seat because I'm so mad I don't know what to say and my Bionator is in the way.

"Just because it happened doesn't make it okay," I yell.

Beth and Taylor start talking about war and short stories and how great being smart is. Jolina stares at them and then she stares at me.

"Don't worry, Utah," she says. "They don't know what they're talking about. Everybody knows it's the white man who starts everything like that."

Taylor says, "I didn't start anything."

Jolina says, "You started this argument."

Beth says, "Dottie started it."

I say, "I did not."

Jolina says, "Hitler was a white man and Stalin was a white man. All the men who killed the black people were white men. All the men who killed the Indians were white men. It's a white man problem. The woman who wrote the story was just telling all the white men how stupid they are."

"Yeah," I say, "that's ironic."

I am very proud of Jolina.

Ms. Webber asks us what all the yelling is about and I say, "White men, ma'am." She looks at us, tosses her hair, and says, "Okay." I look around the room and I see Fat Eddie just sweating in his desk. He's drawing something with a ruler. Fat Eddie is a white man, well, he is white and he will be a man. He's big and damp and embarrassed all the time. He doesn't look like someone who would start a war, stone someone to death, or even ever be mean. I squint my eyes and look closer. He just looks fat and tired. Jolina sees me staring at Fat Eddie.

"You never can tell, Utah," she says. "You never can tell. Think about Napoleon."

I think about Napoleon. I think about Custer. I think about all the dumb white men we read about. I get very angry. I think about Dad and Lyle, but then I think about Pop and Grandpa. Grandpa had to get away from the Nazis because he didn't want to shoot anyone. Pop had to get away from his dad because he didn't want to get shot.

"Jolina," I say.

"What?" she asks.

"Kennedy?" I ask.

She thinks for a minute.

"Hey yah, he was okay," she says.

We have to give speeches in Ms. Webber's class on something we believe very strongly in. I ask Mom if I should give a speech on how McDonald's is killing all the rain forests or how President Kennedy was a decent white man. She asks me which I feel more strongly about and I say, "President Kennedy." She says, "Well, there's your answer."

I work very hard on my speech, but I'm not good at public speaking. I get in front of the class and my knees knock and I feel like I'm going to puke. I kind of stumble through the speech, but I do finally get it over with. I sit down and feel stupid. I've seen Kennedy speak on those documentaries they have on television. He is so wonderful and powerful and it makes your skin get tingly when you listen. I feel bad for him because I basically suck.

I sit in my seat and hate myself because I should have given a speech on some woman who did something instead of some dead white man I don't even know. Jolina talks about Chief Joseph and she is wonderful. She's so tiny and pretty that you can't help but listen to what she says. I just feel lost because I don't really look up to anyone and I'm not lucky enough to be a Colville or a Navajo or a Mohawk. I feel stupid and white and angry. I start to think there really are no good white people besides my grandparents and maybe Gabe.

Beth talks about some dead Mormon guy who made it okay for men to marry like a hundred women and Taylor talks about some fashion designer from France no one has ever heard of. I hitch my sweatpants up to my knees and mutter. I think speeches are stupid. I think I should have stuck with

McDonald's and the beef crisis and all the dying trees. I should have just talked about the worms in the burgers and the lack of oxygen in the air and the melting polar ice caps.

Ms. Webber tells us to all take a slip of paper from the bag in her hand. We all do what she says and sit back down at our desks.

"We're going to have a lottery!" she says.

Beth smiles at me and I hate her.

"Open your slips of paper," says Ms. Webber.

We open them.

"Whoever has an X on their paper instead of an O, please stand up," she says.

No one stands up.

"If you have the X," she says, "you've won the lottery!"

We all look around at each other.

"C'mon," she says, "no one's going to get stoned to death, I promise."

Still no one moves.

"Fine," she says. "Whoever has the X wins this!"

She holds up a bunch of school supplies with different-colored pencils and notebooks and stickers, but still no one moves. Ms. Webber looks defeated. She flips her hair and sighs.

"Class dismissed," she says.

We all get up from our desks and on the way out I crumple up my X and throw it away. I can't help but remember what Jolina said before: "You never can tell, Utah."

≈ Omak

Mom worries when I play.

She goes to my games with Gabe and sits in the stands and worries. She worries because of my asthma. She watches my face turn red and covers her eyes. She covers her eyes and then Gabe worries and tries to pry her hands off her face.

"Dorothy, you get so red," she says.

"I'm okay, Mom," I say.

"But you're so red," she says.

"Mom, I'm okay," I yell. "Leave me alone."

Gabe says, "Red."

"Shut up, Gabe," I say.

I get red when I play, but it doesn't matter.

The season has been amazing. We've only lost to Omak and it's them we're facing in the last game. If we win, we're champions. If we don't, it's the third year in a row we've lost the final game to them. I know we'll win this year. I know it for certain.

The only problem is that we're playing in Omak. It's very difficult to play the final game away from home.

We're all silent on the bus ride to Omak. No one says anything. Dannie has her eyes closed the whole time. I know she's going over her foul shots in her mind. Roz looks pale and she sighs a lot. Willa and Jolina share a seat and they both stare out the window. The cheerleaders sit up front and even they're quiet.

I watch the back of Dawn's head. She has her hair in a ponytail. Once in a while she'll look back at me and smile. I try not to think about her smile. It would make me more nervous.

I concentrate on the caravan of cars in front of the bus. Every girl's parents, aunts, uncles, cousins, and grandparents are going to the game with us. I'm glad Mom had to work because I don't think I could stand her worrying about my red face in the stands.

We get to the locker room and Roz runs immediately to the bathroom. She dry heaves into the toilet while we all get ready. She gets sick sometimes before games because she's so nervous.

The gym is boiling inside.

The heat from all the bodies of people standing on the sidelines and all the breath and nervous sweat and the screaming turns the air to steam and it's hard to breathe. We warm up listening to the cheerleaders scream and the crowd roar.

When the Omak girls come out, the noise is deafening. People stomp their feet on the bleachers and whistle. The Omak girls are amazing. It looks like they're on wheels, gliding across the floor. Their faces are expressionless.

"Bitches," whispers Dannie.

"Shh," whispers Jolina.

The first half of the game is like watching a bad dream. We're down by ten and I already have two fouls. Coach is calm. She tells us to relax, to focus, and to pay attention.

When we're down by fifteen, Dawn starts to smile at me. It's one of those smiles you would give someone who is dying. She doesn't mean to make me feel worse, but she does.

Coach tells us to talk to each other on the court. She tells Dannie to stay out of the key and for Roz to watch her passing. She tells me to stop slamming the girl who's guarding me because if I get another foul, she'll bench me.

We're down by eleven at the end of the first half.

Coach takes us into the locker room. She screams. She throws shoes.

"I don't care what you ladies have to do out there, but you better start doing it," she hollers. "You better throw yourselves on that ball whenever you see it! No more outside shots! Take it inside and draw the foul. Burn this team down, ladies! I mean it."

The second half of the game is a bloodbath. We have no room for any emotion except pure rage. It feels like we're a fist just pounding into them.

Dannie reads my mind and gets open at just the right times. My passes are perfect. Willa spins on the inside, drawing the fouls. Jolina's outside shots sail right into the basket. Roz fakes out Omak's point guard so bad that the point guard trips over her own feet. I steal every ball I can get my hands on.

We tie it up in the second half and go into overtime.

My knees and elbows look like hamburger. Dannie's limping. Willa has actually started sweating. I can't feel anything except my heart beating in my stomach. It feels like a drum. Coach doesn't even talk to us. She knows we are in the game. I look at Dannie, Willa, Jolina, and Roz. I know what they are thinking. I know what they are feeling. I know what we can do. I know every move before they make it.

Everyone in the stands is on their feet. Omak takes a time-out.

We have successfully stopped every single one of their shot attempts and they have stopped all of ours. There are so many fouls on the court the referees have given up calling them. Parents are screaming bad words from the stands. The cheerleaders have been cussing at each other from the sidelines. Dawn threatened to stomp in the face of Omak's head cheerleader and two fat Indian men had to break them up.

It's the best game ever.

Omak has the ball. Somehow their guard gets around Jolina. Something happens to me. I see her going toward the basket and my body turns liquid. Everything slows down. I dive toward her and knock the ball away. My knees leave blood on the court. The girl dives into me and the ball gets loose. We both try to grab it, but she knocks it out of bounds.

It's our ball and there are seven seconds left.

Things speed up and Willa makes me take the ball out. Before I can even worry, the ref blows his whistle and there are bodies everywhere.

Things slow down again. The tall girl in front of me jumps up and down in slow motion. I see Willa get free and she nods at me. I pass it between the tall girl's legs. Willa gets the ball, shoots, and sinks it. The buzzer goes off.

We all stand on the court and stare at the score. We won by a basket. We won.

Willa grabs me and we fall to the court. The noise from the stands finally reaches us. It is deafening. The screams of joy drown out the booing.

We start crying.

Dawn sits next to me on the bus ride home. She shows me the scratches on her arm from her fight with the other cheerleader. No one can stop talking or crying. It's so loud on the bus you have to yell to be heard.

"Do you believe it?" she yells. "You won."

"Hey yah," I say.

I can't think of anything else to say. I can't feel anything except joy. There is no room for thoughts or confusion or anything. There is only the feeling of pure joy.

≈ Quarters and Menstruation

I didn't really think it would happen.

All of a sudden my jeans won't fit over my hips, I start to get boobs, and then I'm in the middle of the Clothes Horse buying bras with Mom. They're small and white and horrible and they ride up and pinch. I leave them on the floor of my room and just wear two shirts to school instead. Mom says they look like dead rabbits just lying there on my floor, "Where they'll do no damn good to anyone, Dorothy!"

I never thought I'd get my period. I just kept thinking I could outrun it. When it first happened, I scrubbed my underwear and put on clean ones. I had to do it again a few hours later. I stood in the bathroom and scrubbed and scrubbed until I started crying like a baby. It's just not fair. I'm being taken over.

Some girls, like Beth and Missy, think having your period is the greatest thing ever. They think they're all cool being crybabies and fat and worthless. They whine about cramps and clothes and boys.

Mom says to use what's under the bathroom sink to fix myself up. Everything's Mom-size, though. The pads are like diapers and they make noise when I walk. The tampons are horrible and there's no way something that huge will fit in me. I ask Mom to get me something else, but she won't. She says, "There's no need for you to get all wound up." All I can do is stand in the damn bathroom like I've been doing all day. I have toilet paper in my underwear and I'm angry.

Grandma always sends me quarters wrapped up in ten-dollar rolls. I keep them in my top dresser drawer. I think about these rolls of quarters I've been saving, all lined up under my T-shirts. I wasn't sure what I was saving them for. I never thought I'd use them to buy tampons. I pack more toilet paper into my pants and begin the walk to the grocery store.

I get in the store and go to the girl aisle, but I'm too embarrassed to take anything off the shelf. I pull my hood on and tie it under my chin. I circle and circle the girl aisle until I know every display by heart, even the prices of the dusty canned stuff that no one buys, like water chestnuts. I'm all hot and sweaty and nervous and ashamed. The paper is chafing and I hate myself. The only thing that gets me to pick up the boxes I need is the thought that everybody else thinks this is normal. No one else is embarrassed by it. Beth had a sleepover to celebrate her period. It was stupid, but we went anyway because Shayla said she was bringing beer and one of her father's dirty movies. Beth stared at the movie, lying on her back with a heating pad on her stupid stomach, and kept saying, "This is disgusting. My mother will kill me if she comes in. This is disgusting, really."

Everybody else has their periods and they all brag about it. Roz was at the river with a bunch of us once and we wanted to throw her in the water. We were all laughing while we carried her, but she started screaming and kicking. She even started crying. No one knew what to do, so we let her down and she went to sit by herself. I went up to her to apologize and she looked up at me all teary and said, "It's okay. It's just that . . ." her voice got all quiet and important ". . . I have my period." I didn't understand how having your period meant you couldn't get wet, but now I know, having circled the maxipad aisle for an hour, that if Roz had toilet paper in her drawers it's no wonder she was screaming.

Even Mom thinks it's no big deal. She wears these huge diaper pads and her big horrible tampons and leaves them wrapped up in the bathroom garbage. She wraps them up all neat and hidden in toilet paper, but I know what they are and it grosses me out. Lyle will ask her to do something sometimes and she'll say, "I can't. I'm too wiped out because of my period." She'll say, "Dottie, my cramps are so bad. Would you do the dishes again? I'm so tired, watch your brother?"

When Beth is supposed to come over, she'll make excuses. "My back is killing me," she'll say. "I can't go anywhere. I have cramps. I'm distended. My face broke out."

I hear it from all of them: "I'm too tired to go to the movie. I'm too bloated. I'm too exhausted. I have PMS. I have a headache. I think I'm dying. I'm dead."

This is the worst thing ever. Now I have to spend my money on crap I don't even want. I hate this. I hate being a girl. I'm in the middle of the tampon aisle, with rolls of quarters in my pocket and a handful of toilet paper in my underwear and I'm thinking hate hate hate. There's stuff on the shelves I've never heard of. There's Vagithis and Vagithat and suppositories and pills and creams and gels. There are boxes that say Stayfree, O.B., and Freedom Maxi. I hold my boxes of Tampax and turn the face of my hate toward Judy Blume and all her crappy books adults gave me. I hate Judy Blume and her *Are You There, God?* bullshit. I hate how everyone in her books is rich and clean and how they all talk to each other about periods and kissing and love and shit. I wish Judy Blume were right here next to me with a wad of Cottonelle up her Vagithis and a suppository in her Vagithat. I wish she were here in a hooded sweatshirt with heavy rolls of quarters in her pockets sweating, ashamed, and all alone.

But none of this gets me anywhere and I have to count out dollars in quarters to a mean checkout lady with a long line of people waiting behind me.

≈ Something Bad Will Happen

I can't eat. Mom asks me why and I tell her it's because of the dreams.

Every time I go to sleep I dream horrible things.

I dream I'm at the kitchen table and about to eat pizza. I take a bite, but the pizza is made of hair.

I dream I'm on a hill and the moon is yellow. It's so dark that I can't make out what's on the table in front of me. When the clouds pass the moon, there's a bowl full of blood in front of me.

I dream that a monster with long blue fangs is gnawing on my foot. The monster smiles up at me, but it has a child's face all covered in fur.

I don't know what to do, so I don't do anything. Mom makes me hot tea and steaming cups of chicken broth. She takes my temperature and worries. She tells me I have to eat something. I tell her I can't.

I dream I'm eating and it tastes so good that I smile. When I smile, food falls out of my mouth, but it's not food at all. Maggots fall out of my mouth. I throw up into my hands, which are covered in fur.

All the dreams make me stay up late and go for long walks. All the dreams make me feel like something bad is going to happen.

≈ Burying Things

Mom's not back from bartending yet because the Moose Lodge stays open late.

"Those Indians drink a lot," said Mom. "There's a Colville man who sits at the bar and eats an entire loaf of white bread. He eats this white bread because he knows he'll be drinking a great deal. The white bread protects us from his fury when he's drinking because it soaks up all the whiskey and the beers. He drinks and drinks and his stomach swells up, but he never gets angry."

I think about this Colville man and his loaf of bread. I think about him and other things because I can't sleep. My light is on and my window is open for the air. It's very cold outside and the crickets are loud. I told Gabe that crickets don't make the noises with their mouths, even though he thought they did. I told him they rubbed their wings together. Lyle said they rubbed their legs together. He may be right. I'm not exactly sure, but Gabe thought about it a little and waddled out of the room, ignoring us both.

On my dresser is a teacup Grandma gave me. It's very thin with flowers on it. I pick up the cup and put things in it. I put an earring in it and some erasers and a piece of wrapped candy. I am still thinking about the Colville man and his loaf of white bread. I am thinking of the Vietnam vet that Mom talked about. She said he is very quiet and his eyes are dark. Mom said, "He served three tours, Dottie, and that means three years in the jungle." She said, "He sometimes forgets he's not there anymore." I ask her what stories he's told her and she says, "Oh no, he never talks about it."

I walk outside with my teacup and I think about a million years from now. A million years from now, when they're digging up this yard, wouldn't it be fine if they found a little teacup with my things in it? The crickets make noise with their wings or legs and the stars are out. I think this is a good thing to do and I go into the house for a spoon. I dig a hole and am careful to lift the grass off in one chunk. I bury my teacup and set the grass clump right over it. You can't even tell I did it. I like that it's there.

I sit outside near my buried cup.

Mom said there's a man at the bar who is very very old. She said he takes his teeth out to drink. She said, "Dottie, now this man is extremely old." She said, "He'll come in without even a hello and plunk his wet teeth right on the bar and order beer after beer." I think about this old man and his false teeth. Mom said, "He told me teeth get in the way and that he doesn't have much time left to waste on trying to get beer past his teeth."

I walk around and around the yard. My cup is in the very middle.

Someone says, "Dottie?"

I say, "Yes?"

"Hello!" says the voice.

I turn toward the voice across the fence. It's Henry, who is my neighbor and a year ahead of me in school. He's very nice but very rich and he has a girlfriend whose name is Polly. He's also Chinese or something and this makes him interesting. I remember when I was at the movies with Beth and Shayla once. Henry was kissing Polly near the front of the theater. Everyone was impressed. Here it is, one o'clock in the morning, I'm burying things, and Henry's hissing at me through the fence.

"What are you doing?" he asks.

"Nothing," I say. "What are you doing?"

"I was just thinking," he says. "I was thinking wouldn't it be nice if it rained candy?"

"I guess so," I say.

He says, "Well, good-night."

"Good-night."

I sit by my teacup and think about the loaf of bread, the jungle, and the teeth that are in the way.

I lie down and stare up at the stars until it feels like the whole sky is swirling.

I close my eyes and laugh and laugh.

≈ *Aunt Claire*

Aunt Claire is Mom's sister who visits from Detroit. She is beautiful. When she kisses me on the cheek, she always leaves a lipstick mark. Gabe gets a mark too and he always runs to the bathroom mirror to check it. It makes him very happy. You always know when Claire is visiting because we all have red marks on our cheeks and run to the bathroom, smiling.

Aunt Claire isn't married and she doesn't have kids and she says it's on purpose.

When she visits, we have the best time ever. Aunt Claire takes me shopping in Spokane. She takes me to fancy stores like Macy's and lets me get whatever I want. She tells me I am a lovely girl and I can get away with wearing anything. She says I have the perfect coloring for spring shades. She also tells me I can wear black and be dramatic if I want. She buys me things and doesn't even look at price tags like Mom does. She says life is too short. Aunt Claire says I am like a daughter to her and I can get whatever I want.

In Spokane we get Chinese food. We eat egg foo young and egg rolls. We eat lo mein and spicy shrimp. She lets me sip her beer. She tells me Detroit is going straight to Hell. She tells me I'm lucky to be where I am. She tells me I have to promise never to live in Michigan. She tells me I have to promise to go to college and not mess around with boys.

I promise.

Mom says Aunt Claire is a very smart woman. I agree. I want to be just like her. I want to have a career and no husband or children. I want to be able to fly wherever and whenever I want to, even though I hate flying. I tell Aunt Claire I will either be a lawyer or a famous jazz musician.

She says, "Good choices."

I tell Aunt Claire about school and basketball and Seattle. I tell her anything can happen in Seattle. I tell her I have dreams and that when I can't sleep I walk all over the world. She tells me how proud she is of me.

She says, "Dorothy, you can be anything you want to be. You can be wonderful. You could even be more wonderful than you are now."

I say, "Thank you, Aunt Claire. I plan to be powerful."

I tell her that because when she's around, I believe it. I tell her that because I want it to be true. I tell Aunt Claire all the things I can't tell Mom because Aunt Claire travels the world and orders egg foo young and drinks beer and smiles. I tell her my plans because she looks perfect all smiling, surrounded by shopping bags.

She says, "Dorothy, never forget who you are."

I tell her I won't, even though I'm still trying to figure it out.

≈ Dad

My father is coming to see me and it's just as well I can't sleep or eat because I wouldn't be able to anyway. Mom keeps running around and moving things and Lyle just drinks and storms out and then in, out and then in.

The basketball season is over, but our All-Star team is playing Tonasket's All-Star team the night Dad comes in from back East. Tonasket is over three hours away and Mom says he and Aunt Claire can meet me at the game and I can drive back with them. I ask Mom if she's going too and she says, "No." I don't remember ever seeing her and Dad together.

Tonasket is an easy team to beat, but I'm off my game because I keep expecting Dad to walk through the door. Coach tells me to take a seat for a while. I sit and sweat and wring my towel and hate that Dad's missing the game. He's never seen me play, not ever. When I see Dad in the summer we play baseball. That's his favorite.

When I see him, I can't move. He's actually here with me. He came to see me. He came with Aunt Claire and drove for hours just to see me play and there's this huge crowd. He hugs me in front of everyone and I kind of start crying because I know no one believed me that he was going to visit. The girls whisper on the bench that my dad is really tall. They say, "Hey yah, Utah. Your dad's real cool, man." And I say, "Ain't it?"

Coach puts me out on the floor after a while and I make a few, but my heart's not in the game at all. Tonasket gets their asses kicked and we all leave. Dad says, "I didn't know how far this place was from you." Aunt Claire says, "Well, if you visited more often you'd know how hard Dottie works to be first string and an honors student." I say, "Hey yah, Dad, you tired?" And he says, "Yeah." I feel bad that he flew out and then drove all the way to Tonasket when I could have told him we were going to win because Tonasket sucks.

When I see Dad see Mom, I can't believe it. Lyle is off getting drunk because it's already one in the morning. I've made Dad a lopsided coconut cake that ends up tasting really good. They eat cake and drink wine and Aunt Claire goes to sleep. I try very hard to stay alert because I want to see what it's like to have both your parents in the same room, but it feels so good that I actually fall asleep for the first time in months.

Mom lets me skip school to hang out with Dad. We go to Electric City and watch the windmills some old guy made swirl in the sun. Dad thinks it's really cool and takes a lot of pictures. I'm bored because I've seen all this so many times. We have lunch and walk around some more. I keep waiting for him to ask me to go back with him. All the summers I've spent with him are so different than this. He came specifically to see me. I'm expecting something wonderful after the windmills and the car ride to Tonasket, whose team sucks. Gabe likes my dad a lot. He always walks up to him and grabs on to his leg and my tall dad swings him around until Gabe giggles and Lyle pouts.

I wait all weekend for Dad's invitation. I fall asleep on the living room floor while Mom and Dad talk about the past. I haven't slept so well or for so long.

The day Dad leaves, I'm crawling out of my own skin. I've even missed school just to show him how much I want to be with him. He's getting a ride to the airport and I've packed my bags.

Dad sits me on the front porch and says, "Dottie, I have something to tell you."

I think, something to ask, to ask . . .

And I keep staring at him and thinking, and and and . . .

He says, "I just wanted to tell you before I left: Cecilia and I are getting married."

Mom comes out and says, "We have to be getting your dad to the airport, Dottie. Are you ready to go?"

I say, "I'm not going."

They look at each other and there's so much silence as I walk into my room and slam the door. See, he wasn't taking me. Never planned on taking me. He just came to say he was leaving. Missy was right all along.

I can't breathe through all the crying and the kicking so quiet behind my door.

≈ Dream of Pop

Sometimes I dream about Pop. I dream the most about him because I think he knows things about dreaming, even though he never talks about it.

I dream Pop is wearing a black suit and we are at a carnival. The carnival is in a huge building. There are tents and rides and animals.

Pop says he is sorry he never got to take me more places. I hold his hand. We look up at the rides.

I tell Mom the dream and she says, "Dottie, how did you know?" And then she cries.

I ask Mom why she's crying. She says Pop is very sick and the dream I had means he wanted me to know that. She says Pop has cancer. After she says "cancer," she cries so hard she has to run out of the room and lie on her bed.

I can't move from the living room. I am terrified. I wish I could fall asleep right away. I wish I could fall right to sleep and dream something good and make Pop better. Instead I sit down on the floor and hug my knees to my chest.

≈ Pop on the Porch

We are in Michigan, even though I should be in school.

Mom just up and put me on the plane with her and Gabe and we flew to Detroit because she said it was important.

We are leaving Detroit and I have missed one month of school. I don't care about school so much, but I'm not sure what to feel.

Pop stands on the porch. He waves good-bye at me. It is very bright on that porch. It is so bright outside, the windows just glare and glare. So bright outside, the grass looks pale and the street shimmers.

In the backseat, Gabe puts his head down and cries. Mom starts the car to drive us to the airport. We're in a white rental car and her eyes in the rearview mirror are black.

I sit backward in the seat and stare and stare until Pop is lost in that shimmery bright place that was a porch and now is just light.

I want to jump out of the car and run back to him and hold on forever, but I don't.

I stare at him until our car turns a corner and he disappears.

≈ What Happened in Minneapolis

I was awake all night, watching light wake into gray, blue, then morning. There was this breathing, this slow, calm breathing that was mine. When I rode the bus to school I thought, something wonderful is going to happen. Something wonderful.

At home, when I heard what had happened, there were two of me. One standing cold and the other curled at her foot, sleeping. I couldn't move when Mom told me. I couldn't move, not until she left. Her face was the worst face I'd ever seen and her mouth was twisted and her eyes were not hers. Her eyes were gone and still there, gone and still there. They weren't my mother's eyes at all but someone else's altogether.

I thought her mouth might even melt until she covered it with her hand and walked quickly away.

I looked down at the sleeping me and fell to the floor and rolled up in her and wailed. I wailed and wailed and wailed until I choked myself. Pop was dead dead dead. He was dead dead dead. Oh God oh God oh God, he was my father.

This was what I screamed in my head, He was my father my father, but he was really my grandfather and I couldn't stand it. I couldn't stand it at all.

When we left him, it was Minneapolis we ended up in. There was nothing wrong with Minneapolis except we had to stay for three days while my eardrums sighed back into themselves and Mom complained about the wind.

Gabe and I sat on the bed in the motel and watched cable for the first time and we fought and I pinched and hit him and he yelled and hit me. Then I would stare at my face and make horrible expressions in the mirror because I was so ugly and then we would fight some more. Mom wouldn't let me wash my hair. I wasn't allowed to get my head wet until we left Minneapolis and I just wanted to die right there in Minneapolis because I couldn't even go outside because of my ears and I hated that. "There's nothing wrong with Minneapolis," said Mom. "It's nice out there and the people are wonderful." I didn't know if she was lying because all I had was cable and Gabe and a terrible fear of airplanes.

Her face would be red with the wind of Minneapolis and her coat would smell of outside and the city and I just sat there in front of cable, eating pills, taking eardrops, hating my greasy head and my terrible face.

"You almost 'ploded," said Gabe. "You almost 'ploded."

My eardrums almost exploded during the descent into Minneapolis, the city I never saw. It was like someone had set a fire in my head and it was coming out my ears and I screamed and screamed. I fell into the aisle, kicking like a girl and holding my ears while the stewardesses held me and tried to put Styrofoam cups over them. While one would try to hold me down, another miserable woman would hold the cups, which had wet, hot paper towels in them, over my ears. I clawed at them until their buns fell around their ears and their pantyhose ripped. In the middle of my screaming there were two of me, one screaming and the other standing, embarrassed, shaking his head.

We stood in line for the next plane and Mom looked like she'd been hit over the head. A man who had been on the plane with us said, "Ma'am, I don't think you should take her up again." And Mom said, "No." The man was a doctor and he helped us while I sucked snot up my nose and wished blood was pouring from my ears for all the mess I'd made of things.

The last day in Minneapolis, the last day of cable, Mom came back, red faced and grinning.

"I bought you something," she said.

The doctors had terrified her. She had bought me a hat, a winter stocking hat with nubs and a ball on it. It was thick and wool and big and it was the ugliest thing in the world because it was pink. I put that big pink hat over my greasy hair and over my terrible ears and it itched. Then I wore the hat and wore the hat and wore the hat until the trees had leaves.

Pop was dead and all I could think of was my shame of the pink hat and the awful awful loneliness. Pop was dead and all I could imagine was nothing and a lot of it. The nothing is huge and dark and terrifying and it opens its mouth and swallows me all up. I rattle around in it and I can't breathe.

I hate myself for not running from the car when I had the chance. I should have run right up to him on the porch and held on so he couldn't ever leave.

It's all my fault that he's gone because I knew we'd never see him again. I knew it and I did nothing.

I should have run right up to him and held on.

≈ *Science Fair*

He is the oldest boyfriend I will ever not have. His science makes no sense and his glasses are foreign looking, like he went somewhere and saw something. Mr. Dawson tries to explain the universe and I buy macaroni and cheese for lunch.

"You can tell me," he says. "You can talk to me, Dottie."

He thinks I can talk to him as if all the science in the universe wasn't guarding him, a black wall with stars that stare at my cheap, too-big T-shirt and my old shoes. "How are you? How are things at home?" he asks and then Shayla and her friend walk by and laugh at me in the hall. I lower my head because I am on the outs, as Mom would say. I keep thinking Mr. Dawson Mr. Dawson Mr. Dawson knows knows knows.

You cannot go to the East for twenty-seven days and watch someone dying real slow like summer and come back to your life all put together.

Mr. Dawson is tall and handsome with the bluest eyes and blackest hair of any boy. He doesn't mind that I don't have the answers to what he asks. Tall, blond, Mormon Beth pushes up to him after tests asking, "How did I do, how did I do?" I know it's all he can do to stop himself from telling me how she doesn't interest him. He's very much in love with me. I think if only I was sixteen and a girl we could go away to Detroit where things happen instead of where we are which is nowhere.

Shayla and her friend make faces at me in the hallway and laugh and run holding their books. Mr. Dawson finds me and tells me about science and leaves and rocks like igneous. I tell him about the Mayans and volcanoes and when he listens he cleans his glasses and squints at me.

"You can tell me about home," he says, "and where you went."

Pop watched me hula-hoop for almost an hour while he smoked his pipe. And the sun went down over our square of lawn, the cherry smoke in the air, his slow laugh. Squirrels sat on him while he fed them stale peanuts and he said, "Never make friends with a squirrel because they're filthy and they bite. But I can," he said. "I can because my skin's leather and they know who I am."

In Detroit, where things happen, for twenty-seven days I hula-hooped and counted the black crescents of mascara on my mother's pillow multiplying like sad butterflies. She never cried in front of me because she didn't think I knew. All four feet of Nana smoked Chesterfields and made Lipton with milk and sugar. All seven pairs of her beige shoes lined the steps leading inside. Pop just smiled and smiled and swung Gabe around, calling him "old man."

"Hey, old man," he would laugh.

Gabe would giggle and giggle and say, "I'm an ol' man!" Gabe would point at Pop's tattoos and smile and nod. He liked the anchor the best.

I don't remember talking for twenty-seven days except for agreeing about squirrels and the challenge of the hula-hoop. Gabe refused all food except McDonald's, crying and hanging on Mom, but he crawled into the sawdust-smelling arms of Pop who smoked his pipe. Pop would say, "McNugget! McNugget!" until Gabe laughed.

I wore my armadillo sweatshirt that Lyle let me buy when we all went to Seattle.

I like it because it reminds me of the ocean, even if it is only a picture of an armadillo. Mom hated the sweatshirt because it was too expensive and whenever I wore it at home she would yell. She didn't say anything when I wore it around Pop. In Detroit she was very quiet and left rooms quickly. She made meals for Pop and us and we ate things he liked like duck and potatoes.

I opened the foil of my potato and placed it on the plate. I cut the potato and dropped cubes of butter on it. I salted and peppered it and added cool spoonfuls of sour cream on top. I stared at it, perfectly on my plate. I took my knife and began to saw it into cubes, skin and all. I took my first salty, buttery, creamy bite. At the end of the table, Pop put his fork down and laughed. He laughed and laughed until I was embarrassed.

He said, "You eat your potato like an Irishman."

I knew that was a good thing.

"McNuggets, McNuggets!" said Gabe. "McNuggets!"

And we all laughed and the duck just lay there crisp and easy.

Standing in front of Mr. Dawson, with all his science and his impressive glasses hiding those deep blue eyes, all I feel is lousy and in love. Am I supposed to tell him about the duck and the hula-hooping and reading *The Guinness Book of World Records* to put myself to sleep? Am I supposed to tell him how I ached for his smile and thought of him every night while I lay sleepless in bed listening to Mom cry?

Before I tell him everything, because it's on the tip of my tongue, I realize Mr. Dawson knows already. He knows knows knows because I love him.

He just has to know because I can't ever tell him all this.

≈ *The Dance*

Beth says dances make everyone a better person. She has a
theory that the dark is best and I believe her because Shayla
loved the dark. When she would come over at night we would
play Mad Libs and she would tell me about her father's porno
collection, how a man wore a rubber with a devil's head on it.
He had horns and chased women and they liked it. I asked her
for an adverb.

Beth says it's the Indian boys you have to be careful
about. They only want one thing and it's not good because
they're not Mormon and are known for cooking outside. I
went to Beth's house once for dinner and we had to do the
dishes. I dried them, but her dad got mad. He said, "Let's
show Dottie the proper way to dry dishes." And he took the
towel so that his hands were covered completely and then he
dried the plate. Without touching the plate with his bare
hands, he put the plate away. He smiled and said, "Never
touch the plate. Never touch the glass. Never touch the clean
forks with your hands because germs happen." Beth knows
about germs.

"Taylor will be there," she says.

Mr. Dawson will be there, all tall and gentle with his questions making sure no one kisses anyone. Mr. Dawson will stand
in a corner and watch us dance and it will be dark and different from school and we can talk and maybe I can tell him
about the twenty-seven days that made Shayla hate me and
made my mother cry, the days that passed in Detroit, so far
from here. I could tell him about the squirrels and how life
goes away from you when all you did was take a plane and
almost die yourself. I could tell him about Minnesota and what

happened in Minneapolis. I could tell him how I can't sleep or stop walking and why I am so thin and ready to disappear.

He could dance with me.

I tell Mom about the dance and her eyes open wide. She takes me to the Clothes Horse store, where girls go when they have dances. The sale rack has a blue and white striped dress. She says I can wear my white shoes Nana bought me. She keeps telling the saleslady I'm going to a dance and the lady says, "That's special." It's not special because it's the sale rack and I'm ashamed, but I pray to look right. Mom bleaches my shoes in the washing machine.

The gym is dark like Beth said it would be and at first no one's dancing except one couple who sneaked in without their parents knowing. "She's fast," says Beth. But I know the girl's just in love with the boy she's dancing with. Beth dances with an older boy and I stand alone in the sweat smell of the gym thinking about the outside and not wearing dresses and how we play our games here. How hundreds of people watch us here and we're popular.

Mr. Dawson stands in the hallway with our English teacher and she laughs too loud at the things he says. I watch her flip her long hair and when he laughs, he takes a step back. I smile. She leaves and I go talk to him. He smiles and says, "Dottie, you're here." And I know he loves me so, only in this fluorescent light, it's just like class and he's only smiling at me instead of telling me how much he loves me. "It's good you're here," he says. "You're here with friends?"

I know he thinks I'm okay because I'm at this dance, which is the last place I want to be, and I'm only here because he loves me. All the things I wanted to tell him dry up in my throat and I feel myself, my alone boy self, in a stupid striped dress with my pointy white shoes in fluorescent lights and Mötley Crüe playing in the background.

In the gym, fat, red-faced Eddie asks me to dance and his sweaty hands freeze in the middle of my back. It is all I can do to even bear it. All I want is for the song to be over so I can run away. I look out into the gym and I see Dawn. She's standing with some of her cheerleading friends. I am so embarrassed to have her see me in a dumb dress, shuffling around with Fat Eddie and wearing pointy girl shoes.

When the song is over I try to get out of the gym, but Dawn follows me so I have to stop. She smiles at me in the dark and the little scar on her lip is covered with pink lipstick.

"I hate dances," she says.

"Me too," I say.

"I don't know why I came here," says Dawn.

"Me either," I say. "I mean, I don't know why I came here either."

Dawn winks at me.

"You want to go smoke a cigarette?" she asks.

We go behind the school and sit in the grass. We share a cigarette and make fun of all the dumb dresses the girls were wearing. We don't make fun of each other.

Mom gives the dress away when I tell her I hate it.

≈ The Walk Home and Mom Tells

It was just to get groceries was where we went.

Pop had been dead for months and I had started eating a lot.

We had nachos when Pop died because you could order it and pick them up and Mom didn't have to cook and I ate those nachos and ate them. I kept eating. I ate carrots dipped in Italian dressing, chocolate milk on my cornflakes, pizza, big pieces of cheese, and cookies. This is what I did because I missed Pop and no one cooked and we all just wandered around in the house.

I went to sleep with the film of the foods I had eaten on my teeth to remind me what I had felt. When I thought, I thought about food. Pop and duck, Mom and nachos, Gabe and McDonald's, Lyle and fried walleye. I ate and ate and ate and Mom got skinnier and skinnier. Her eyes got bigger and bigger and then we had nachos again. I said, "This is what we had when Pop died." Gabe stared at me and put his head on the table. Mom covered her mouth and went to the basement. Lyle said, "That's great, that's just great." And I kept eating and eating. When it was over, I scraped the cheese from the tinfoil, ate it, and cleared the table.

We went to get groceries and I was thinking about gym class while we walked. It was warm and the sun was going to set soon.

I remembered how I was going to gym and at the bottom of the stairs leading into the girl's locker room there was a full-length mirror. When I looked into it as I passed, there was this girl, so ugly I should have known her. She was fat, really fat, like embarrassing. But it was me in this mirror I was only trying to pass. It was me and the top button of my jeans was unbuttoned. I was ugly and fat and not there at all, but really there. I was afraid because I didn't know who I was with all this death around me.

We walked to get groceries and my thighs were rubbing together. We got the groceries and were walking home. I thought about Dawn and how she'd never love me because

I had let myself become a fat girl instead of what I was before.

Over the rough edge of the bag, Mom started talking. She said how Pop was dead and how sad it was. And I walked. She said how lung cancer is so terrible. And I walked. She said how the doctor stared at his gold Rolex and swore he could cut it out, he could cut the cancer out. She said how Pop laughed because the cancer was the size of a baseball. I walked. She said how Pop walked out, away from the doctor, laughing. She told me the doctor didn't know what to do. "They want money," she said. "They want money and eternal life."

I just walked and thought about Pop laughing because he heard the truth in what the doctor said. He knew he was going to die. He knew it would be expensive.

Then Mom said, as I kept walking, "He killed himself, Dottie. He shot himself in the head and then he died."

I kept walking walking walking, but all I wanted to do was to fall on my knees with the groceries and roll down the hill. I wanted to howl and scream and pull out my hair. I wanted to be in a war far far away from where I was. I hated that Pop had done what he did. I hated him so much for leaving us when all he had to do was suffer a while longer. We walked and walked, but I couldn't feel anything through all the hurt. We unpacked the groceries. We breathed in and then out while we moved from room to room.

There was all this dark quiet inside my head when I went to bed. It crawled over me and shut my eyes. It weighed and weighed on me. I cried and cried and my hands ached for something to hit, but there was nothing big enough. I heard Pop laughing inside my head. I saw him smoking his pipe. I watched him watching me.

I couldn't help it. I loved him for laughing. I loved him for leaving. Then I just hated and loved him and curled into a tight, warm ball.

That night I dreamed dogs were chasing me and they howled and howled. I ran from them, through the dream and through the dark. I wasn't fat in the dream. I wasn't hungry. I was mean and fast and didn't care about anything.

≈ *Mannequins/Voices*

When I start hearing voices, I get the mannequins. They are at a garage sale and Dawn helps me drag them back into my room. There are three lady mannequins and they're kind of scratched up. I place them in my room in poses that make them look like they're talking to each other. I put clothes on them. I put sparkly scarves around their necks and long skirts on them to cover their legs. I take all the posters down from my walls. I even take down the poster of Prince where he's in purple and leaning against a motorcycle. What's left is my bed and dresser and the women.

The voices keep me up all night. I can't make out what they're saying. It just sounds like a buzzing crowd and laughing, like everybody's at a party. If I do fall asleep, I wake up to the voices and it takes an hour for them to go away. I don't like to go to school anymore. I don't care about practice or grades or anything. I tell Mom I have stomachaches and cramps and headaches. I lie to her and tell her I've been throwing up. I sleep all day and wake up as soon as the sun sets. I stay up and wander around the house. I don't eat. Mom makes me mugs of hot chamomile tea, but I pour them in the sink when she's not looking. I feel myself start to melt away. The sight of food makes me sick. I sneak out at night and take long walks in the dark.

I walk all over the neighborhood and walk until I'm dizzy and feel like I can fly. I get skinnier and skinnier. Mom worries.

I spend hours taping music off the radio with my tape recorder. I empty my dresser drawers and fold my clothes perfectly. I go outside and walk for miles. I walk to the basketball courts. I walk to the store which is closed. I walk to the sand hill and climb it in the dark. I walk to Dawn's house and stare at the front porch. I want to tell her things, but I don't know what to say.

One night I decide to take the longest walk ever. I will walk to the dam. The dam is huge and sits in the middle of everything and I decide to walk there.

I walk and walk and I'm not afraid at all. The night is warm and there are the sounds of crickets and faraway cars. I don't hear the voices on my long walk. I make up things in my mind. I make up how my life will be. I think of how beautiful I will be and how tall. I imagine the car I will have and it's a blue Mustang convertible. I will have a house with a porch all the way around it. I will have two dogs and my friends will stay with me whenever they are in town. I will be a rock star or a saxophone player in a jazz band. I will be a movie star or a lawyer. I will be something amazing.

I'm on the bridge and I'm staring at the dam. Underneath the bridge is the Columbia River and it smells sweet, like candy. The dam is huge. I stare at it and stare at it. The water pours from it. The dam gates are open and it looks like a wall of white. The stars are so bright that the white water on the dam looks like it's glowing. Everything is blue and gray and black and white, like a dream.

I lean over the railing of the bridge and into the wind. I close my eyes and smell the water. I feel like I'm floating.

I feel like me, but far away.

≈ *Utah, I Had a Dream*

Dawn says, "Utah, I had a dream about you and Mom told me to tell you about it."

Dawn and I take the same bus home from school. We walk the first three blocks together. She is so beautiful and smart and I don't want her to get too close to me.

She says, "We were older and sitting in the grass by a pond. We were drunk and laughing. There were a million stars out."

"What were we laughing at?" I ask.

"I don't know," she says, "but you stood up and told me you had to leave."

I see Dawn out of the corner of my eye. She is so lovely and perfect. I don't like to look into her eyes because I wouldn't know what to say. I watch the scar on her lip.

"Then what happened?" I ask.

"Nothing," she says. "I woke up."

Dawn takes the right turn to her house. I go to the left, stop, and watch her walk away.

I don't know why she talks to me. I don't know why she dreams about me. I want to tell her things, but I don't know what to say or how to say it.

I want to tell her about Shayla and how I feel like a boy sometimes. I want to tell her about Pop and how he left me all alone. I want to tell her about Lyle's beers and how Mom's quiet and how Gabe is perfect and how it makes me jealous.

I want Dawn to be with me forever, but if I let her close she'll leave. Everybody leaves and when they're gone, there's nothing. Just the shadow of them is left and it's worse than nothing.

I want to disappear.

I want to kiss her and disappear to Seattle with her kiss on my mouth.

≈ I've Walked a Long Way

I'm so sad and I can't stop sleeping. I miss a lot of school and Mom is worried. She brings me tea and cold washcloths for my head. She sits on the side of my bed and stares at me. I look at the wall a lot because I don't know what to say to her. Sleeping too much is worse than not sleeping at all.

When I wake up, I'm more tired than when I went to sleep. I feel so heavy all the time. I feel dizzy. When I close my eyes, I feel dark, mean things gather themselves up all around me. They push me into dreams.

I have a gray fur coat on and I'm walking in the cold. There's snow everywhere. I know I have been walking for a very long time. I walk until all the pine trees are gone. I walk until the rocks turn to piles of sand, then dust, then snow. I walk until the snow blends in with the sky and I feel like I'm walking in a very pale world.

Ice hangs from the fur hood around my face and then there's a river in front of me. I want to walk into the river and freeze and disappear. Instead something makes me leap over it. When I land, there is nothing. There isn't even the pale place anymore.

It feels like shadows are moving all around me. They brush into me. They are warm all over and they pass through me. I can't move. I smell Pop's cherry pipe smoke and I taste snow in my mouth.

I cry out to Pop and ask him to help me. I ask him to come with me. I hear him inside my head and he's laughing. He says he'll carry me back and he'll be there when I wake up. I feel him pick me up and I know everything is okay. When he puts me down and I open my eyes, there's no snow. Everything is green and yellow and bright and you can smell the leaves in the sun. I look for Pop because he promised he would be there.

I see him everywhere without really seeing him.

When I wake up from this dream, I'm not tired anymore. I sit up. I want to take a shower and go for a walk. I open my bedroom window and breathe in the air that's cold and clean and real.

≈ Wheel in the Sky

There is going to be a carnival and a stupid parade and we all look like assholes just marching around the school for practice. Mr. Smith says it looks as if we are marching toward the Russian front. He says he can tell from the smiles on our faces. I wonder why it is okay for a band teacher to be sarcastic, but it isn't okay for us. We try and try to care about practice, but we just can't. No one wants to march. No one wants to play our stupid school song. All we want to do is go home and clean up and go to the carnival. Everybody knows you could fall in love at a carnival.

Nothing much happens in the Coulee, but when the carnival comes it's like the whole world is there all at once. After marching in circles and getting yelled at, we all go home. I can't wait to go to the carnival because I know Mr. Dawson will be there. I know it is going to be one of those nights where anything could happen. Beth is going to come over and we are going to get ready together. Mom complains about Beth's parents. She says, "Dorothy, what is wrong with those people?" She says, "So the girl wants to date. So what? So she wants to wear makeup, so what?" I tell her she has to be more understanding of religion. Mom just looks at me.

Beth comes over and she brings a huge bag with her. I look at Mom and she gets a scared expression on her face. I know she's thinking Beth may never leave. We go into my room and Beth opens her bag. Inside the bag are clothes that are very small and a lot of makeup. Beth starts squeezing herself into the clothes. She talks to me while she does it.

She says, "Dottie, it's not like it's a real sin. You know? I mean, life is just this way and you have to go with it or else you're just out of the loop. I know a good Mormon wouldn't do these kinds of things. Dottie, I know I shouldn't. Let me just tell you, I feel terrible. I think I am very misunderstood here. I mean, it's not like I'm doing anything really wrong. Right?"

I don't say a word because I realize none of this has anything to do with me. The fact that Beth looks like a prostitute has nothing to do with me. All I want to do is get out of the house and away from my family. I want to see Mr. Dawson and hold his hand while I tell him how important the periodic table is.

The carnival is just as beautiful as I knew it would be. All the high school people are there. They hold hands and kiss under the bleachers. It smells like corn dogs and cigarettes and cherries. The only thing I wish is that I was alone. I don't want to be here with stupid Beth in her stupid hooker outfit. I feel dumb even walking with her. She eats corn dogs the boys buy for her. She drinks Pepsi after Pepsi. I end up following behind her and whichever boy has bought the latest corn dog. I feel ridiculous. I want to run far away. Beth laughs a lot at the bad jokes the high school boys tell her. The boys look at me and squint. I squint back. I hate them and their stupid jokes.

After Beth's fourth corn dog she decides we should go on one of the rides. I hate her and her corn dogs and her short skirt and her long blond hair and her dumb long legs and small shoulders. I tell her it's about time we went on a ride. She laughs and says, "Dottie, you're such a good sport." I really hate her. We decide to go on the Wheel, which spins you around and around while you're standing up. Beth thinks it's a good ride because everyone can watch you while you spin. I think it's a good ride because I won't have to hear her stupid mouth anymore.

We get strapped into the ride and stupid Beth is looking around at who sees her being strapped down. She keeps pulling her skirt down and saying, "Boy, this skirt sure is short!" I just keep hating her and hating her. When the ride starts, Beth smiles and says, "Oh!" When the ride finally gets going, Beth turns green. I think it must have been all the boys and the corn dogs. She screams, "I feel sick!" I can't help it, but I start laughing. There's old stupid Beth in her hooker outfit all green and crying.

It's really funny when she throws up and they have to carry her off the ride. Two of the carnival guys take her and lay her down on the grass and she keeps puking and puking and cursing God. The part that isn't funny is all her puke ended up on my shirt. She really let me have it. I climb off the ride covered in asshole Beth's corn-dog puke, and I'm trying to get to a bathroom when I run into Mr. Dawson.

"Beth threw up," I say.

"She sure did, Dorothy," he says.

"It's corn dogs," I say.

Mr. Dawson smiles. "It sure is."

"I have to go to the bathroom," I say.

He says, "I'll go with you."

We walk to the bathroom and I want to die. I waited all night to see Mr. Dawson and when I finally do, I'm covered in throw-up. I hate Beth so much I want her to die right this second. I want her to throw up until she dies. I know it can happen. Mom said Janis Joplin did it.

When we get to the bathroom, Mr. Dawson tells me to wait. He goes into the men's bathroom for a minute. While I wait, I think things. I think beautiful things. I think he's in there trying to figure out what to say to me. I think he's in there trying to get up the nerve to tell me he loves me. When he comes out, he hands me a white T-shirt.

"I was wearing this under my sweatshirt. Do you want to wear it?" he asks.

I say, "Thanks."

In the bathroom I put the shirt to my nose and breathe. It smells just like him. It's still warm when I put it on. I shake and shake with the thought of wearing Mr. Dawson's T-shirt. He is so beautiful. He is so in love with me. I throw my puke shirt in the garbage. I walk outside. He smiles at me.

He says, "Have a good night, Dorothy."

"Okay," I say.

When he walks away, my heart aches and aches. I don't even have the energy in me to think about stupid puking Beth all alone on the grass with the carnies. I hope she dies. I wrap my arms around myself and walk back to the carnival.

"Utah!" yells someone.

When I look, it's Dawn and her mom just smiling at me. I walk over to them and we all stand there.

"This is my mom," says Dawn.

"Hi," says Dawn's mom.

I say, "Hey."

Dawn looks wonderful. Her strawberry-blond hair is tied up into a ponytail and her eyes sparkle.

"Wanna go on the Zipper?" she asks.

I say, "I do."

Dawn's mom laughs and gives me a big hug. At first I want to pull away from Dawn's mom because I don't know her. After a few seconds I just let her hug me. She smooths my hair down and gives me a kiss on the top of my head.

She says, "I'll meet up with you girls later."

She stops hugging me and looks right into my eyes.

She says, "So you're Dorothy."

"Yes, ma'am," I say.

She smiles and says, "Don't 'ma'am' me, honey. I'm not that old."

Dawn and I walk toward the Zipper. It's the best night ever, just like I knew it would be. I don't really care where Beth is right now. I figure she's probably making out with a carnie and thinking how she's a misunderstood Mormon.

≈ It's a Very Small Town

Beth puts eyeliner on me. I borrow Mom's clothes.

I still can't eat, but I actually slept the other day and woke up humping my big stuffed hippo Grandma bought me.

Shayla's been looking at me funny. She's been telling me to grow up all along, but I don't think she expected it. I don't tell anyone about the hippo.

When Gabe was smaller, the hippo scared him. I used to put the hippo in his bed when he was sleeping. He was much smaller than the hippo. When he opened his eyes, there was this big gray hippo staring at him. He would scream and scream and then run.

Now the hippo scares me a little. I mean, it's not right waking up and having these rubbings going on, even if you didn't mean to. I put the hippo in the back of the closet.

Mr. Dawson hasn't said anything for a while, since the dance and the eyeliner and the general confusion of my breasts. I haven't talked to him much either. On the weekend I work on being a woman like in the music videos. Every Sunday I swear that I will tell Mr. Dawson how I feel on Monday. He's sure to feel the same or why else would things be so quiet?

It's a very small town. Mr. Dawson has been away on the weekends a lot. The Indian girls say he has a job in Seattle and they tell me he's leaving the Reservation to work with rich white kids. The white girls say Mr. Dawson's gay. I don't know why being gay would make him leave on weekends, but I prefer the Indian girls' version. This way he can take me with him when I tell him how I feel.

Beth says Mormon girls can get married whenever they want. I think I could be Mormon for Mr. Dawson, but I'll wait until I talk to him. There's no sense in being Mormon and being queer about cleanliness and bigamy before I have to be.

Since I don't sleep much, I have all night to plan my outfit. There isn't much to choose from and in my mind things are different. There's no mouthful of retainers and my hair is longer and blond. There's music playing, like Journey, and Mr. Dawson and I are all alone. The sun is setting and I'm very pretty. I tell him how bad things are and how lonely I've been. He threatens to kill Lyle and I tell him that he doesn't have to because then Gabe wouldn't have a dad.

Mr. Dawson holds my hand, takes off his glasses, and his dark blue eyes stare into mine. I've never noticed before, but he has a few freckles across his nose. I push his black hair out of his face and tell him how much I love him. He tells me how much he loves me and then we move to Seattle away from Mom and Lyle and the basic nowhere that is our very small town.

In the hall on Monday, Mr. Dawson walks toward me. Everyone else in the hall kind of disappears when I realize he's walking toward me on purpose. I forget for a minute my dream isn't true, but then I remember and slip my retainer into my hand while he stops in front of me. He's smiling really wide and I have never loved him more. I forgive him instantly for all the weeks he hasn't been paying attention to me.

He says, "Dottie, I want you to meet someone."

I realize he isn't alone. There's this woman with him and she's very tall, almost as tall as he is. She has brown hair and a big stupid face and she's smiling at me

He says, "Dottie, this is Jessica, my fiancée."

She sticks out her big man hand and says, "It's so nice to meet you. I've heard so much about you."

She wants me to shake her hand, but I can't because my retainer is in my right hand and I think I'm going to throw up.

All I can say is, "Hi."

It's a very small "hi" and I hate myself and I hate Jessica and I hate Mr. Dawson. Now I'll never get away from any of this and he never loved me even a little if he could go out and find this horrible woman and bring her back.

I turn and run and run outside, down the street, past the tavern Mom works in and past the tavern Lyle drinks in, past everything I'm sick of looking at because it's a very small town and I have a broken heart.

≈ The Deer Head

Gabe's watching *The A-Team* and eating an apple fritter. Directly above the television is Lyle's deer head. When we watch television we also watch the head. When we watch *Ripley's Believe It or Not*, we watch the head. When we watch *Night Tracks* on Friday, we watch the head. During commercials we look up at the head just hanging there.

The head isn't very big, but it's very important.

Many years ago Lyle killed the deer and took its head for himself. Since the murder Lyle has been dragging the head around with him. He dragged it into apartments he shared with his buddies and they would drink and watch the head. He took it with him when he married his first wife and she sat and watched the head with him. He took it from their home when he left her and Missy and kept the head in his van.

When he found Mom, we watched him take the head from its bed in the van. He brought us to this house and went and hung the head right above our television. He is very attached to the head after all of this moving it around and rescuing it from the body of the dead deer. Gabe says, "Where deer? Where deer?" And I have to remind him that a long time ago his father killed the very small deer with the very small head and it's never going to finish what looks like a great jump through the wall.

This used to make Gabe cry, but now he just eats his fritters in the damp basement and doesn't worry about it.

Things are exploding on *The A-Team* and helicopters whir and buzz. I am on the phone with Dawn and very happy she called. She is watching *The A-Team* too and while we watch our televisions, we talk on the phone. I lean against the wall and play with the hair on the deer head. I comb it up and smooth it down. I ruffle it and pat it. I just talk and watch television and pet the deer the whole time.

The A-Team is over and Dawn hangs up. I go to my room and Gabe is put to bed and this is the end of the evening.

It is very late at night when Lyle comes home. I hear him stumbling around and dropping his keys. It doesn't take too long before I hear a yell and a stumble, another few stumbles, and a few more yells. My bedroom door slams open and he starts yelling at me.

"The head! The head!" he howls. "What have you done to the head?"

Mom shows up and yells too. She yells about all the yelling until Gabe starts crying and toddles out, dragging his banky.

"Dottie pet head," says Gabe.

He doesn't mean to rat me out, but he does. Lyle tries to lean against the wall, but he misses and falls into the wall instead.

"You're gonna fix the fur," he says. "Right now you're gonna go downstairs and fix the fur."

We all go into the basement and I stand there with a brush and brush the head until all the fur lies flat and Lyle stops yelling. Everybody goes to bed and I am just left there, staring at the head until I have an idea.

After school Dawn comes over to my house. We hide in my room and open her backpack. This part is Dawn's idea and I cannot say no to it. We reach into the pack and pull out beer after beer. They're very warm. We open them, squint, and chug. Soon we feel fuzzy. No one is home.

I tell Dawn the head is downstairs. We are ready.

"And how will we carry the head?" she asks.

I say, "We will put the head in a garbage bag."

Dawn says, "This is a good plan, Utah. A very good plan."

We hiccup and bag the head. We sneak outside, though there's no need to sneak because no one is home. Between us we half carry and half drag the bagged head for several blocks until the sand hill is in front of us.

Dawn says, "It's a great plan, this plan of yours. Now, will we climb to the very top of the hill with the head? Or should we drink our beer and think about it?"

I say, "We will go to the very top of the hill and we will bury the head. While we bury the head, we will drink the last of our beers and that will be a fitting end to it all."

She agrees and we climb.

We collapse at the top of the hill and open our beers. The sun is setting and we're loopy on warm beer and the deer head sits between us. Dawn leans her arm on it and gestures to the lights of our very small town with her beer. She says, "There's the junior high and there's my house." I stare at the lights. I stare at the dam squatting in the middle of our town. We drink and drink and stare at the head.

"It's a shame to bury her," says Dawn. She says, "She wasn't very big, was she, I mean, when he killed her."

I look at the furry head and into the brown glass eyes. I sigh and think about how it's not fair to bury the head when it could just sit here at the top of the hill and stare out onto the town. The head could just look out onto everything and just be. I tell Dawn we won't bury her.

Dawn leans over and kisses me on the cheek. She takes a drink of beer.

She says, "It's a shame, Utah. She's so far from the rest of her."

When Lyle notices the head is missing, he sits me down in front of Mom and yells and yells, "Where is it? Where is it?

Where is it?" And Mom yells, "Where's the head, Dorothy? What have you done with the head?" And I say, "I don't know where it is. I just don't know."

I say this over and over and over. Gabe comes and sits on my lap with his banky while they yell. He wraps his fat arms around my neck, turns to them, and says, "Head go bye-bye."

They stop yelling eventually.

≈ Running, Asthma, and Hairy Legs

I should never have joined the track team.

The reason I joined is because it's the only sport in the spring. Mom says my school is different because it never has more than one sport at a time. She says they keep sports going all year so the Indian kids will come to school. She says, "They'll come for sports but not for class." I don't believe her, but I'm glad there are sports all year because they keep me out of the house. Mom can blame the Indians all she wants as long as I'm not home having to listen to her and Lyle argue.

I'm not a good runner. Basketball is hard too because I have asthma. It's better than it used to be, but it's only because I work really hard not to have an attack. Sometimes when we're running drills at basketball practice, I'll have to stop and put my head down and be calm because it feels like my lungs aren't working. Coach yells and yells, but I don't tell her why. I just stay late sometimes and run more drills on my own. I never had a problem during a game, though. It's just that practice is really hard because we're the best.

I don't like the track practices. There are all these people and even though they say we're a team, it just doesn't feel like it. There's no huge crowd screaming, no cheerleaders, and no smell of an old gym floor. It doesn't feel like a team. I don't know what to try out for, so I try everything. I try hurdles, but I'm too slow. I try the high jump, but I'm too short. I try and try, but I suck. I'm about to give up when the track coach makes me try the shot put. I'm very good at the shot put. He says, "Dot, you have the shoulders for the shot put. This is mighty good." Now I feel more like part of the team because I know I can become tremendous.

At meets I watch the Colville girls run. They run for miles, they run like leopards. Their braids fly and their faces show nothing. They run and run and move like the wind and never seem to sweat. I stand there with that heavy iron ball in my hand and feel rooted to the ground. I want to run like them. I want to have long black hair and no shoulders and feel like I'm flying. I would give up basketball and softball, my powerful arm, and even my impressive hand-eye coordination to be a runner. When people ask me what I do, I want to be able to say, "My name is Dorothy and I'm a long-distance runner." I want to go to the coast and run all the way to Alaska and all around the edge of the continent with my long hair flying behind me.

I think about being a powerful runner so much I believe I am one. I forget about the asthma because it doesn't matter. I begin to believe God has taken away my small lungs and given me huge lungs and long legs and some Indian blood. At one track meet I get my chance. Coach says, "Dot, we need you to run the mile. Willa couldn't make the meet and we'll be disqualified if we don't have one more body out there." I say, "Coach, I will run the mile." He says, "Now, Dot, I know you're not a runner, so take it easy. We just need a body out there."

Coach doesn't know the power of mind over matter. He thinks he does, but he doesn't. In my mind I've already won. He says, "When you run, kiddo, just pretend you're holding a potato chip between your thumb and forefinger of each hand." Coach believes it helps with wind resistance.

We all line up and I've never felt so alive. I feel like I'm made of air. They shoot the cap gun and I leap forward. I run and run and feel so light. I look up and there's no one there. All the Indian girls have passed me. I'm the last one. I try harder and pump my legs as fast as I can, but they're all too far ahead of me. My throat starts to close and my eyes get dark. I keep going. I run and run, but I collapse. I can't breathe and I dig my nails into the dirt of the track. I try hard to be calm. There are people all around me. Coach is saying things. I look up to see Jill and she's rubbing my back. I try to shake her off me. I can't breathe when she's there. She pats me on the knee and I look into her eyes and she's laughing. I look at her hand on my knee.

In the locker room I am very sad. I feel like a failure. I hate God, my small lungs, and my heavy shoulders. I hate my short legs, my tall father, and my lousy luck. I hear girls talking behind the lockers. Jill laughs and says, "Well, it was very funny. The gross thing was that Dorothy doesn't shave her legs!" I look at my legs. It's true, I don't shave them. I didn't know you were supposed to shave your legs when you're twelve. The Indian girls don't. I don't want to shave them. What's wrong with not shaving?

Jolina sees me. She sits down next to me. Her long hair is unbraided. She's so small she's barely there. She's the best runner, a guard on the basketball team with me, and a straight-A student. She's also a Colville girl. She says, "Hey yah, Utah. I could never throw the shot put."

≈ Braces

"Dorothy, wake up."

When I open my eyes, Mom and Aunt Claire are standing over me. They're smiling. When I see them smiling, I smile too because I remember.

Today I get braces.

Gabe is worried. He thinks the braces will cover my face. I tell him braces are a good thing and that retainers like the Bionator are much worse. Gabe nods when I tell him this.

"Dottie?" asks Gabe.

"What, Gabe?"

"I'm glad braces are good and you are good too then," he says.

"Thanks, Gabe," I say.

Aunt Claire and I get in the car. She pats me on the knee. Mom and Gabe wave from the porch. I am so excited I can hardly stand it.

By the time we get to Dr. O'Donnell's office, I feel like I'm crawling out of my skin. Aunt Claire is excited too. She keeps ducking out of the office to smoke cigarettes and pace back and forth.

One of Dr. O'Donnell's assistants sticks me in a chair and puts a bib on me. I wait and wait until I hear Dr. O'Donnell running down the hallway.

"Dorothy!" he yells. "We're getting braces today!"

He blows into the office, rubbing his hands together. He has a huge smile on his face.

"Let me see," he yells. "Let me see!"

He always says this to me. I point my chin at him.

"Look at that chin, lady!" he says. "That is the finest, strongest chin I have ever seen."

"Yes, sir," I say.

Dr. O'Donnell sighs and puts his hand under my chin.

"Spit!" he says.

I spit the Bionator into his hand. He sits and stares at it. He pinches it and twirls it. He nods and smiles at it. He likes the Bionator very much and I know he's sad to see it go.

"Tell me, Dorothy," he says.

"Yes, sir?" I ask.

"Will you miss it at all?"

I look into Dr. O'Donnell's eyes. His eyes are sad and hopeful all at the same time.

"Yes," I lie, "I will miss the Bionator."

He sighs and smiles.

"It gave you a chin," he says.

"Yes, sir," I say. "It certainly did."

Within hours I have braces from Dr. O'Donnell and a new haircut, black turtleneck, and black jeans from Aunt Claire.

"Dorothy," says Aunt Claire over beer and egg foo young.

"Yes, Aunt Claire?"

"I think you're ready to be a beatnik."

"Absolutely," I say.

She smiles and tells me what that is.

≈ Earaches, Rashes, and IQ Tests

I have a lot of allergies. It's the worst in the summer. Every summer when I go to Cleveland I swell up and throw up and my ears pain me. The summer of the IQ tests is the worst summer of all.

I eat cheese sandwiches while Dad asks me questions. He's a teacher, like Cecilia. She teaches retarded kids. She says, "They're not retarded, Dorothy. They're children with special needs." Dad has decided to teach retards too. He used to teach gifted kids. Because I'm gifted, Dad tries a lot of tests on me. I take tests all summer. I eat cheese and drink lemonade and he asks me questions and shows me pictures. He shows me a picture of a phone. He asks me what is missing from the picture. I can't tell him. The phone looks fine to me. Cecilia walks in and out. She talks about the food drive for her church. She looks at me. She looks at Dad. She folds laundry on the couch while I try to answer Dad's questions.

"I don't know," I say.

"Look again, Dottie. What's missing on the phone?" he asks.

"I don't know, Dad. I just don't know," I say.

"Okay," he says. "It's the cord. The cord is missing."

"Oh," I say. "The cord, right."

Cecilia leaves the room with her folded laundry.

"Dad?" I ask. "I think I'm getting an earache."

"Do you want to stop?" he asks.

"It sort of really hurts," I say.

"Try to lie down for a while," he says.

When I wake up it's like someone has set fire to my head. My ear is pulsing. It feels like liquid fire is pumping out of my ear. I lie on the couch for two days, crying. I hold my ear and rock. I get sort of delirious. I remember Cecilia sticking her face in mine. I remember her saying, "An old Irish cure is to pour warm urine in the ear." I remember her laughing. Dad looks worried. He sticks his bearded face into mine. "Dottie?" he asks. "Dottie?" I say, "Daddy?"

He takes me to the ER. The doctor looks in my ear and gasps. They lay me out on a bed-type thing. The doctor talks to Dad over my head. Everything is so white and very bright and this makes my ear hurt more. There are silver instruments everywhere and it smells like rubbing alcohol. I start screaming.

"You're going to have to hold her down," says the doctor.

Dad pins my shoulders down. I scream at him to leave me alone. The doctor keeps sticking something into my ear. I scream and scream.

"Her eardrum is about to burst," says the doctor. "I have to take out all the wax in there or the drops won't get to the eardrum."

"It's okay, Dorothy," says Dad. "It'll only be a second. I promise."

The doctor twists a metal scoop into my ear and Dad has to fight to hold me down. The doctor pulls out a huge chunk of wax and wipes it on some gauze. I curl up and cry. I see him start writing on a pad of paper. His mouth is pursed. He looks very angry. He peers down at me and places his hand on my shoulder.

"Dorothy," he asks, "how long has your ear been hurting?"

I can't stop crying so I don't say anything.

"It's only been a couple of days," says Dad.

The doctor is very quiet and he looks at Dad.

"Shame on you," says the doctor.

I have to put drops in my ears and wear special earplugs. I have to take antibiotics and decongestants. The doctor tells Dad I have weird eustachian tubes. He says they don't drain properly. He says I should take Afrin and Sudafed every time I fly on a plane. He says I should see an allergist. He says a lot of things to Dad. Dad tells Cecilia all of this and she shrugs. She says, "How were we supposed to know?"

We go swimming in Lake Erie and I am careful not to get my head wet. I keep my earplugs in and wear a hat against the wind. It doesn't help. I get a rash all over my body. The doctor says, "Damnit, I said to take her to an allergist!" Dad covers me in calamine lotion and Cecilia reads Roald Dahl stories to me all night. I wear socks on my hands to keep from scratching. While I lie there in the humidity, tears just roll out of my eyes.

When I get better, Dad tells me George's girlfriend is a teacher too. He says, "You remember George? My old roommate?" He tells me George's girlfriend, Margaret, wants to give me an IQ test. I feel like a sick, stupid guinea pig.

I can see the answers to the test from where I sit because Margaret is not as careful as Dad. I cheat. I give her every right answer and throw a few wrong ones in for flavor. When it's all over, I can't sleep. I know I have cheated and that I'm not as smart as what the tests say. I stay up all night. I feel bad, but I can imagine what Cecilia would say if she knew. I decide I don't care at all.

≈ Summer of Cheese

All I want for my birthday are Izod shirts. That's what everyone wants for their birthday. Kelly says I should ask for something else too. She says I should ask for a hat like Prince wears and cowboy boots. She says I should ask for a Walkman and all sorts of stuff. I tell her I don't care about all that. I just want Izod shirts, in green and blue.

Kelly is my Cleveland friend. Dad moved in with Cecilia and Kelly lives in the house down the block. We're the same age and Cecilia said being friends with Kelly would help me "lighten up" and help stop my constant complaining. I wanted to tell Cecilia I had plenty of friends in Washington and I didn't need her stupid help. The truth is I like Kelly and I'm glad to have her. Kelly has a really cool haircut with steps shaved into the sides. She brags about having had sex once. Actually she said, "I think I had sex." That's close enough.

Kelly helps me bug Dad and Cecilia about the Izod shirts. Cecilia says we could just go and buy little green crocodiles and sew them on normal shirts and it would be the same thing. She says the shirts are too expensive to buy. She says Izod is stupid. Kelly and I look at Dad, but he just reads the paper.

"Dad?" I ask.

"Sir?" asks Kelly.

"Dad?"

"Sir?"

"Dad!" I yell.

"What?" he says.

"Can I have Izod shirts for my birthday?"

"We'll see," he says.

Kelly and I go to summer school together. She goes because she has to and I go because Dad thinks it will be good for me. He has me taking typing and pre-algebra because he thinks these things will prepare me for something important. I have to take the city bus all the way to the school. Kelly says summer school is a waste of time now that she's had sex. She says, "After all, I'm practically a woman and who ever heard of a grown woman going to summer school?" I like summer school, but I don't tell Kelly. I like to get away from Cecilia because she says I complain too much. I like to get away from Dad because he likes Cecilia.

Kelly's mom has twin boys and they're always covered in snot and dirt and poop and they cry. Kelly hates her house, but we always go there for money. Her mom gives us ten dollars and we go out to eat. Kelly takes me for sub sandwiches and pizza and McDonald's. She says there's no point in trying to

eat at her house because her mom has the twins and everything is covered in dirt and snot. She says there's no point in
trying to eat at my house because there's only cheese and
bread and eggs and a bunch of weird stuff. I am thankful for
Kelly and her mother's money. Since Dad moved in with
Cecilia, there's never any food. She always rides her bike and
swims and walks and carries on like she's fat. There's never
food except cheese sandwiches and I have to make them. I ate
and ate cheese sandwiches until I couldn't poop at all. Cecilia
said I was eating too much cheese. I didn't know what else to
do because they ate kibbeh and boiled chicken and curry with
raisins in it.

All summer I eat cheese mixed with real food and I go to
summer school. It's my first summer with black people.
There's a boy named Fred in my pre-algebra class. He says he's
an actor. He says he's a better actor because he's black and
then he asks me what two white girls are doing at summer
school. He says this is a black school and Kelly and I shouldn't
be here. He says white people have their own schools. Kelly
says she had sex with a black guy. I don't say anything.

It's a hot summer and we all sit sweating in our pre-
algebra class. Fred passes me notes. Our teacher has an Irish
accent and one arm. I get straight A's on all my exams.

My typing teacher's hair looks like it just gave up. It's a
round brown bowl that sits on her head, but in all the humidity it just falls. It kind of slides to the side. I nibble cheese
sandwiches during class, trying to stay awake. The black girls
crack their gum and scream, "Bitch, please!" I am hopeless in
typing class. I can't make my fingers do what they're supposed
to do. I just stare at the black girls. I love their hair and all the
bright ribbons and barrettes. They wear orange and purple
skirts and shirts with lemon flowers on them. They tie pink

scarves around their necks and wear clear jelly sandals. They have grand names that mean something. Names that combine their aunt's name with a planet with a star with a color. I hit wrong keys and sweat and nibble cheddar in pita with mustard for a kick.

Fred asks me to go on a date with him. I tell him I'll have to think about it. I'm too nervous to say yes right away. I think he's very handsome, but I don't know if I want to date an actor. I tell Kelly that Fred asked me out. She laughs and says he asked her out too. I feel stupid. She asks if I really thought about going. I tell her I never considered it because I knew he was that type of guy.

I stare at Kelly and her cool haircut and her pink Izod shirt. I think I wouldn't be very good in the city with all the buses and the Izod shirts and all the boys who ask you out when they just want to see what you'll say. I miss the Coulee, where no one has any money and there aren't any cool haircuts and people just walk where they want to go.

For my birthday I get an A in pre-algebra, a C in typing, and two Hawaiian shirts that are too small.

≈ The Gap

Grandma takes me to the barn to teach me about my period.

She hands Grandpa a chicken and he chops its head off with one hand holding the feet of the chicken and the other hand holding the ax. The head doesn't come off completely. The chicken dances around with its head flopping.

"Show-off," says Grandma.

Grandpa grabs the chicken again and really lets her have it. The head flies to the right and the dog runs and grabs it.

The body goes to the left and Grandma takes it. She takes a knife and opens the belly of the chicken. She fishes out the ovaries and pinches them.

"This is inside you," she says.

Grandpa says we should bake the chicken and make fried potatoes. He says it can be my good-bye dinner before they drive me to Nana's house. I am thankful Nana doesn't have chickens.

Sometimes I forget Pop is gone. The house is still there and looks exactly the same. It's very hard to fall asleep because I keep thinking about what Pop did. I don't know where it happened. I don't know if it happened in the house. His hats are still hanging in the hall by the back door. I stare and stare at them. I wait for him to come inside the house and pick me up and laugh. He's so tall and his hats are still there. I want his eyes to crinkle up when he smiles and I want him to laugh. I walk into his room and *The Guinness Book of World Records* is still by the bed. I feel sick and lost. Nana and I play a lot of cards and drink a lot of tea. We stay out of the house as much as we can.

Nana takes me to the Gap and buys me sweaters for fall. One is blue and one is green. She buys me shirts and shoes too. We have lunch at McDonald's and when she bites into her Filet o' Fish, her dentures come loose. She laughs and says, "Don't tell anyone my teeth almost came out."

That night I dream about chickens as big as people. They have teeth and they laugh because they're on the *Carol Burnett Show*.

I dream a giant dog is chasing away chickens.

I dream Pop is laughing and laughing because he's riding a horse. I ride with him and we circle the ocean.

13 Years Old

Dorothy, Daredevil

≈ Montana

Lyle has a story.

"I'll tell you a story. Hell, we were out in Montana and there wasn't shit around. Well, you know how those wildfires can get. Anyway, we had us one of them and boy, was it hot out. You could feel the heat just cookin' you where you stood. We get this call up in the office from Barney. Barney was the barber and he lived right up on a hill where he could see just about every goddamned thing. Barney tells us he can see the damn fire comin' right his way and we should get up there and take a look-see.

"We joked around with him and then told him to hurry up and get his ass off of that mountain. He laughed and joked back sayin' that he was just gonna put his whole house on a flatbed and drag it into the river where it'd be safe.

"Well, now, we put out that fire and it was fast and hot and strong. We put out that fire and it damn near killed us. Come to find out, Barney never made it.

"We found him burnt up as Hell in his car with his hands stuck on his steering wheel. Thought he could outrun the fire. Everyone knows you can't.

"Had to get a new barber."

Mom says, "You shouldn't tell the kids that."

Lyle says, "Aw, hell."

≈ *Football*

I decide to do it only when the announcement echoes out of the PA system. The announcement says, "Anyone interested in trying out for the football team, please go to room 107." I get up and I grab my books and I leave. People look at me. White girls giggle. White boys nudge each other with their elbows. Mr. Dawson remains silent. I go into the hall. Mr. Dawson follows. He says, "Dottie, these boys will be running into you." I look at him and into his dark blue eyes and I still love him so, even though he went and married that bitch, Jessica. I say, "I know, Mr. Dawson. I know they'll be running into me."

The truth is I hadn't thought about it. I just heard the damn announcement and got pissed off. I got mad when I saw all the scrawny boys get up and make smug looks at us and take their books and go. There's no reason I should sit through science class if I don't have to. The boys' football team is the only sport the school loves besides girls' basketball. I decide I want to be a part of it.

I get to room 107, which is really just the home economics room. I sit at one of the desks and all the boys stare at me. I stare back. I see Duncan and Nacho and John Garvey and they stare. I stare at each one. I shift my weight. I sigh in a manly way. I appear bored. I come off as very cool. They like this. They say nothing. Brandon is in the corner and I hate him. He's fourteen and very popular. He's rich and stuck up and stupid and cruel. Brandon's girlfriend, Jill, is one of the worst girls in the school. She has perfect hair and perfect teeth and she's rotten as Hell. Brandon and Jill waltz through the halls, make out by the lockers, and come up for air when their faces are red. They squint and glare and shrug and sigh all the time. They're assholes. Brandon looks at me and smiles. I don't know what to do because I never saw such a mean smile. He leers at me and I just breathe slowly and remain calm.

The door opens and Dawn comes in. My heart skips and I love her like I've never loved her before. She sits on the floor near my feet because all the desks are taken.

"Utah," she whispers, "I thought you'd be here."

I love her so much. I love how she knows these things about me and we never have to talk about it. I watch her look around the room at the boys. We're bigger than at least a third of them. I watch her smile to herself. Dawn is not really into sports. She's a cheerleader by nature.

"What about cheerleading?" I ask.

She says, "Fuck cheerleading."

I think about what she says and I like that she's said it. I like that she's sitting at my feet and that I don't have to go through this alone. Dawn is so much prettier than Jill. I look at big, mean old Brandon and smile. It is my first very evil smile. He crosses his arms at me and looks away.

Coach comes into the room and all the boys sit up at attention. They begin posing for Coach, flexing their muscles and jabbing at each other. Dawn and I stay quiet, watching. He outlines the tryouts and what practice will be like. I think football practice seems a lot easier than basketball practice.

It's shorter by an hour and a half and it's outside. I think these boys are pretty soft if this is all they have to do.

The next day a few of the guys talk to me. I am told I'm wasting my time. They tell me I'm an embarrassment to the sport. They tell me there's no way Coach will ever let me play. They tell me I'll be sitting on the bench all season. The Indian girls don't say anything to me, but I watch them cluster around when a white boy throws threats at me. I watch the Indian boys take cues from the Indian girls. The white boys are in a frenzy. Roz talks to me. She talks about football and teams and strategies. John stands next to her. He's a football star. He pats me on the back. The white boys calm down. They stop yelling at me. They listen to John. John listens to Roz. I'm going to be okay. Because I'm okay, Dawn is too.

Practice is easy and slow. Dawn and I hold our own, even though neither of us has ever thrown a football before. Coach tells us there is one more cut we have to make and that is we have to run the mile in under twelve minutes. Dawn looks at me. I stare at the ground.

She says, "You can do it."

I say, "I can't. I can't run that far."

Dawn stares at me. She looks up at the nothing all around us. She stares at me.

"You can do it. Just follow me," she says.

The day of the twelve-minute mile comes around. We all stand there, nervous and wondering if we'll make it. Dawn is next to me. I stare at her blue and gray Nike running shoes. She seems so powerful. She's so thin and wiry and her strawberry-blond hair is tied into a ponytail. She smiles at me. I smile back. We run.

I follow Dawn. I refuse to think about anything. I just pretend I'm chasing her. I pretend I'm trying to stop her because

I have something important to say. There's a point where I feel like I'm going to die. I think I will collapse and die right there in the middle of football tryouts. All of a sudden, I feel like I've had three beers. I feel high and light and amazing. I follow Dawn and we run side by side until we hit the finish line. She smiles at me and I run up to her and wrap my arms around her shoulders. She hugs me back. We just stand there hugging each other and I can breathe like I've never breathed. I feel better than I've ever felt before.

≈ Lyle's Friend Whose Penis Hangs Out

If Mom hadn't fallen down the stairs on account of Gabe's girlfriend, I probably would have never seen what I saw.

Frank shows up around dinner claiming he's Lyle's buddy "from way back," so we have to let him wait. I tell Mom, while we are hiding in the kitchen, that she should just go ahead and call the police. Frank doesn't look very good. He looks kind of gray all over and keeps running his palms along his thighs. He keeps saying stuff like, "Boy, sure have been on the road a while" and, "It's powerful hot out there." Mom finally asks him if he's thirsty and he says, "Yes, I am mighty parched." He actually says that.

Gabe and his girlfriend, Stacey, are out front helping each other look into Frank's car window. I suppose it wasn't really a car because it looked more like a van with the back part hacked off. The car is gray like Frank. He says, "Hell, I mean, just call me Frankie," and then Mom does. The third time she asks, "Now, how do you know my husband?" I go outside. I figure if Mom's going to let some gray stranger with sweaty palms into her house, then she deserves what she gets.

Stacey is a little taller than Gabe and I think they met in school. There's really nowhere else for six-year-olds to meet, I guess. Stacey has bright red hair in short curls and freckles all over her face. She squints all the time, like she's always thinking real hard. She bosses Gabe around and he seems like he's trying to keep at least one room between them most of the time. He calls her his "gorefriend" because it's still hard for him to say "girl." They're staring into Frankie's truck and elbowing each other and giggling. They whisper, "Look, cigarettes," and "Hee hee, dirty magazines." I go and look into his truck and they're right. Frankie's truck looks lived in. It's filthy and weird like some gross old guy's bedroom. I think that this is just the kind of friend I expect Lyle to have. Mom's all alone in the house with him and it makes me worry.

Stacey and Gabe run into the house screaming that they want to watch *The Smurfs* on television. I follow and hear Mom saying they need to go down to the basement to watch. Gabe starts to go down the stairs, but Stacey doesn't move. She whines and says, "Couldn't we watch it up here?" I know she wants to stay close to dirty old Frank and hear what he has to say. She's one smart six-year-old. What Stacey doesn't know is that Mom hates the television. She blames cancer and juvenile delinquency on the TV. She makes us watch it in the basement because she doesn't want it cluttering up her living room. She says she'll be damned if the television drowns out her Miles Davis albums.

Stacey finally convinces Mom to bring the TV upstairs when she says, "It's so cold downstairs and I have allergies." I've never seen a healthier girl in my life, but I think Mom's afraid of Stacey's parents. I heard her call them "asshole yuppies" once. Mom lugs the TV upstairs while Frank drinks his third beer. The kids watch *The Smurfs* in black and white. I see Stacey's ears twitch every time Frank opens his gross mouth.

It's pretty informative watching *The Smurfs* and listening to Frank. Come to find out, he worked with Lyle back in West Virginia. They worked somewhere called Job Corps and used to "get shitfaced skunked, pardon my language" together. Lyle finally comes home and you'd think he and Frank were long-lost brothers. They stutter and stare and paw the floor with their feet. They run their hands through their hair and stare and clear their throats and say stuff like, "Goddamn, boy," and "Who woulda thunk it?" Mom stands there too, looking relieved, until they start drinking.

She clears the dinner that no one eats and Stacey finally gets picked up. Gabe looks very tired and goes to his room to play with his Masters of the Universe toys. I help Mom with the dishes and listen to the men at the table. I have never seen so many beer bottles in my life. They keep saying they'll go out "after the next one" but they never do. Lyle weaves into the kitchen and I see Mom cringe. He opens the special cabinet he keeps the whiskey in. She says, "You better not be planning to drive," and Lyle says, "Hell, woman, there's nothing to hit but dirt and Injuns."

Lyle says, "Hell, remember that transvestite in Baltimore?"

Frank says, "Jesus Christ on a cross."

"Shit," says Lyle, "what a godawful sick thing."

Mom goes into her room downstairs and I go into mine upstairs. I sit a while, but the television is blaring and the cigarette smoke is coming under my door. I climb out my window and go for a walk. I think how awful it is that Gabe has a girlfriend and I don't have anyone. Even Lyle found someone to marry him. I think about what it means to be a transvestite. I think it's when you're part man and part woman all rolled up into one. I know I'm not a transvestite, but if I was I can't imagine anyone worse than Lyle to tell.

When I get home, it's late. I climb back in through my window and I hear the television blaring. I shove my dresser against my door, just in case, and crawl into bed. I don't know what time it is because I've dozed off for a while, but I wake up because I hear a huge bang and a lot of yelling. I run to the top of the basement stairs and see Mom at the bottom. I go to help her and I see the television on the floor of the basement. She looks stunned but okay. Lyle runs out of his bedroom, completely naked, screaming, "What the hell? What the hell?" Mom stands up and says she's okay and that she hates the television and the hurt it has caused her. I look at gross naked Lyle and run upstairs. I look toward the living room couch and there's old gross Frankie with his shirt on and his pants off. The blanket's slipped off him and he's snoring to beat the band with his penis in his hand. I run into my room and climb straight out my window.

I walk and walk all barefoot to the basketball court. I just sit against the pole that holds the basket up. I just sit and sit. I think that they'll never be in trouble for what happened. I start wishing someone would just kill them for what they've done.

Dawn would laugh if I told her about it, but I don't think it's funny.

≈ Game Over

My mom and Dawn's mom, Nancy, are mad. Dawn and I have given them the permission letters they are supposed to sign so we can play football. They have herded us into my mom's living room. Their faces are red and angry.

Mom says, "I told you about Rudy."

"Yes, Mom," I say.

"Who's Rudy?" whispers Dawn.

"Rudy," screams my mother, "is a boy I knew in high school who was paralyzed from the neck down because of a football game!"

"Shit," says Dawn.

"Watch your mouth, girl," yells Nancy.

"Yes, ma'am," mumbles Dawn.

We sit for an hour while our moms scream and yell and carry on about how if we play football, we will surely die a terrible death. Or worse, be paralyzed and traumatized and pulverized. Dawn rolls her eyes at me and the mothers scream more.

"If it wasn't a deadly sport," says Nancy, "we wouldn't have to sign these forms."

"Yes, ma'am," we say.

Dawn and I sneak looks at each other. She shrugs. I know what she's thinking. She's thinking that if we really wanted to play we would have faked their signatures anyway.

"And don't think you're forging my signature," yells Nancy. "I'm calling this Coach What's-his-face right now."

"That goes for you too, miss," says my mother.

"Yes, ma'am," I say.

When they finally let us go, Dawn and I walk to the basketball court for a smoke.

"Fuck football," she says, exhaling smoke, "just fuck it."

She's right.

≈ Too Old for Halloween

I decide to be a bum and Nancy helps. She says, "Honey, we could do better, but if this is what you want, so be it." Nancy smokes really long, really thin cigarettes. She wears lots of clothes all at once, but they're all different colors. She has red hair and huge green eyes and she says, "My mother, Linnea, was from the old country and she knew everything." Nancy says she's a Buddhist because they know everything too.

It's Halloween and Dawn and I are going out. It's like a date. Nancy gives us red wine in juice glasses and does my makeup. I ask her what I was in a past life. She says I am a very old soul, she can see it in my eyes. She says I am well traveled. I like that. I ask her who I was and she gets very quiet.

She says, "A long time ago I think you had a farm and it was beautiful. There were green apple trees and rows and rows of grapes and you were very strong. Dorothy, the grass was so green that it hurt to look at it."

I say, "That sounds like my grandpa's farm in Ohio."

She says, "Maybe it is. Maybe we'll talk another night when it isn't so witchy out."

Nancy draws black whiskers on my face and says, "Dorothy, you won't always feel like this. Okay?"

I say, "Okay."

I'm not sure how Nancy knows what I feel. I believe she does, though. I think maybe being Buddhist and full of past lives and Karma can help in understanding things. When Nancy looks at me I feel a little embarrassed about being a boy and a girl and alone, but she doesn't care. I guess when you've lived a thousand times it's possible to have lives crowding up inside you all at once.

Dawn is wearing her BMX outfit. It's purple and she has a helmet. Dawn likes to ride her bike on ramps. She's getting pretty good. I'm too afraid to do that. Nancy had someone build a ramp in the backyard for her and I've watched her practice.

One time Dawn said, "I'm going to the Olympics one day and I will ride my bike down ramps ten times higher than this old thing." Dawn said, "One day this will be an Olympic event, Utah. Not like all that gymnastics bullshit."

I believe her.

We drink our wine and stare into the fireplace. Nancy's doorbell rings and, when she opens the door, we hear kids scream throughout the neighborhood. Nancy has friends over and they're all dressed up. One woman is a cat and there's a man dressed like a dead guy. There's a woman in a bunny suit and she keeps smoking and saying, "Hell, I love Halloween!" One man is very tall and he's a Vampire. I can't help but stare at him. His hair is black and slicked back and he's very pale. He has blood running down his chin and on to his white T-shirt.

He says, "I need a drink."

He's very convincing and he drinks red wine. Nancy pushes us out the door and into the street. I wish I was a Vampire too, but I'm just a bum.

Dawn carries her pillowcase by tucking it into her purple pants. She looks very cool. When she talks to me, she tilts her helmet back. We're kind of drunk on red wine and I like it. Dawn struts when she walks. She starts to sing a Doors song. She sings, "People are strange, when you're a stranger."

I sing, "Faces look ugly, when you're alone."

We strut down the street, ringing doorbells and grabbing handfuls of cheap candy. We hide behind a house and she says, "Hey, Utah, I took the rest of the wine." When I look over, I see that Dawn has hidden a small thermos between the waist-band of her purple pants and her baggy purple shirt. We move down the street drinking thermos wine and smoking Nancy's long cigarettes. We laugh and talk about movies. Dawn talks about boys. She says, "Mr. Dawson is so sexy!" I don't have much to say to that. I mean, I have a lot to say, so I don't say anything.

I ask her if she remembers her past lives. She says, "Sometimes."

She says, "I don't remember walking on hot coals, but I do remember charming snakes."

I say, "I don't remember anything at all."

She says, "That's because you weren't ready to come back."

I say, "What do you mean?"

She says, "That's what my mom said. She said that we knew each other. Me and you, Utah. We've known each other a long time."

All I can think is that I love Dawn so much it makes my throat hurt. We ring a doorbell all drunk and laughing. Jill answers the door. Jill's a sophomore. This is very embarrassing. She's one of the cool girls that Dawn and I make fun of. She has big dyed blond hair and an evil face.

"Well, trick-or-treat?" she says all nasty.

This is terrible. Jill's boyfriend, Brandon, is on the couch staring at us. I feel like an asshole. Brandon is cool and mean and lousy. He beats up everyone. He even beat up Martin just because Martin plays the flute. He always trips girls in the hall at school. He snaps bra straps and laughs at people with retainers.

I can't think of a way out of this. We can't pretend we're not trick-or-treating because we're all dressed up. I think about just sitting on a couch for Halloween and having a boyfriend and being all grown-up and horrible. I would never be so boring. All these thoughts are going through my head really fast and there's big stinky Jill, just holding a bowl of candy at us and sneering because she thinks we're stupid kids.

I look at Dawn and she turns her purple helmet head at me in slow motion. I know what she is going to do. I like what she is going to do. After all, it's the only way out.

Dawn punches Jill right in the face. We run.

When we finally stop running, we sit and sip thermos wine. Dawn lights another cigarette.

She says, "Did you get real candy bars or just a bunch of suckers and crap?"

I say, "I got a Baby Ruth."

Dawn says, "Hey yah, Utah. What a night."

≈ Daredevils Sledding the Hill and the Pink Hat

Dawn says she doesn't ever want to die. She says she just wants to come close.

Her Buddhist mother from Pittsburgh told her past lives determine Fate. Dawn thinks if Fate is just waiting for her she might as well have fun. I have decided to believe this. I don't believe it for me, but I do for Dawn. She's the one with the perfect jeans, the tiny scar on her lip, and the red-blond hair. It makes sense that she has Fate.

Nancy says Dawn was a fire-walker in a past life. She says Dawn was an Indian man from India who healed the sick and brought dreams to poor women and made his living charming snakes. Nancy also said she'd have to get to know me better before she knew what I used to be.

Dawn decides our Fate is to sled the Hill. This is dangerous. The sand hill is frozen solid. A layer of ice covers it. No one has ever tried to sled it. There was a rumor that three seniors in high school tried once. They had been drinking

Busch from cans all day. They climbed the frozen sand hill with borrowed cookie sheets from their mothers.

Everybody knows what happened. Everybody knows they were all paralyzed from the neck down, ruined for life, and never able to drink beer again. I didn't believe the not drinking beer part, but Dawn said no one wants to buy a cripple a drink for fear of bad Karma.

The day arrives and we stand in the frozen neighborhood, staring down the block. The Hill just sits there. We walk toward it, dragging our blue plastic sled, which scrapes across the icy gravel in the road. My mother screams.

"Your hat, your hat, your hat! Goddamnit, goddamnit, goddamnit!"

The Hat. My mother screams about the Hat. This is the Hat that may never be removed from my head from the minute I step outside. She makes me put it on before the screen door is opened. This is the pink, nubbed wool piece of Minneapolis shit my mother picked up in the middle of a windstorm, in a store somewhere, in the world of Minnesota when my ears almost exploded.

My mother believes my ears could go at any time. When she looks at me she sees blood pouring from my ears, sign language, and Helen Keller. Mom believes the pink hat will somehow protect me from the wind in the world, the cold in the world, and all the earaches that ever were and ever will be. The Hat has become a shield from all that is terrifying. The Hat protects me from leukemia and worms and pregnancy. The Hat is a sign to God not to strike me down in prime sledding season.

I cringe. Dawn stares at my pink nubbed head. Dawn sighs and says, "How Karmically unfortunate." I know she heard that from her mother.

We start walking again when Gabe and Zack roll toward us, all bundled in their snowsuits. Trailing behind them is Zack's older brother, Martin. Martin eats his boogers, plays the flute, and still doesn't know how to ride a bike.

Martin says, "Sledding?"

Dawn is upset. She pinches my arm. I am embarrassed. I'm with a beautiful, cheerleading Buddhist and here are all these losers following us.

"Of course we're sledding," I say.

Martin digs into his nose. Gabe sits on my sled. Zack sucks up snot. I know that soon he too will be digging for boogers. Martin snuffles, flicks, and paws the gravel with his moon boots. He asks, "Where're you going?" Dawn pinches me again and I decide to lay it out.

"We're sledding the Hill," I say.

Martin looks up from the top of his moon boot. "The Hill?" he asks.

"The Hill," I say. Dawn and I turn away. We walk and walk and the Hill gets bigger and bigger. We stare up at the Hill. The sky is gray. We stare at our sled. We look around. The boys have followed us to Fate. Martin pulls up his left moon boot and clears his throat.

He says, "I will sled the Hill with you, Dottie. I will sled the Hill with you because I hate the flute. I hate the flute and if I break my arm I will never have to play the flute again. I will play the trumpet instead. There's nothing wrong with the trumpet. There's nothing wrong with people who play the trumpet."

Martin makes his speech and I feel bad for him. I play the saxophone and I know the shame of the flute. I think maybe Martin should break something. After all, he followed Dawn the Buddhist to Fate. I look at Dawn and she understands. Gabe and Zack watch us begin the climb. They try to toddle up the Hill, but the weight of their snowsuits tips them over and onto their butts. They try again and again and fall again and again. Finally they sit and start eating snow.

The climb is tough. Dawn wants to go all the way to the top. Martin does too. I am terrified. I look toward the top and there's a gray fog. I try to think of how to stop them. Dawn has Fate and Martin has his hatred of the flute, but I have nothing to make me want to go to the top.

I say, "Now, wouldn't it be smart to stop here? We're halfway up and this is quite a ways. I think we should try sledding from here. We can develop a strategy. We can get a feel for the Hill. We can sled now and climb up again."

Dawn and Martin stare at me. I sweat. I pray. They agree with me. I think at that moment, Martin must be weighing the pain of the flute against his life. I think Dawn may be thinking about paralysis and beer. I know Dawn likes beer. I know she'd like to keep drinking beer, and maybe one day have a few by a fire out in the woods with the Colville girls.

No one speaks as we take our places on the sled. Dawn is in front and I am behind her. Martin sits behind me and grips the blue plastic. Gabe and Zack look like fat puppies at the base of the Hill. We push off.

Nothing could have prepared us.

No one could have explained the power and speed of plastic on ice. No one could have explained the pain of cold wind at such a speed. Together we dig our moon boots into the Hill. The Hill spits ice and gravel into our faces. We choke on frozen sand behind closed eyes. We try to stop. We dig our mittens into the Hill and the Hill sprays us with gravel and snow. We cannot stop. Martin is screaming.

We hit a bump in the sand and, in slow motion, I watch Martin sail through the air and onto his ass. We have stopped, finally, at the bottom in front of Gabe and Zack. Martin lands and immediately leaps to his feet. He clutches his ass and runs howling down the block toward his house. He screams, "My butt! My butt! My butt! My butt!" while Dawn and I listen as his screams grow fainter the closer he gets to home.

For a minute I think of poor Martin. I think of the power of the trumpet, the horror of the flute. I think briefly of the health of his arms as he held his ass and ran screaming.

I look up and see Mom. She screams, "WHERE IS YOUR HAT?"

Somewhere, in the middle of the frozen Hill, somewhere pink and nubbed, somewhere far away, is the Hat.

Mom leads Gabe and Zack away with promises of hot chocolate and kittens. Dawn turns toward me. She says, "Fate, Utah. Now you have to believe."

⇌ Lost Luggage

I refuse to spend another summer away from my friends.

Mom says if I don't go to my dad's for the summer, I have to go this Christmas. I tell Mom I will only stay a few days and not through Christmas. I tell her I refuse to spend Christmas with Dad.

Mom looks at me and raises her eyebrows.

"What's going on, Dorothy?" she asks.

"Nothing," I say.

"Is there anything you want to tell me?" she asks. "Is there anything I need to know?"

I think about all the things I could tell her, but I don't say anything. I wouldn't know where to start. I wouldn't know who to blame for everything. Maybe it's all my fault anyway.

I get on the stupid plane and my ears burn and I hate it and then I land in Cleveland.

The airline loses my luggage and they say it will be sent to us in three or four days. I have to borrow Dad's clothes because Cecilia's clothes are too small and too tight and too girlie. I don't have anything of my own and it's freezing in Cleveland. Cecilia says I should stop complaining because it's no big deal. She's a Unitarian and doesn't believe in material possessions. I think that I'm not a stupid Unitarian and it's my stuff missing, not hers.

Cecilia takes us to a church potluck one night. Her church is out in the woods and there's no Jesus stuff hanging all over the walls like in Grandma's church. Cecilia says Unitarians believe in different things like freedom and peace and moments of silence. I meet her Unitarian friends and they're weird. All the women have hairy legs, no makeup, and smell like mothballs. They talk a lot about all the good stuff they do for other people. We sit in a circle and I wait for something to happen. Nothing does happen. They all bow their heads and sit in silence. I bow my head and stare at my knees.

Once in a while someone will say something. They talk about what is on their minds, what they are thankful for, and what the holidays mean to them. Cecilia pipes in and says how thankful she is that I'm with them for the holidays. My face gets all red because it's so embarrassing. I want to stand up and scream that Cecilia is full of shit. My nose starts running. It runs and runs. I want to stand up and yell that I need a stupid Kleenex. I don't know if I'm allowed to stand up and get a Kleenex, so I wipe my nose on the back of my hand. I want to stand up and say I am thankful for the back of my hand.

I'm bored and uncomfortable. I want to say something important, but I don't know where to start.

I think about Kelly and how we saw a guy's penis when all we wanted were cheeseburgers. We saw the penis after we had gotten McDonald's and were walking back to her house. Two boys came up and started talking to us. Kelly was flirting and flirting. I just held on to the food and stamped my feet against the cold. All of a sudden one of them grabbed the bag out of my hand and they both ran away. I was really mad at Kelly for flirting with criminals. We were out of money and just kept walking. When we crossed over the North Avenue Bridge, some man leaped from the bushes and, in the freezing cold, whipped out his stupid penis. We went back to her house and I let her put makeup on me.

This is what I end up thinking during the time we're supposed to be praying. I think about my lost luggage and penises and stolen cheeseburgers. I wait for God to give me deeper thoughts, but they never come. My stupid nose just keeps running. I don't think I could ever be a Unitarian, what with the silence and no Kleenex and having to be thankful.

Dad wakes me up one morning. He asks me if I want to play racquetball. I say okay. I realize I don't have a bra with me. I have gotten into the habit of only wearing a bra during sports. I didn't wear one on the plane, so I don't have one with me. I usually wear two T-shirts. I put on my two shirts at the YMCA and go to meet Dad for racquetball. I realize early on that two shirts do not make up for one bra. I feel gross and embarrassed. Every time I swing the stupid racquet, my stupid chest bounces. I'm all embarrassed and disgusted and ashamed. Dad asks me if I want to keep playing and I say I don't. I tell him I have a headache. We come home early and

Cecilia asks why. Dad tells her I had a very bad headache. She says, "There she goes, complaining again."

My luggage arrives. I have brought all my nicest clothes. I want to look good. I think if I look good and grown-up, maybe Cecilia will get off my back. Dad says we're all going cross-country skiing. I put on my nicest clothes. I wear long underwear underneath. I go downstairs. Cecilia looks up and laughs. She says, "Dorothy, it's not a fashion show." Dad tells me to change. When we go to ski, I really suck. I can't get my feet to go in the right direction. I fall a lot. Dad says it's normal to fall. He says it's tough for baseball and basketball players to ski because they're used to using their upper bodies. Cecilia laughs and says, "Well, I guess you'll be complaining about this later. Won't you, Dorothy?"

I want to tell Cecilia to kiss my ass, but I don't. I figure she'd just bring it up during one of her meetings and all the hippies would hate me. I think she's only a Unitarian to make my life miserable.

I'm just happy I get to spend all summer with my friends and play softball, eat real food, and have nothing to complain about.

≈ Page Seventy-six

I hate Christmas. I hate Christmas so much people tell me to shut up when I talk about how much I hate it. There's never any money and there's never the right present. I ask Mom why we have to celebrate Christmas at all. I ask her why it's so damned important when we don't even go to church or anything. She sighs and says we celebrate Christmas because it's a beautiful thing. She says Christmas isn't as important as

Christmas Eve. She says playing Bach and lighting candles and watching the lights on the tree the night before Christmas is the most important part. She says when Gabe and I go to bed, she sits alone in the living room and watches the lights. I tell her I think that's a fine idea, but I ask her why she can't light candles any old time. I ask her why she has to only do it during Christmas. Mom sighs again and tells me it's because of the Virgin and why don't I just calm down and look through the catalogue.

When you live in the middle of nowhere, the Sears catalogue is a window to what's going on in the world. If it wasn't for the Sears catalogue and music videos, I would never have known you're supposed to be wearing long sweaters with belts tied around your waist. If it wasn't for Sears, I wouldn't know about acid-washed jeans. If it wasn't for Sears and the fact that Spokane is so far away, I would have never gotten my brand-new winter coat.

Every Christmas Nana sends money for me and Gabe. Mom decides what we need the most. This year Mom decides I need a winter coat. I tell her it's true, I do need a winter coat. I also tell her I'm growing up and fashion is something to consider. I tell her I want something stylish. She tells me to look in the catalogue. I tell her I want something flattering. She tells me to look between pages eighty-two and eighty-six. I tell her I want a cool coat and not something girlie. She tells me to look on pages seventy-four through seventy-eight. I tell her I don't want a dumb boy's winter coat. She tells me to calm down and pick something.

The Sears catalogue is not only important for what you get for Christmas, it also determines what you get for other people. Every year I pore over it looking for the perfect gift for Dad and Cecilia. I don't really care about Cecilia, but I think if she likes the present I pick out she'll like me too. This Christmas I decide on sweaters. I pick out a blue one for Dad and a purple one for Cecilia. Mom says I made very good choices and she's sure they will love their sweaters. Then she smiles at me and says, "Did you pick your coat?" I smile too because I found my coat on page seventy-six. It's a boy's coat, but it's very cool. It's dark blue and warm looking with zippers all over the front of it. Mom says it's a very fine coat and Nana will be pleased I picked it.

When Christmas Eve comes, I stay up with Mom. She does exactly what she said she would. She lets me help her light candles. We sit on the couch and she sips wine and we listen to Bach. We don't talk, we just watch all the lights. It's very late when I go to bed. I feel happy and calm and peaceful. I start to rethink my feelings about Christmas because just sitting with Mom in front of the tree is the best thing ever. I fall asleep right away and don't dream and wake up early, feeling hopeful.

It smells like bacon and coffee and toast when I wake up. Gabe is in his baseball pajamas and his bowl cut is messed up. He drags his banky with him while he walks back and forth from the kitchen table to the tree. He hops up and down and his eyes shine.

He says, "Santa, Dottie! Santa came!"

We open our presents and I put on my coat. It is definitely the coolest coat I have ever owned. Mom says it really complements my eyes. I tell her it's not about my eyes. I tell her it's all about being stylish. She smiles. Gabe gets so excited over all the toys that he starts crying. He sits and sobs in the middle of a mound of wrapping paper and boxes. He doesn't know what to do. He is overwhelmed. Mom tells me I have one box left.

The thing I really hate about Christmas is this last box. The last box is always from Dad. I save it until the end because it makes me nervous. Every year he sends me things I could never like. He sends me books on science experiments to do at home. He sends me weird puzzles to put together. He sends me small boxes with projects in them. The projects are on how to make things with household items like pipe cleaners. The things he sends me are never what I want or even care about. This year I get a mobile kit. Inside the Young Scientist box is all the crap you're supposed to use to put the mobile together. It's not even a cool mobile with butterflies or dragons. It's a stupid geometric hanging thing made of wood you're supposed to paint.

Mom and I clean up the living room. She tells me we need to call Dad and Nana and Grandma and Grandpa and thank them for what they sent. I hear her in the kitchen dialing the phone. I hear her talking to Dad. I hear her tell him that if the sweater is too big he can return it. I hear her get mad and say, "Dorothy picked it out herself." I put on my new coat and leave the house. I hear Mom call me, but I keep walking. I walk and walk and before I know it I'm at Dawn's house. I knock on the door.

Dawn opens the door and smiles. She lets me in and her mom laughs and laughs. Dawn runs into her room. I don't know what they're laughing at, so I just stand there like an idiot. Dawn's mom gives me a juice jar of champagne. She smiles down at me. Dawn comes running out of her bedroom wearing my new coat.

"We picked the same coat, Utah," she says.

"Only yours is red," I say.

Dawn's mom asks, "Who wants pizza for breakfast?"

≈ *We're All Going to Die*

We're all hoping Jimmy Carter can fix it. Lyle says there's nothing Jimmy Carter can do because he's from Georgia and only knows things about peanuts and not volcanoes.

I tell Gabe he shouldn't go to school. I tell him he should pretend to be sick like me because Mount St. Helens could explode any day. Gabe gets worried. He poops a lot. He carries around his banky and follows Mom wherever she goes. He puts all of his Masters of the Universe toys in a box. He thinks he'll be able to ride the hot, molten lava all the way to the river, carrying his box of toys. I tell him there's no way that will happen. I tell him the lava will finish him off. Mom yells at me to stop scaring my brother. I don't know why she's not worried.

"We made it out of West Virginia, Dorothy. We'll make it through this. Besides," she says, "the volcano is hundreds of miles away."

I take out my book on Pompeii and point to the pictures of the people covered in ancient lava. I show her the picture of the woman bending over a basket. I show her the picture of the child sleeping in its bed.

"That's how fast it can happen," I say.

"You're terrible, Dorothy," she says.

"You all just better hope that Jimmy Carter can do something about this," I warn.

Lyle gets mad. "There's nothing a damn peanut farmer can do about a goddamned volcano!"

I can tell I've made them think. The truth is, I'm not worried at all. I just like making them mad. There's no way the explosion will affect me. I have a weird sense of happiness. I like it that at any moment my family will be swept away by a huge lava flow. I figure I'll save Gabe, but Mom and Lyle are on their own.

For days I have been watching the news and following the progress of Mount St. Helens. It all started with the earthquakes they reported on the news. They waited almost a month before telling us about them. When they saw the smoke, they had to tell us something. When the bulge showed up on the side of the mountain and the National Guard was called, I was more than ready. It's not like I really did anything to get ready, but I was ready in my mind.

Gabe wakes me up very early. He sits on my bed and pokes me with his chubby fingers. His green banky is wrapped around his neck like a scarf. His baseball pajamas are on inside out. I stare at him.

"It said on the TV that it's going to 'plode," he whispers.

"Now?" I ask.

"After the 'mercial," he whispers.

Poor Gabe, I don't think he's slept for days. We run downstairs to watch TV. Gabe's box of toys is on the couch. He curls up next to his toys and sticks his thumb in his mouth. He looks at me. I feel bad for scaring him. I really didn't mean to. I just meant to get him excited. I realize I shouldn't have shown him the pictures of Pompeii.

"We're not going to die," I say.

"Okay," he says.

"Gabe, seriously, we're going to be okay. The volcano is far away. I just said all that stuff to scare Mom and Lyle," I say.

He unwraps his banky from around his neck and stares at his thumb.

"I know," he says. "You were just kidding us."

I can't tell if he believes me or not.

"I wouldn't ever let anything happen to you," I say.

He nods at me. The television says that Mount St. Helens has exploded. Gabe farts.

The next couple of days are gray. There is no light. A little sticky ash falls here and there. No one talks about anything except Mount St. Helens. Jimmy Carter goes on the television and says it's the worst thing he's ever seen.

"I told you he wouldn't do anything," Lyle says.

I didn't want President Carter to stop it. I just wanted him to say it was the worst thing ever, and he did. A bird flies into our window and dies. No one else is hurt. Gabe smiles and unpacks his toys.

≈ *Races, Rodeos, and Stampedes*

"She's dating a cowboy," sighs Dawn.

"A real cowboy or a drunk with boots?" I ask.

"A real goddamned yahoo. A shit-kicker. That's what he calls himself," says Dawn.

Dawn is upset because Nancy's dating a cowboy. She told me she didn't mind the sculptor guy, she thought the computer guy was nice, and she even liked the jazz musician, but she doesn't know about the cowboy yet. Dawn says cowboys have a tendency to break hearts. She says Nancy's wearing a lot of turquoise and is listening to Emmylou Harris late into the night. Nancy has started having visions of a farmhouse in what she thinks is Montana.

"She said it's either Montana or Wyoming," says Dawn. "Shit, she might be falling in love. She only has visions when she falls in love."

I've been staying with Dawn and Nancy a lot. Nancy lets us drink watered-down wine while she reads our Tarot cards.

She doesn't make real dinners, just a lot of appetizers. We all sit around on her Oriental rug and eat liverwurst and tomatoes on crackers, drink watery wine, and listen to Willie Nelson. Dawn tells me her mother doesn't understand her all the time. Dawn says Nancy was against the BMX racing at first because she thought it was too patriarchal. Dawn told me patriarchal means that boys do it.

"For example," said Dawn, "peeing standing up is patriarchal."

Dawn wants to join the Navy when she's older and Nancy doesn't want her to. Nancy says the military is the worst example of violent capitalism. I ask Dawn what that means exactly and she says it means when you make too much money you get angry. I don't say anything to Dawn, but I agree with Nancy. I don't want Dawn BMX racing because she might get hurt. I really don't want her to join the Navy because I'll never see her again and then I'd have to join the damn Navy, which would suck completely. Dawn tells me how wonderful it would be to float around on a huge ship and go to amazing places. I tell her we could float around on a normal boat and go see amazing places. She said, "That's true, but we couldn't wear uniforms or blow things up."

It's hard for me to imagine that Dawn was a cheerleader when she first moved here. Nancy says I'm a good influence. No matter what Dawn wants to do in the future, she's upset that she has to deal with the cowboy now.

She says, "Things were really starting to mellow out. We even sold the jazz guy's trumpet and now she has to go and be a cowgirl."

One Friday night, while I'm staying at Dawn's, the cowboy shows up. He's short and all full of muscles. He smiles a lot. Nancy makes a real dinner and we all sit around the table.

Dawn is seething because we're going to have to miss our Tarot reading. She drops her napkin and when she goes to get it, she kicks me. I drop my napkin and meet her under the table.

She whispers, "We have to get rid of him."

I think for a minute she means to kill him. I don't think we could get away with it. After all, Darrell is a cowboy and he'd most likely be missed.

"Will we kill him?" I ask.

"No!" she says. "Just embarrass him so much he leaves for good."

Back up at the table, I watch her out of the corner of my eye. Her strawberry-blond hair is pulled into a loose ponytail. Her cheeks are flushed from the watery wine. She starts chewing her fingernails. I want to tell her Darrell's not so bad. I want to stare deep into her beautiful brown eyes and tell her it could be so much worse, but I don't.

"So, Darrell," she says, "are you a real cowboy or just a drunk with boots?"

I am horrified because she stole my line and this isn't the most subtle attack. Darrell picks up his glass of whiskey and smiles. He looks at Nancy and Nancy looks at Dawn. Dawn stares at Nancy and I pick at my casserole. I wish I had the guts to do what Dawn's doing.

"Well, honey," says Darrell, "I wouldn't consider myself a drunk, though my father had quite a problem."

"So," says Dawn, "your father was an alcoholic."

"He shore was, honey," smiles Darrell.

"Do you have horses?" I ask.

Dawn looks at me as if to say, what a stupid and not-mean question. I meant to sound smug when I said it, like, "Do you, lame Darrell, even have horses or are you just a lying loser?"

"I have six horses out there near Nespelem," he says.

"What do you do all day?" asks Dawn. "Just sit around with your horses?"

"I made my money some years back, so I do just sort of sit around with them," he says.

"Gambling?" I ask.

Dawn nods at me as if to say, that's a better question than the first one.

"Nope, don't gamble," he says.

All through dinner we try to catch Darrell in a horrible and embarrassing truth, but we can't. Nancy stops glaring at us and begins to smile. She clears plates and brings dessert. Over ice cream Darrell tells us about the Suicide Race in Omak.

"Y'all got to come with me tomorrow and take a look," he says. "It's a race and a rodeo and damn near a stampede. These guys ride their horses down this cliff, cross the Okanogan River, and race on to the finish line. Some men have even been killed."

"What about the horses?" I ask.

"Some of the horses get hurt, honey," says Darrell.

I decide to let Darrell have it.

"I think that's disgusting," I say. "It's fine if men die because they have a choice, but it's not okay if horses die."

I look at Dawn because I think she will agree with me. There's a sparkle in her eye and she's leaning forward.

"Are you going to do it? Are you going to race?" asks Dawn.

"Sorry, honey," he says. "I'd like to stick around for a little longer."

He winks at Dawn and it enrages her. I can tell she's decided to try and get him killed instead of just embarrassing him.

It's hot on Saturday, exactly one hundred and four degrees. At least that's what they say on the car radio. When we get to Omak, the dust rides up into our faces and the river is clear and ice cold. Indians from all the Colville Confederated Tribes are there. Some are dressed in ceremonial clothes, some wear cowboy hats and blue jeans. Darrell seems to know everyone. They all shake his hand and slap him on the back. Dawn and I sit by the river with our shoes off and our feet in the water. We chug Diet Pepsi and squint our eyes against the light on the river.

"Looks like diamonds," she says.

"Why do you hate him so much?" I ask.

She doesn't say anything. She buries her feet in the wet sand. She sighs and burps.

"What if it works out?" she asks. "What then?"

There's nothing for me to say because I know how she feels.

We walk through the festival watching the Indian stick games, the dancing, and Nancy's jewelry buying. Darrell runs up to tell us the Suicide Race is going to start. We stand in a crowd of people and stare up at the cliff. There are about twenty men on horses at the top of it. When the gun goes off and the men start coming down the hill, Dawn's face lights up. She is mesmerized at the danger. She clenches her fists and screams with the crowd. I know she wants to try this. I can almost hear her in my mind saying, "Hey yah, Utah. I can do this." The men come crashing down the cliff. Two horses fall and their riders are thrown. The others cross the river and the water sprays up into the heat and dust of the afternoon.

The man who wins is Nez Percé and one of the most beautiful men I have ever seen. He's tall and bronze with long black hair that he ties up with a leather strap. People gather around him, slapping him on the back. He stares at his horse, who's heaving and scared. He moves his horse through the crowd and squats in front of it. He strokes its head and nose. When I stop staring at the Nez Percé man, I realize I'm all alone. I see Dawn riding on a horse and laughing. Darrell is leading the horse. Nancy stands to the side with the sun glinting off her turquoise necklace.

Nancy walks over to me and puts her arm around my shoulder. She gives me a quick hug.

She says, "See, Dorothy, he's not so bad."

I say, "I didn't know Dawn liked horses."

"Her father had horses a long time ago," says Nancy.

"Oh," I say.

"Would you like to ride one?" she asks.

"I can't," I say. "I'm allergic."

"Would you like to meet the man who won?" she asks.

I can only nod at her because I am so nervous. I didn't know she knew him. I didn't know anyone knew him. She leads me over to the tall, beautiful Nez Percé man.

"He's beautiful, isn't he?" she whispers to me.

"He's Nez Percé," I whisper.

"How did you know that, Dorothy?" She smiles.

"I don't know," I say. "He looks different."

Nancy laughs. The man comes toward us. He looks down at me and smiles. His teeth are bright and his eyes crinkle up.

"This is Dorothy," says Nancy. "Dorothy, this is Mike."

The man reaches out his hand toward me. His hand is huge and his fingers are the longest, most beautiful fingers I have ever seen. I shake his hand. I fall in love. He laughs and laughs because somehow he knows everything about me and it's okay.

"Where have you been?" he laughs.

I don't say anything because I am in love in the weirdest way. I know him. I know him.

Darrell and Dawn ride over to us, and Darrell helps Dawn off the horse. Dawn's eyes are shining. She looks at the Nez Percé man and back at me.

"You should ride," she says.

"I can't," I say. "I'm allergic."

I'm very embarrassed Mike heard this. It's not cool to be in love with someone who's so good with horses and not be able to ride one yourself. Everyone knows that.

Mike laughs and I look down because I'm sad he's laughing at me. All of a sudden his arms are around me and I'm in the air and then on the back of the horse with him. I think he must be an angel.

We take off and ride and the wind is amazing and you can smell the barbecue and the whiskey and the river. We ride and ride and I feel his arm around my waist. He's so beautiful that I don't ever sneeze and my eyes don't even itch.

When we get back, Nancy gives me and Dawn a beer and matching turquoise bracelets.

We all sit by the river and laugh at things Darrell says.

I sit near Mike and feel perfect.

I steal looks at him in between sips of my beer. I feel like I know him.

Dawn holds my hand and smiles.

≈ We Make a Great Team

Every time you come in first, you win money. It's not a lot of money, only a few bucks here and there, but it all adds up. Dawn and I win almost every single event.

The Moose Lodge picnic happens every year. All the members and the employees get to go. They barbecue steaks and deer meat and the women make all kinds of salads. They make macaroni and potato salads. They make corn salad and coleslaw and Jell-O salad. There's slaw with raisins and Jell-O with carrots. There's a lot of meat and sauce and macaroni and cheese. There are ten kinds of rolls, all hot and buttered. There are biscuits, fry bread, and baked, mashed, and sweet potatoes. All the food that ever was is at the Moose Lodge picnic. Mom takes us and we love it.

They have contests for the kids. I bring Dawn and we make a great team. We've already won at least ten dollars apiece. We beat the stupid boys and even the drunk adults. Dawn tells me this is a fine and important thing we are doing. She tells me she wished her mom worked for the Moose Lodge too.

Dawn wins the fifty-yard dash and I win the tug-o-war. Dawn wins the obstacle course and I win the girl's baseball throw. We count our money and laugh. We take plates of macaroni and cheese and coleslaw and sit under a tree. We eat and laugh and make plans for our strategy in the three-legged race.

"It's five bucks, Utah," she says.

"I know," I say.

"We should practice," she says.

We tie my left and her right leg together with a purple bandanna we borrow off the guy pouring beer. We run and run in circles. We plan and plan our maneuvers.

"I'm full," she says.

"Me too," I say.

We sit under the tree and stare at the river. It is so bright and beautiful out. All the money we've won sits heavy in our pockets. I steal a look at her out of the corner of my eye. She is so beautiful. Her hand is resting on her stomach. There are leaves in her hair and barbecue sauce on her chin. I want to reach over and wipe it off for her.

"Who is that?" she asks.

I look over to where she's pointing her chin and I see a very thin boy. I look all over to see what she's looking at, but there are only a few trees and the very thin boy.

"The trees?" I ask.

"No, silly," she says. "Who's that guy?"

I look at the guy and I don't know who he is. He's very thin and that's all I know. Maybe she thinks he's weird and ugly.

"He's so cute," she says.

"He's weird and ugly," I say.

Maybe she thinks he's staring at her and she hates it.

"I think he's staring at me," she says.

"Should I punch him?" I ask.

"No," she says. "I'm going to talk to him."

I can't believe it when she actually gets up and walks toward him. I watch her do it and I feel sick all over. I feel like I'm going to puke macaroni and coleslaw all over the tree.

I watch them talk and they actually start laughing. She points over to me and the thin boy waves in my direction. I look around, but he's really waving at me. I don't wave back. I hear Dawn laugh and I wonder what she's saying to him. I yell over to her that the race is going to start soon. She pats him on the shoulder and walks toward me. I want to throw up so bad I can taste it in the back of my throat. The thin boy puts his hands in his pockets and whistles. I hate him for whistling.

While Dawn and I walk toward the race, she starts telling me about the boy. She tells me he's in high school and he's on the debate team and isn't that so cool? I tell her winning the race is cool, but her new friend is definitely not cool. I tell her there's something wrong with a boy who stares at girls when he's all alone with his hands in his pockets. I remind her of Ted Bundy and how nice everyone thought he was. I remind her of the high school girl who we heard got pregnant and then died. I tell Dawn her new friend was probably the one who got the poor girl knocked up. Dawn tells me I'm being stupid.

"He's just a boy, Utah," she says.

"I don't see what's so great about a skinny, weird, hands-in-his-pockets high school boy," I say.

We tie our legs together and glare at each other. We lose the stupid race because we're both too mad to focus. Two stupid boys win the five dollars. Dawn rips the bandanna off our legs and heads toward the macaroni and cheese. I follow her. When she gets to the table, the High School Boy starts coming toward us. My hands start to itch and sweat.

"Let's go swimming," I say.

Dawn looks up and sees him coming. She smiles and loads up her plate.

"I don't feel like it," she says.

I see him coming closer and I want to just die right there next to all the weird Jell-O salads.

"C'mon," I say, "let's go."

"He's just a boy," she says. "We don't have to run away."

I stare at her and her plate and her eyes and her red-blond hair all messed up with leaves in it. I feel my heart just stop.

"It's okay, Utah," she says. "He's just a boy I met."

When I look up, he's there. He's just standing there, looking at her and smiling.

≈ *Does He Have to Be Here for This?*

"It's not going to be that bad, Utah," says Dawn.

I am holding a box full of candles, books, and towels. The bottom of the box is falling apart already and I haven't even gotten it loaded on the truck yet.

Dawn doesn't think moving all the way out to Nespelem is going to be bad. There's no reason for her to feel it will be bad. She'll have Nancy and Darrell and the horses. Mike will probably visit and they'll all sit around watching horses and drinking beer and laughing. I'll be stuck in the Coulee with Gabe, listening to the *Thriller* album and watching *Night Tracks* on the weekends. Dawn is going to be a cowgirl and I'm going to have to get used to only seeing her in school when we pass each other in the hallway. She will forget about me and make new friends and ride horses all weekend. When I'm finally old enough to drive, she will have joined the damn Navy and I'll have to drive my blue Mustang to different ports trying to track her down. The worst part is the High School Boy who likes her. He's carrying boxes too, but they're not falling apart.

"Does he have to be here for this?" I ask.

"He wanted to help and Mom said he could," she says.

"Well," I say, "I don't like him. He smells funny. He walks weird and he keeps staring at you. He's too old and too ugly and completely in the way."

"I barely noticed he was here," says Dawn.

I hate the High School Boy. He wears too much cologne and laughs too loud. I keep warning Dawn she'd better watch out because she could get pregnant. One day it's just a movie date and the next minute you're eating government cheese and changing diapers. Dawn says she's not even sure if she wants to go out with him. She says he may not be mature enough.

Nancy tells us all to quit working so we can have lunch. She puts Kentucky Fried Chicken buckets on the picnic table and Darrell brings out a cooler of beer. He wipes his forehead off with a bandanna and offers the High School Boy a drink. I can tell it's probably the first beer the stupid guy has ever been offered. He kind of stammers and stutters and turns red. I look at Dawn to see if she's noticed this uncool behavior. I stride on over to Darrell and stick my hand deep in the ice of the cooler. I pull out a beer, open it, and hand it to Dawn. I stare at the stupid High School Boy and put on what is my coolest glare.

He says, "Drinking alcohol is against my religion."

What a loser.

"What religion is that, dear?" asks Nancy.

"I'm Mormon," he says.

Man, what an asshole. I nudge Dawn and whisper, "That means a lot of babies" in her ear. She walks away. I can tell she's mad at me, but that's just because the first guy who's really been into her is an asshole, moron Mormon. I decide I'll stop bugging her about it. After all, every time the guy opens his mouth he digs himself a deeper hole. He doesn't need my help to look stupid.

I grab a seat under a tree and eat my chicken and drink my beer. I watch the stupid High School Boy talk to Dawn. I throw a chicken bone into the bushes. Nancy comes over and sits next to me.

"Dorothy, you're always welcome at the house. You know that, right?" she says.

I say, "Yah, I know."

"Just because we're going to be farther away is no reason for us not to see you," she says. "You can come out every weekend and stay through the week. You girls can take the bus in to school together. I've already talked to your mom about it, okay?"

I say, "Yah."

"Dawn knows that she can do the same over at your house," she says.

I say, "Okay."

"Dorothy," she smiles, "just between you and me, I don't think it'll work out between them."

We both look over at Dawn and the High School Boy. Nancy starts laughing.

I say, "I think he sucks."

She says, "Yes, I think so too. Don't tell Dawn I said it, okay?"

"Okay," I say.

I hope and hope Nancy's right. I really hate him. I just can't believe Dawn thought it was okay for him to be here on what is a very important and upsetting day. I decide there's nothing I can do to stop this, so I may as well let it play out. This goes against everything I really want to do, but I know it is the smartest thing. Dawn comes over to me, sits down, and puts her head on my shoulder.

She says, "I'm going to miss you this weekend."

I tell her I'm going to miss her too. The stupid High School Boy is looking at us. He must be mighty jealous of Dawn's head on my shoulder. I smile. He smiles back.

Dawn says, "He's going to take me to a movie on Saturday. He can drive."

My stomach lurches.

Saturday rolls around and I keep pacing through the house. I have tried to go on walks, but I keep walking to Dawn's house and she's not there anymore. I found the chicken bone I threw in the bushes and I was so bored that I buried it in the dirt near their driveway. I felt so stupid burying bones like a stupid dog that I went home and stole a beer from the fridge. Gabe keeps running in asking me if we can watch *Night Tracks* together. I yell at him to stay out of my room because I'm trying to get drunk and I don't want Mom to find out. He says he'll leave me alone if he can taste the beer. I tell him he's too young and that your heart has to be broken before you can really appreciate beer.

He says his heart is broken. I ask him how the heartbreak happened. He says he just woke up with it. I tell him his heartbreak is not real. He cries and says it is. He cries so loud that I let him sit on the floor of my bedroom and play my 45s. He spins around.

It takes me a minute to realize my worst fear is coming true. Dawn is on her way to a date with a stupid Mormon and I am drinking alone in my room with my baby brother.

I sit straight up in bed. My heart is pounding. I realize I can't let her go out with this stupid High School Boy. I decide I will stop the date. I will do anything to make this not happen. I know I have to be sneaky and sly and conniving. I don't know exactly what I will do, but I figure something will come to me. I start to put on my shoes when Gabe gets wise.

"Where are you going?" he asks.

"I just have to go," I say.

"But where, Dottie?" he asks.

"I have to go to the stupid theater and do something really important," I say.

"You gonna see a movie?" he asks.

"I might have to, but I don't know yet," I say.

"I'm going too," he says.

"No way."

"Yes way."

This cannot happen. It's late and I have things to do and I can't go to the movies with my little brother on a Saturday night. Everyone knows Saturday night is date night. I tell Gabe he can't come with me. He tells me if he can't go, he's going to tell Mom I was drinking a beer. I stare at Gabe. He wraps his banky around his neck and smiles. I cannot believe he's smart enough to come up with this. He waddles off to get his shoes.

I tell Mom I'm taking Gabe to a movie and she looks at me weird. I tell her the movie is *Nine to Five* and Gabe doesn't have to go if she thinks it will be too adult for him. She continues to stare at me. She sees Gabe all dressed in the living room with a stuffed dog and his banky wrapped around his neck like a scarf. She tells me he can go because she saw the movie and it wasn't bad.

She says, "Make sure you never let go of your brother's hand."

We make our way to the movies and I tell Gabe he can let go of my hand. He tells me Mom said he could hold my hand the whole way. When we get to the movies, I really want to die. Gabe looks like some kind of circus geek and I have to hold his hand. All this because of one beer. I make him hide behind a car with me.

He says, "Are we peeking?"

"Yes."

He says, "Who at?"

"I'm trying to find Dawn."

He says, "There she is! There she is!"

"Shh! That's not her."

He says, "There she is!"

"Shut up, Gabe! That's not her either."

When I do finally see her, I feel like puking. She gets out of a blue car and her hair is down. She has makeup on and even a skirt. I can barely recognize her. She looks a lot older.

"Is she here?" asks Gabe.

I point her out to him.

"That's not Dawn, Dottie," says Gabe. "That's a grownup."

I am starting to think my brother is gifted and must be watched very carefully from now on. I make a mental note to tell Mom to get him tested just so I know what I'm dealing with. While I'm thinking this, the stupid High School Boy takes Dawn's hand and leads her to the ticket window. Gabe pulls on my coat, saying he wants to go inside and sit down. I tell him if he waits a little longer I'll buy him a hot dog. He sits on the curb.

When we go in I buy Gabe's hot dog and get us seats in the back. Eventually Gabe falls asleep with half of the hot dog in his hands. I keep staring at the backs of the seats trying to find Dawn. When I find her, I see that the stupid Mormon High School Boy has his arm around her. I get angry, but I don't know what to do. I think I should throw Gabe's hot dog at them, but then they'd know I was there. I decide this is the dumbest thing I have ever done and I need to get out as soon as possible, but I can't seem to move.

Gabe is snoring a little and I slump down in my seat and wait. I pick Gabe up before the movie ends and carry him outside. He wakes up after I put him on the grass and then finishes eating his hot dog. I see Dawn and the dumb Mormon come outside. They're talking and holding hands when all of a sudden he kisses her. Gabe's eyes get really big and he starts to open his mouth. I clamp my hand over his face, pick him up and carry him away.

At home Gabe tells Mom we had fun and he got to eat a movie hot dog. I think he's already forgotten about the beer and Dawn and the kiss. He hugs me and goes to bed. Mom tells me I'm a good sister and she can tell that Gabe had a lot of fun. I feel sick and guilty when she gives me a kiss on the cheek. I go into my room and lie on the bed. I stare and stare at the wall. I know this will now be my life. Now that Dawn's been kissed, the world has ended. There is no hope. I sigh and sigh and stare at the wall. I decide to listen to my Stevie Wonder 45. I sing along to "Tuesday Heartbreak" even though it's Saturday.

There's a tapping at my window, so I turn the music down. The tapping becomes a banging. I pull back the curtain and see Dawn's face and it's a very angry face. I open the window and she climbs inside.

"What an asshole," she says.

I don't know what to say. I feel like God has finally paid attention to me.

"He said girls had no business riding BMX bikes. He said God made women to have babies and stay home. He said there's no way they'd ever let me in the Navy because women weren't allowed on boats. Did you ever hear that?" she asks.

"No," I say.

"What a jerk!" she yells. "I have to use your phone to call my mom. I'm staying over."

"Okay," I say.

Dawn calls her mom and tells her what happened. Dawn gives me the phone and says her mom wants to talk to me.

"Dorothy?" asks Nancy.

"Yes?"

Nancy laughs. "I told you it wouldn't work out."

When I hang up the phone, Dawn asks me what her mom said. I tell her Nancy said she could stay the rest of the weekend. Dawn says, "Cool."

⇒ Enough Whiskey

I suppose there's just not enough whiskey in the world when your dad dies. Lyle's trying to find out how much there is.

He wanders around the house barefoot, holding a bottle of Jack Daniel's. His eyes are bright red and he can't stop smoking. He'll light one cigarette with the other and smoke and smoke until he wheezes. Mom runs around opening windows and offering glasses of water, but he doesn't want them. He circles the house and the yard over and over. He walks until he stumbles and then stumbles until he falls and then Mom covers him up wherever he stops.

Gabe says, "Somebody died, Dottie."

And I say, "Gabe, your dad's dad died."

"Like when Pop died?" he says.

"Kind of," I say.

Gabe and I watch Lyle stumble in his circles and we wonder why he doesn't leave the house. I think he's trying to get up enough speed to just fly into the air. Gabe thinks he doesn't remember how to leave. Mom doesn't say anything much. I ask her why we never met Lyle's dad.

"He wasn't a very good man," she says.

I think he must have been pretty terrible if even we didn't meet him because we meet everyone and most of them are horrible.

One morning Lyle is gone and Mom sits at the table all day, drinking coffee and smoking cigarettes. She jumps every time the phone rings. Later in the evening, she tells me to watch Gabe and to stay in the house. She gets her coat and her car keys and leaves. I do what she says. Gabe and I play with his Masters of the Universe toys and listen to 45s on my record player. He likes Superfreak the best and tries dancing, but he mostly just spins in circles.

An hour later there's a lot of noise at the front door. I tell Gabe to stay put while I peek. I can't make out exactly what's going on, so I squint my eyes against the dark. There's a very tall Indian man standing in the living room, holding Lyle like a baby. Mom is leading him toward their bedroom. She looks terrible and Lyle looks dead. He's gray and small and the man holding him seems like a giant. They take Lyle into Mom's room and when they come back upstairs she says something to the tall man. The man pats her on the back and she cries a little. When he leaves Mom sits down very suddenly and puts her head in her hands. I think I should go out to her, but I don't.

I stare out the window at the tall man. I am embarrassed because I know it is Mike. I am embarrassed but then I don't care. I know Mike is amazing in all sorts of ways. I know he is powerful. I am happy he saved Lyle from the horrible tavern, the whiskey, and the going around in circles.

The next day Lyle is gone. Mom says he went back home for the funeral.

I used to think I'd be really happy when Lyle left, but I'm not. Mom isn't any fun and Gabe is quiet. He doesn't realize Lyle is coming back. Gabe is afraid his dad is walking in circles somewhere and can't find the door. I tell him his dad will come back because it's not right to joke about something so important with a little boy who's missing his father.

For Gabe's sake, I decide to talk to Mom about what's happening. After Gabe goes to bed, I sit up with Mom while she listens to Fleetwood Mac on the record player. She's drinking wine and has quilt squares laid out all over the floor. I recognize some of the squares as having once been parts of my old clothes.

"That's my old shirt," I say, pointing to a blue square.

She kind of wakes up a little and smiles.

"That's part of your old sweatshirt," she says, pointing to another square.

"I wondered what happened to it," I say.

"Don't tell Gabe, but that green one is from his old banky," she says.

"He likes his yellow banky better," I say.

Mom kneels on the floor and starts arranging the squares. She tells me it is going to be a beautiful rainbow quilt with parts of all of us in it. I tell her that's a fine idea. She looks me straight in the eye.

"How are you?" she asks.

I don't know what to say.

"I'm okay," I say.

"How's Dawn?" she asks.

"She's okay," I say.

"You know, I ran into her mom at the grocery store the other day," she says.

I don't say anything. I don't really know how to have a conversation with my mother. It makes me kind of uncomfortable. I'm worried Nancy has told her things about Tarot and watery wine and dreams and past lives.

"She's a very sweet woman," says Mom.

I figure Nancy must have kept her mouth shut. I feel better.

Mom says, "You and Dawn are such pretty girls. I'm glad you found a friend like that. You love her a lot, don't you?"

"Yes," I say.

"Good. I didn't like that Shayla girl you used to hang out with," says Mom. "She seemed a little destructive. You know what I mean?"

I just stare at Mom and she looks back at the quilt squares. I didn't know she even paid attention. I didn't know she ever saw me.

I say, "What did Lyle's dad do that was so terrible?"

Mom pours more wine and leans against the couch. She looks around a little and smiles. She looks at me.

"It's not what he did. It's more like who he was," she says. "He was a very abusive man. He drank a lot. Lyle and his mom and sister put up with a lot of hurt."

"Oh," I say.

"Sometimes," she says, "people that hurt you have a hold on you for a long time. Sometimes you don't realize how strong that hold is until they are gone forever."

"Is Lyle going to be okay?" I ask.

"I hope so," she says.

She stares at the scraps of fabric on the floor.

"You know, it's hard to imagine this is going to be the most beautiful quilt in the world," she laughs.

"It's not that hard," I say.

When Lyle comes home, he looks quiet. It's hard to explain someone who looks quiet. I mean, Lyle is quiet and he looks quiet. He looks calm. He doesn't walk in circles or get loud when he talks. He just kind of moves around the house slowly. He looks at things and asks about them. He asks if the lamp is new. Mom tells him the shade is new, but the lamp is the same. He says things seem brighter. He drinks a lot of iced tea.

He makes sun tea on the porch and asks us all to tell him what we think of it. There's a lot less beer around and there's no whiskey at all.

Lyle makes dinner one night and we have to eat it even though it's some kind of fish casserole with potato chips on top. I suppose it's good if you like fish casserole, but I never ate a fish all mushed up in stuff. Gabe looks at me and I look at him and nod. He eats as much as he can and makes sad faces at me in between bites. Lyle must have seen us staring at each other and he asks what's wrong. I don't say anything because I don't want to make him mad. Gabe takes his spoon out of his mouth.

"Daddy, is the head in there?" he asks.

Lyle actually laughs and takes the casserole away. There's noise in the kitchen and he comes out with two bowls of ice cream. He gives us our ice cream and tells us we're good sports.

After a while, we all get used to Lyle being in the house. He got in the way more when he wasn't there. I don't really know what to make of it all. Mom just smiles and works on her quilt.

≈ Gabe Was Sick Once/Dreams of Kittens

Brandon's dead.

This is what I tell Mom.

Brandon's dead and he was never nice, but then he was sick and then he got nice and he swelled up and now he's dead. I don't tell Mom that part though.

She says, "I feel sorry for that boy's parents. Leukemia is a sin. Sickness in children is a sin and it makes me feel like God isn't listening."

People are saying Brandon was an angel and God called him home because God thought big, mean old Brandon was such a prize. I think God has more sense than that. I think God knew Brandon was a rich bully and struck him down in the prime of his nastiness and swelled him up and now he's dead and gone and won't bother anyone anymore ever. I don't tell Mom that part either.

Gabe and Zack are running in the backyard with kittens stuffed in their shirt fronts. I think soon there will be the boiling of the poisons and the hanging of the quilts and general swearing. I look up at Mom and she's just staring at the boys.

She says, "Your brother was very sick when he was born. He was in the hospital for a long time. He could very easily have died in that hospital and you would have never known him."

I think about not knowing Gabe. There's not a lot to know really. He's fat and smells weird and carries cats around and thinks he's invisible when he closes his eyes. Gabe's afraid to wipe his own ass when he poops. He sits on the toilet and yells, "Mom! Mom!" until she comes running to help.

The other day he was squatting over the toilet and screaming for Mom, but she had gone to the store.

I was in the living room and I yelled, "She's not here."

There was a pause.

"Dad?" he yelled.

"Your dad's gone too," I said.

There was a long pause.

"Dottie? Will you wipe my butt?"

"Hell no!"

"Dottie, wipe my butt. Wipe my butt!"

"Go to hell, Gabe!"

I peeked in after a while and Gabe was still perched there, arms shaking, trying to keep from falling into the toilet completely. He was nearing collapse. He climbed down from the toilet, wrapped half a roll of toilet paper around his hand and forearm, and began to dab his ass. After becoming completely disgusted, he threw the wad into the toilet and flushed. The toilet overflowed and Mom came home. There was yelling, Gabe was traumatized, and I was blamed.

I think about not knowing Gabe. Not knowing that he rocks himself to sleep so the bed creaks until he's out cold. I think of not knowing how he loves slices of cucumber and how he won't eat meat on a bone and how he follows me around trying to dribble my basketball. I think about not knowing how when Gabe was really little, if you hugged him and patted his back, he would hug you and pat your back.

I fall asleep for a few hours that night and I dream about Gabe. In my dream he's in the backyard, but it's really bright and glossy. He's laughing really hard and rolling around. He's covered in kittens and he's just so happy to be playing with them.

The kittens are clean though, not like the ones next door.

When I wake up from the dream it's morning and I still can't really care about Brandon.

≈ It Just Happens Sometimes

We're going on a vision quest. Nancy told us girls were supposed to go on quests after they got their periods. Nancy talked to my mom and Mom agreed Dawn and I could skip school on Friday and go on a quest. Nancy convinced Mom it was necessary for our spiritual growth.

Dawn says, "That sounds like a crock of shit. They just want us out of the house."

I tell Dawn it really isn't a crock. I tell her I've talked to the girls on the team. Some of them have done it. Dawn tells me it sounds cool and all but asks where in the hell are we supposed to go? I tell Dawn we have to go to a mountaintop. Dawn just stares at me and shakes her head.

The closest thing to a mountaintop is the sand hill and we decide on that. Nancy packs us food for our quest. I tell Nancy we're supposed to go without food. I tell her we just need water and sleeping bags. Nancy says we don't have to eat the food if we don't want to. She says she knows how important a vision quest is, but she'd feel better knowing we had something to eat just in case.

Dawn says, "Just don't make anything with mayonnaise. We don't know how long this will take and if the stuff goes bad and we eat it, we'll die."

Dawn isn't as excited about our vision quest as I am. Dawn's idea of a vision quest is going to Las Vegas.

"Can you imagine, Utah?" she asks. "Can you imagine what it must be like with all the lights and champagne and money and glamour?"

"No," I say.

"Vegas, Utah," she says. "One day we have to go to Vegas."

I tell her this weekend we're going to the top of the sand hill and our spirit guardians will be revealed to us. I tell her Vegas will have to wait.

"As far as I'm concerned," says Dawn, "it's up to my spirit guardian to show itself to me. I don't see why I have to go freeze my ass off on a sand hill."

I say, "It'll be fun."

She says, "Fine."

Nancy loads us up and gives us a ride to the hill. We climb slowly because we each have a backpack, a sleeping bag, and a cooler with us. It takes an hour to get to the top. When we finally do, we're covered in sand and sweat and our noses are running. Dawn collapses and readjusts her ponytail. I collapse next to her.

"Utah?" she asks.

"Yah?"

"I'm sorry," she says. "I'm ready for a vision quest."

"Okay," I say.

"My dad called this morning," she says.

I sit up and put my arm around her. I don't ask her what her dad had to say. I don't ask her anything about her dad. I know there's no point. She knows we're okay not talking. We stare out at the town together.

"We need peyote," she says.

"What's that?" I ask.

She tells me peyote is very important when you want to have visions. She smiles and starts digging in her backpack. She pulls out a tape recorder, sets it against a rock, and hits the play button. Music fills the air.

"The Doors, Utah," she says. "The Doors."

I know about Jim Morrison and I know about the Doors. Lyle loves them and so do I. Whenever we drive around in the van, Lyle likes to put his Doors tape in. Jim Morrison is the most beautiful man besides Mr. Dawson. I begin to think our vision quest will work out after all. I decide to show Dawn my big surprise.

I unroll my sleeping bag and Dawn watches. I pull out a bottle of Wild Turkey. Dawn smiles. I pull out two big bottles of Pepsi and Dawn smiles some more. I open my backpack and Dawn watches. I pull out a bottle of Pinot Grigio and smile because I think it must be a very fancy wine if I can't pronounce it.

Dawn says, "Utah, I am impressed."

I got the whiskey from our neighbors. I had to go next door and get Gabe for dinner. He and Zack were playing in the yard. I waited for Gabe to get his jacket from Zack's house and, while I waited, I wandered into their garage. Inside the garage were three liquor boxes. One of the boxes was open and the whiskey was just sitting there. I didn't think too long about it, I just grabbed the bottle and shoved it inside my coat. I got Gabe and ran while he toddled behind me screaming, "Wait, Dottie! Wait!" I feel bad about the wine because I actually lifted it from Nancy. She has a huge wine rack in her basement and I just took it. I figured Dawn would get blamed anyway and I was mad at her at the time.

"I stole the wine from your mom," I say.

Dawn says, "That's okay, Utah. I don't care. I'm just mad I didn't think of it myself."

We lay out the tarp and put our sleeping bags on top of it. We put the coolers on the edges of the tarp to keep it down. Dawn pulls out the candles Nancy has given us and sticks them in the sand all around the tarp. We light the candles and they smell funny because they're the kind that are supposed to keep bugs away. Dawn pulls out two huge plastic tumblers and fills them with ice from the cooler. I open the whiskey and pour. Dawn laughs and adds the Pepsi. We toast right there on top of the sand hill.

"What should we toast to?" I ask.

"Jim Morrison!" says Dawn.

We toast to Jim Morrison of the world-famous Doors and I think about the vision quest. I toast secretly inside my head to a beautiful guardian who can see me even when I feel all lost.

Whiskey isn't like beer. Maybe a little bit of it is okay, but we don't do that. At one point Dawn says, "Oh my God oh my God oh my God, everything is spinning." She's right. We can feel the earth itself spinning and it's going the exact opposite way of the stars. There's sand everywhere and all we want is a toilet.

We stumble around the top of the hill, laughing. Dawn trips over something.

"I tripped," she says.

I stumble over to her and start laughing so hard I may just die.

"What?" she asks.

All I can get out is, "The head!"

Dawn tripped over Lyle's deer head. We're laughing so much we're forced to crawl back to the tarp. We drag the head with us. We set the head next to our camp and scream at the tops of our lungs.

Saturday is pretty bad. Dawn spent most of the night throwing up and I had to hold her hair back. I threw up too, but not as bad as Dawn. It's weird throwing up all over the top of a sand hill. Dawn said she felt like a cat. All she had to do was kick sand over the puke and move on. We spend most of Saturday feeling sick and staying in our sleeping bags. Around two in the afternoon, Dawn has an idea.

"I have an idea," says Dawn.

She smiles and drapes her arm around the head.

"What?"

"What is it you want right now?" she asks.

"I want to die," I say.

"Besides that," she says.

216

Dawn digs around inside her backpack. She pulls out four beers and smiles. She sticks them deep inside one of the coolers and lies back down.

"You had those all along," I say.

"Well," she says, "I knew you felt all proud of what you did, so I decided to wait. I have eight more in the bottom of my sleeping bag."

"Where did you get them?" I ask.

Dawn laughs and looks down.

"I stole them from Lyle," she says.

We laugh and laugh and drink beer until the sun starts to set.

"Have you had a vision yet?" asks Dawn.

"No," I say.

Saturday night we just drink beer and eat the peanuts Nancy has packed. We talk and talk and laugh and make a lot of noise that no one can hear. We stare out into the lights of the town and make fun of everything that bothers us. We decide beer is good, whiskey is dangerous, and wine is stupid. Dawn says even though wine is stupid, we should probably drink the bottle before we go down the hill on Sunday. Dawn says Pinot Grigio is a breakfast wine.

That night I dream I'm running after Dawn because I want to tell her something very important. I run and run after her, but she won't turn around. The next part of the dream is that I'm in a cave in the woods and I'm holding a puppy. Dawn sticks her head inside the cave and yells at me to hurry up and leave. I start to cry because I don't know what to do. If I leave the puppy, it will die.

In the morning, when we open the wine, Dawn asks me if I've had any visions. I tell her about my dream. She looks at me funny and says she had a dream where she was running through the woods. She said in the dream she was really angry. She tells me she kept looking for me because she wanted to save me from something, but she couldn't find me anywhere. We sit in silence and drink our wine.

We pack up and move on down the hill. When Nancy picks us up we are very tired. We are also very hung over.

"Dorothy," says Nancy, "your mom called."

I start thinking Gabe is dead or Dad is dead or someone is very dead and it's my fault because I went on a vision quest.

"Your mom said we could all talk about this," says Nancy.

Dawn and I drop all our stuff and sit on the couch. I look at Dawn and she shrugs. We stare at Nancy. Nancy looks at us and sighs.

"Your friend Shayla is pregnant," says Nancy. "Her mom called your mom, Dorothy, because she knew you two were close. She wanted you to know why Shayla wouldn't be in school anymore."

Dawn starts asking Nancy questions about where Shayla is going, but I can't say anything. I can't tell anyone what I'm thinking because I don't even understand it myself.

All I can remember, all I can think of, is this one time Shayla and I were together. We had beer and cigarettes and a thick wool blanket. We lay out in her backyard and watched the stars get bright.

She told me about where she was going to go and what she was going to do. She told me she was going to Hollywood and that she was going to be a movie star. She kissed me and held me close and swore she'd always write.

Dawn looks at me and takes my hand.

"It happens, Utah," she says. "It just happens sometimes."

14 Years Old

Dorothy Coyote

≈ I'm Not Going Anywhere

"Dorothy, you're not going anywhere!" yells Mom.

"I am," I scream. "I am going somewhere. I'm staying with Dawn this weekend and you can't stop me!"

Missy is coming to visit and I don't want to be there. She's not my real sister and she hates me and she won't care whether I'm there or not. She's old and eighteen and I haven't seen her in a long time, so what's the big deal?

"What's the big deal?" I scream. "She hates me anyway!"

"She loves you, Dorothy," says Mom.

"Bullshit!" I scream.

Mom comes at me and I run outside. I run all the way to the basketball court. I lie on the grass and stare up at the sky.

Cecilia is going to have a baby. I am going to have a new brother or sister.

Dad called the other day and told me. He was very excited and all full of himself. I was quiet while he talked because I didn't have anything good to say. What I wanted to say was very bad and mean and hateful.

Everything is half of what it should be. I have a stepsister and a half-brother and a stepmom and a stepdad. There are people related to me just because someone got married or divorced or pregnant. I don't like any of them except Gabe. I have to be nice to people I don't like and pleasant to people I don't know and give up my room to relatives I've never seen before and get shipped around every summer because stupid people decided to get divorced.

I hate everyone and I especially hate their babies.

By the time I get back home, Missy's already there. Mom doesn't swat me or yell, she just stares at me.

Gabe crawls all over Missy because he loves her very much. They spend their summers together and he has gotten very attached. She tosses him around and he giggles and I decide I don't like Gabe either. If he's that easily won over, then I must not be very important to him.

After dinner Gabe wants to go to the park. Missy says she'll meet Mom and Gabe there after she unpacks. I don't know what to do because I don't want to go to the park with my horrible mother and traitor Gabe, but I don't want to stay with Missy either.

"This will give you and Dorothy a chance to catch up," says Mom.

Mom must hate me.

After they leave Missy starts unpacking. I sit on my bed and watch her.

"How's school?" she asks.

"Fine," I say.

"Do you have a boyfriend?" She smiles.

"Gross, no," I say.

"I was thinking of going to the mall tonight," she says. "Do you want to come with me?"

"The mall's two hours away," I say.

"It'll be fun," she says.

"I don't like the mall," I say.

"Oh," she says. "I thought maybe you didn't like me."

I don't say anything because I like making her feel bad. It feels good to have everyone hate you. It feels good to be mean and horrible and have no one like you.

"You know," she says, "I am sorry I was so mean to you when I was younger."

Missy looks at me.

"I was jealous of you," she says.

"Jealous?" I ask.

"You got to be around Dad all the time and I didn't," she says.

I never thought of that. I never thought anyone would want to be around Lyle.

"My dad's going to have another kid," I say.

"So," she asks, "maybe you know how I feel?"

"It sucks," I say.

"I know it does, Dorothy," she says. "Don't think I don't know."

I feel so bad that I start to cry.

"I'm sorry," I say.

"I'm sorry too," she says.

Missy hugs me.

When we get to the park, Gabe runs up to me and hugs my leg.

"Dottie!" he yells.

Missy smiles.

⌐ Moses Lake and Chief Joseph

"You can't make me go!" I scream. "There's no way in hell I'm going!"

"Oh, you're going, Dorothy!" yells Mom. "It's not as bad as you're making it out to be."

"If you make me go," I say, "I'll run away and hide and go live with my dad."

Mom doesn't say anything. She just sits on my bed and stares at her hands.

"Please," she says, "just do it this once. Maybe Dawn can go with you?"

I know she threw Dawn in there to make it seem like it could be fun, but there's no way I want to go stupid camping on Moses Lake with stupid Lyle and Gabe. I hate camping and I hate Moses Lake. I actually love camping and Moses Lake, I just don't want to have to spend an entire weekend with Lyle. Mom says she needs a weekend to herself and that it would be fun for us.

"I'm not going," I say. "I will run away."

On the ride to the lake, Dawn and I sit in the back of the van. We drink Diet Pepsi and argue about who'll get to sit in the front of the canoe. Dawn wants to sit in the front, but I tell her it really doesn't matter much in a canoe. By sitting in the front, you only get to wherever you're going a second before the person in the back. She doesn't care. She wants the front anyway. I tell her she can have the stupid front. We're only arguing because she didn't want to go with me, but she had to. I begged her and begged her, but she wouldn't go. She said Lyle was an asshole and I should run away and live with her. I was so desperate, I did what no person should do and I ratted her out to her mother. I told Nancy Dawn wouldn't go and I needed her and my heart was breaking. Nancy told Dawn she had to go with me because that's what friends do. Now we're fighting.

"Fine," I say, "take the front. I don't care. I like the back better anyway."

She says, "Maybe I'll take the back. I haven't exactly decided yet."

"Fine," I say.

"Fine," she says.

Gabe climbs into the back of the van with us. He looks green.

"I don't feel good," he says.

"Lyle," I say, "I think Gabe's getting carsick."

"Are you carsick?" he asks.

It's too late because Gabe throws up all over the carpet in the van and then he starts crying. Dawn and I start laughing so hard we feel like we're going to puke. We try to get away from the throw-up, but Gabe keeps moving closer because he doesn't feel good and he wants a hug.

"Stop laughing," he says. "Stop laughing at me, Dottie."

I tell him I'm sorry and I put him on my lap. Lyle pulls into a gas station and we get Gabe cleaned up. When we get back into the van, Gabe falls asleep. Lyle sings along to Elton John.

"Do you girls like Elton?" he asks.

Dawn and I look at each other. Dawn smiles and my stomach drops.

"No," she says. "We like Prince and Mötley Crüe and really cool music."

The truth is, we do like Elton John, but she doesn't want to tell him that. We also hate Mötley Crüe.

"Did you girls bring a tape to listen to?" he asks.

Dawn stares at me. She is confused at the new Lyle. I shrug. "I was just kidding," she says.

We help Lyle set up camp. When we're done, he lets us go anywhere we want. We don't even have to be back at a certain time. He doesn't have any rules except "Don't get hurt." Dawn and I run all over Moses Lake looking for trouble or to get hurt, but we can't find any trouble anywhere. We go swimming in the clear water and try to get suntans. She tells me Lyle isn't half bad.

All weekend we swim while Lyle and Gabe fish. Lyle cooks the fish right over the fire and it's the best thing I've ever eaten. He also lets us drink as much Pepsi as we want and eat potato chips for breakfast. He just tells us not to complain if we have a stomachache.

I'm talking to Dawn in the tent quietly because Gabe's already asleep. I can tell Dawn is tired, but I'm still wide awake. I'm not used to going to bed before midnight anyway. I keep talking to Dawn, but I can tell that she's sound asleep. I get out of the tent and Lyle's just sitting beside the fire and staring at the lake.

"Not tired yet?" he asks.

"No," I say. "I usually stay up late."

"Go for walks," he says.

I don't know what to say.

"I won't tell your mom," he says. "Sometimes you just need a long walk."

We stare at the lake. The side of me pointed toward the fire is very warm. The rest of me is cold, but it evens out somehow.

"You know about Chief Joseph?" he asks.

"Yes," I say.

"What do you know?" he asks.

"He's a hero who tried to save his people when the white soldiers were killing all the Indians," I say.

"Do you know what he said when they finally caught him?" he asks.

I shake my head no.

"He said, 'I am tired, my heart is sick and sad. From where the sun now stands, I will fight no more forever.'"

Lyle looks at me. He smiles.

"What do you think he meant by that?" he asks.

"I think he meant exactly what he said," I say.

"I think you're right."

"What do you think he meant?" I ask.

Lyle smiles at me.

"I think he meant he was sorry for all the pain. I think he meant he was sorry for all the hurt," says Lyle.

There are a million stars out and you can almost hear the beavers gnawing on things.

I know Lyle isn't talking about Chief Joseph anymore.

I know Lyle is sorry for being awful. I know what he means, but it will take a while before I can really trust him.

I think about earlier in the day, when Gabe didn't want to put a worm on his hook. He said it would hurt the worm. Lyle told him worms don't feel the way people do and if you break a worm in half you have two living worms. Lyle said the only way to kill a worm is to have a fish eat it. Gabe said he didn't want to kill worms. Lyle asked him how he was going to catch a fish without a worm. Gabe said he didn't want to kill a fish either. Lyle just laughed and let him hold a fishing pole in the water without a hook or a worm and with no hope of catching a fish.

"There's a monument in Nespelem for Chief Joseph. Would you like to go sometime?" asks Lyle.

The sky opens up and all the stars fall into my eyes. The cold disappears somewhere. I am warm and hopeful.

"Okay," I say. "I'll go with you."

≈ *Lyle, Darrell, Mike, and Bob*

"I think they met drinking, Dorothy," says Mom, "so stop bothering me."

"But when, Mom? When did they meet?" I ask.

"They just met," she says. "People meet each other when they're drinking."

I don't know how to feel. Lyle knows Darrell and Lyle knows Mike and now Gabe is going to know them all too. I don't like it when you know people first and then other people meet them and you never knew that they met and all of a sudden they all know each other.

They're all going fishing and I don't like it one bit.

I don't like it when you know people one way and tell them things and then they get together and say things to each other when they're fishing.

Gabe runs through the house singing "Beat It" and dragging a fishing pole. He stops and stares at me, so I stare back at him.

"I am Bob," he says.

"I know, Gabe," I say.

"Bob, Dottie," he says.

"I know, Bob," I say.

Mom is upset that Gabe hates his name. For weeks now he's been carrying on that he wants to be Bob. Bob's teacher called and said Bob was driving her to distraction. She said Gabe's signing his name "Bob" and it's making her crazy because there's already a boy named Bob in the class.

"I am Bob. I am Bob. I am Bob!" yells Gabe.

"If you were Bob," I say, "you wouldn't have to yell about it all the time."

"I am Bob," whispers Gabe.

I pace around in my room because I'm worried about the fishing trip. I just don't know what to think. I'm not even really sure what it is I'm worried about. It's just that I like to have everyone separate. It's easier. Dawn says I'm overreacting and I should be happy that everybody gets along. She says it would suck if they all hated each other. She says it'll be great to have all the men away so we don't have to deal with them for a weekend.

I sit on the couch and wait. I watch Lyle dragging his tackle box around. He drags a cooler around. He drags sleeping bags around. He piles stuff on the lawn and then loads some of it into his van.

"How did you meet Mike?" I ask.

"Met him drinking beer one Saturday," he says.

"When your dad died?" I ask.

"I knew him before that," says Lyle.

"What kind of beer?" I ask.

"What?" he asks.

"What kind of beer were you drinking?" I ask.

"Coors, I think," he says.

"Oh," I say.

"Would you tell Bob to get his butt out here?" asks Lyle.

I like that Lyle calls Gabe "Bob." I think it's a good sign. Mom hates it because she doesn't want to encourage Bob. She says Gabriel is a beautiful name and one day he will learn to appreciate it. Gabe just smiles and says Bob is better.

"Dottie has two names," said Gabe.

"She has one name and a nickname her friends gave her," said Mom.

"My friend called me Bob," said Gabe.

"Which friend called you that?" asked Mom.

Gabe starts crying and says he can't remember and that it just happened. He cries, hides his face behind his hands, and screams, "Don't look at me!"

A pickup truck pulls into the front yard and Mike and Darrell get out. Bob hides behind Lyle and stares at Mike. I want to run and hide in my room, but I watch from the living room window instead. Darrell and Lyle talk and stare at all the stuff on the lawn while Bob just stands there. Mike kneels down and smiles at Bob.

"Hey, old man," he says.

Gabe says, "I am Bob."

"Hey, old man Bob," says Mike.

Mike laughs and laughs. He picks Gabe up and puts him on his shoulders. Gabe's eyes get bigger and bigger.

"I am Bob!" he yells.

Mike laughs and laughs and spins Bob all around. I walk outside because I just can't help it. I want Mike to say something to me. He is so tall and beautiful with his long black hair and his light blue shirt. The leather cords around his neck have feathers and beads hanging from them. His eyes are so dark.

"Hi," I say.

"Dorothy!" says Mike. "I had a dream you were flying around the moon! What are you doing here?"

"You know," I say, "not much."

Mike laughs at me. I try very hard to be cool and beautiful. Bob hangs on to Mike's leg and stares up at him.

Gabe says, "We're going fishing!"

Mike says, "That's right, old man."

I look at them. I look at Darrell and Lyle already drinking beer from the cooler. Lyle comes up to me and puts his arm around my shoulder. He smiles at me and winks.

"There's another six-pack in the garage," he says.

"Should I get it for you?" I ask.

"No," he says, "and I won't care if it's missing when I get back." He smiles.

I wave when they pull away and I end up thinking Dawn is right after all. This is a good thing.

≈ How Will I Find You?

When I get home from school, Gabe and Stacey are already hard at work building a fort in the living room. I step over couch cushions and blankets to get to the kitchen for a Pepsi. On the way to my room, I warn Gabe he'd better not knock one of Mom's lamps over or he and Stacey will be in big trouble. He tells me it doesn't matter what he does in the living room because we're moving to a new house anyway.

"We're not moving to a new house," I say.

"Yes, we are, Dottie," he says.

"No, we aren't," I say.

Stacey sticks her freckled face out of a pile of blankets and pillows and squints her eyes at me.

She says, "You're moving to Pencil . . ." she thinks for a minute.

"Far away somewhere," says Gabe from under cushions.

My feet aren't moving. I know Mom is downstairs and I should go and ask her what's going on so we can laugh about how it's a mistake. I want to go and laugh about the mistake, but I can't move from where I'm standing. I feel sick to my stomach and I can barely breathe. This is how it happens every time. It happens all of a sudden when you least expect it. It happens when you get comfortable and safe. I feel voices buzzing in my head.

Gabe and Stacey knock over a lamp.

Mom comes upstairs, yelling at them to be careful. She sees me. I look at her. Lyle comes in from outside and we all stare at each other.

"We're not, right?" I ask.

"I'm sorry, Dorothy," says Mom. "I wanted to tell you myself."

Lyle runs his hand through his hair, making it stick up. He shifts his weight onto his left foot. He puts his arm around Mom.

He says, "There's not much difference between Washington and Pennsylvania. In Washington it's a tavern," he smiles, "in Pennsylvania it's a pub!"

Mom looks at him and shakes her head.

"I'm sorry, Dorothy," says Lyle. "I am so sorry."

Stacey yells, "Pennsylvania!" from under blankets.

Gabe emerges from the fort and jumps up and down, yelling, "We're moving! We're moving!"

I start crying and Mom comes over to me. I back away.

I say, "I can't!"

"It'll be okay," she says. "Don't be dramatic, Dorothy."

Stacey turns to Gabe and says, "But how will I find you when we want to get married?"

Gabe turns to Mom and asks, "How will she, Mom? How will she find me?"

I stare at Lyle and Lyle stares at me. My legs are shaking so bad I can barely stand. I want to die.

"I'm so sorry, Dorothy," he says. "I am. I really am."

Mom starts crying.

I run out of the house.

≈ *Divorce*

I didn't really know it would come to this. Mom and Nancy are sitting at our kitchen table drinking wine and talking. Dawn and I are sitting on the couch just staring at them. Once in a while Dawn looks at me. I can see her look out of the corner of my eye. I can't look at her or I'll start crying.

I even had to talk to my dad this week and it was terrible.

He asked, "Dorothy, are you certain staying with your friend is what you want to do?"

"Yes," I said.

"Won't you miss your mom? Don't you want to be with her?" he asked.

"No," I said.

"If you stay where you are, it'll be hard for you to see your mom a lot," he said.

"I know," I said.

I was starting to cry on the phone, but then I got really mad at Dad.

I said, "I hardly ever see you and it doesn't bother me."

He didn't have anything to say about that. He said Cecilia wanted to talk to me. I told him I didn't want to talk to Cecilia. He put her on the phone anyway, so I hung up. I just didn't care.

What happened was I told Nancy I wanted to stay with her. First I had talked to Dawn and she said it was a really good idea. She said it was so horrible and mean of them to take me away from the people who really cared about me. She said everybody thought it was mean. By everybody, I knew she meant her. I cried a lot and Dawn and Nancy tried to make me laugh. It really didn't work. Nancy said she promised to talk to Mom if that was what I really wanted. I told her it was. Dawn piped in and said, "Mom, this is really important. After all, we're about to start ninth grade. Everything changes in ninth grade." I nodded. Everybody knew ninth grade was crucial.

When Nancy and Dawn came over, I was really nervous. Mom had a horrible look on her face and Nancy told us to go outside and walk somewhere. We walked to the backyard and listened in through an open window. At first Mom was really mad at Nancy. She said it was none of her business and there was no way in hell she was signing me over to a stranger. After half a bottle of wine Mom started crying and said she knew it was hard on me, but she didn't realize how hard. She kept saying, "I've tried to make it good for her, but things have been tough for so long." She said, "Lyle's finally getting a promotion. I won't have to work as much. Things are getting better."

Nancy calmed Mom down and asked her if she had said any of these things to me. Mom must have shaken her head or something because Dawn and I didn't hear anything for a while. They talked and talked for a long time. Finally Nancy said, "I respect whatever you choose to do here. I really do. Let's just remember that no decision has to be forever. If Dorothy stays with me, she can go back to you any time she wants." I guess Mom nodded or something. We waited until it got real quiet before we went back in and sat on the couch.

Mom and Nancy look over at me. Nancy smiles and Mom blows her nose. Mom tells me to come over to her. Nancy gets Dawn and the two of them walk outside. I sit next to Mom and start sweating. I am nervous and sad and sick to my stomach. Mom sighs.

She says, "I want you to come with us."

I start crying.

"I don't care. I don't want to go," I say.

"I know, Dorothy," she says. "I'm not going to make you, okay?"

Mom says this and then she starts crying. We both sit there crying.

"We have a few months to figure what we need to do," she says. "I just want you to know that if you ever need to see me or if you want to change your mind . . . "

Mom starts crying so much that she has to get up from the table and go to the bathroom. I just sit at the table alone and cry and cry. I can't believe she's not taking me. I wanted to stay, but now that I can I hate that she let me. I think she must not love me at all.

≈ It Hasn't Rained in a Long Time

It hasn't rained in a very long time, but it's raining now. You can smell the wet sagebrush and feel the dust being cleaned off the trees. Outside it's warm and cold at the same time. If you listen hard, you can hear the water rushing over the dam, miles away. You don't realize how quiet the hot is until it rains. When it rains, everything is alive again. Even the cement, which isn't going anywhere and can't feel anything, even it changes in the rain somehow.

I'm walking and walking in the rain with hurt worse than someone dying. I'm walking to Dawn's old house, which is empty and full of the smell of rain. I'm walking to the sand hill, which is settling with the water in it. The sand hill, which is so much mud right now, only still huge and hulking like someone's shoulders against a sky full of stars. I'm wondering how far I can walk. I'm wondering if I can walk all the way to Dawn's new house because I am homeless.

I have a crazy thought that I will walk on over to the Moose Lodge and order a whiskey. I will tell them I'm Mom's daughter. They will see I'm old and wise and they will give me a whiskey. They will welcome me and tell me I don't have to ever go anywhere. They will see I'm almost fifteen and full of ideas. They will tell me how horrible it all is and ask, "Have another whiskey on the house?" I will buy a pack of Vantage cigarettes and smoke them with my drink. I will tell them how I plan to be a jazz musician who only plays in very dark clubs. I will tell them how I rarely sing, but if I'm begged I'll wail out an old song, maybe Billie Holiday or Ella Fitzgerald. They will see that this is possible and very important. I am walking and convince myself this can happen. I start the long climb up the hill leading out of the Coulee.

I think time will stop if I keep walking. If I walk long enough, maybe time will go backward. By walking I am reversing all things that have ever been said. When I get to the Moose Lodge I lose my courage and conviction. I am soaking wet and confused as to who I am. I want to be a grown woman with her own apartment and a car. I stare at the door of the Moose Lodge. I think about Dawn. I think about Seattle and the ocean. I think about how there's no way I can leave this place and survive. All I want right now is a beer and a cigarette and I don't really smoke or drink.

I sit in the alley across from the Moose Lodge. I watch the drunk men come in and out. I know some of them because they were Lyle's drinking buddies. It's very late and I'm very tired. It is impossible for me to think anymore. I can barely move.

When the door opens, there's a burst of light. A tall man walks out. I know him. I don't mean to, but I stand up and walk toward him. He smiles when he sees me and waves me over to him. He leads me to his pickup truck and we sit in the back. Mike stares at me and grins. I feel stupid being all wet and alone and outside a bar. I tell him we're moving again and it may kill me. I tell him I might die and it would be everybody's fault. I tell him about the sand hill, basketball, Gabe, and even Dawn. I tell him Lyle used to drink, but now he's nice. I tell him Mom knows who I am, but we never talk. I tell him about the walking and not sleeping. I tell him I am very tired.

He sighs and smiles and takes a flask from his coat. He sips from it and then offers it to me. I drink and it is sweet and wonderful. It's an umbrella against the rain and the damp. He laughs at my face and takes back the flask. He lights a cigarette and gives it to me. He asks me what my name is and his voice is like whatever I just drank. I tell him he already knows my name.

He says, "Not that name." He smiles. "The name *they* gave you."

I know he means the Colvilles, so I tell him.

"Utah," I say.

I am embarrassed because I think Mike must have a beautiful name. He smiles.

"It's a good name," he says. "They gave it to you for being brave?"

I nod, yes.

"Then it's a good name," he says.

Mike makes me think of Pop, but I'm not sad about it. He reminds me of Pop with a smile just as bright. He knows things without me having to explain them.

"I will tell you a story," he says. "I will tell you one of Coyote's stories. It is how the Great Spirit makes tests for everyone.

"One day a Monster came to a village and swallowed all of Coyote's friends. Coyote was so busy making the world, he didn't know his people were gone. The world he was making had to tell him. The tall yellow grass told him. The wind whispered it to him.

"Coyote said that if his people were gone, he might as well stop making the world for them. He lived and lived and talked to the trees and the birds and the water. He lived and lived and was lonely. He decided to find the Monster and be swallowed so that he could be with his people and be lonely no longer.

"He found the Monster, and the devil was huge. He stared at the Monster. He said, 'Hey yah, Monster. Now swallow me, my friend.' The Monster was full with Coyote's people and didn't want him. Coyote thought and thought. He asked the Monster if he would play a game. The Monster was full and sleepy but interested in the game Coyote spoke of. He said, 'Yes, I will play a game with you, Trickster.'

"Coyote said, 'If I can swallow you, I will give you the world! Mr. Monster, if you can swallow me, you will have eaten the world!' Monster laughed and laughed. He did not see how he could lose this game. He said, 'Come, Coyote, swallow me!' And Coyote took a deep breath and stood his ground. His jaws opened and he tried to suck the Monster in. He failed. The Monster laughed and laughed and in a huge breath, breathed Coyote in.

"Coyote rattled around inside his fear and searched for his people. He found them hiding against the Monster's heart. He said, 'Now, my people, let us build a fire against the heart of this devil and free ourselves.' They built that fire and burned the Monster from within and were free to make the world."

Mike tells me his story and I feel the steel of his pickup against my spine. I feel all the questions I had raise themselves again, only now there are more. I feel my heart on fire. I tell him I am not Coyote. He laughs and says we are all Coyote or nothing. I start to cry because I feel like I am the nothing.

He says, "No, Utah. You are Coyote and everything."

I fall asleep in his truck while he takes me home. I feel him knocking on my door and I hear Mom crying. I feel him carrying me to my bed and I hear Mom say she loves me. I feel my heart well up so strong I can taste the future, but I don't know what it will be.

≈ What Gabe Says

"Dottie, a long long time ago you ripped gum off the back of my neck, but it was okay and I didn't get mad. Once you locked me in my room, but that was okay too. One time you took me to the movies. Remember when you let me play in your room? Remember when it was that bad movie and I couldn't sleep and you stayed up with me? Remember when you went on a walk really really late and you said that it was okay for me to sleep because you were outside making sure nothing bad happened?

"One time you lied to Mom when it was my fault what happened. And Dad wasn't here, but that one time you said he was because I was scared. Then Zack hid your book, but you found it? Stacey took your shirt and then you gave it to her. Remember when Mom said that you and Dawn could stay here? I think Dawn can come with us. I think that would be better because what about my banky?

"I think you should go with me and Mom and Dad because I had a dream where you were riding a big dog and the dog was laughing. The dog told me in my head that you are supposed to go to Pennsylvania because we love you very much."

I say, "I will go with you, Gabriel. I will."

≈ Light as a Feather

It's the biggest party I have ever been to and it's all for me.

Dawn and Nancy have invited everyone and everyone is there. There are lights all around the porch of Darrell's house. There are tiki torches and candles floating in water. Nancy is burning sage and sandalwood to help cleanse the air so I have a safe journey. She reads Tarot cards and Darrell makes sure that no one drinks so much beer that they get sick. They've put the stereo on the porch and we all take turns playing our favorite records. We sing along to Emmylou Harris and Stevie Nicks. Dawn plays Prince and she spins me around laughing and laughing.

Everybody has brought me something to remember them by. Jolina hands me a team jersey with everyone's signature on it. Willa gives me a pink and purple dreamcatcher she's made. Roz and John Garvey give me a football helmet they stole from the supply room. John had the entire team sign it. Nacho and Duncan even show up, and they give me a baseball hat with the school name on it. Nacho gets me alone and hands me a couple of brand-new *Mad* magazines. He says, "Here, I just found these."

After a while I go into Dawn's room and some of the girls are giggling on the bed. They say we should play Light as a Feather. I don't know what that is and neither does Dawn.

They tell me to lie flat on the carpet, so I do. Jolina tells the five girls to kneel around me. They place the tips of their fingers just under my shoulders, hips, and ankles. Jolina kneels at my head and starts talking.

She says, "You're light as a feather. You're floating. You are weightless and your bones are hollow like a bird. You are full of light and air and can float. You're light as a feather and stiff as a board."

She says these kinds of things for a long time and makes me keep my eyes shut. I hear one of the girls take a deep breath and say, "Oh, my God." I open my eyes and I am three feet off the floor. Jolina says, "I never saw it work before." Suddenly I am on the floor and my elbows hurt from the drop. They all stare at me.

Dawn smiles. We all file out of the bedroom and go back to the party. I grab a beer and stare out at the night. I start walking toward the pond Darrell has on his land. I see a beautiful horse in the dark. It's nibbling the greenest grass that grows on the edge of the pond. I hear Mike laugh. I sit next to him.

"I like the lights you put up," I say.

Nancy told me Mike brought the lights and strung them just so.

"I'm glad you like them," he says.

"Why didn't you come up to the house?" I ask.

"I knew that you would come here," he says.

I stare at Mike and I love him very much. I love how he's so much like Pop and so much like no one ever was.

"I'm going to miss you," I say.

"Hey yah, Utah. Don't you be sad. We've known each other for a long time. We'll still know each other for a long time," he says.

"What's your name?" I ask.

Mike laughs and laughs until his sides ache and he has to lie flat down in the grass.

"My mother used to call me Mikasi from the dreams she had." He smiles. "Do you know what that name means?"

"No," I say.

He stands up and smiles at me in the dark. I can see the flash of his teeth. I don't know what to do, so I put out my hand. He grabs me and hugs me tight. He kisses me on the top of my head. When he lets me go, I stare up at him.

"Mikasi," he says, "means Coyote."

"Coyote," I say.

Mike laughs while he climbs onto his horse.

"Utah," he says. "Dorothy Coyote."

I watch him ride away. I feel something tugging at my heart, but it's okay. I know I will see him again, somewhere.

I hear someone coming down to the pond and when I look it's Dawn. She has two beers with her and we sit on the dry grass.

"What will I do without you here?" she asks.

"I'll come back," I say. "I swear I will. I can always come back."

She turns to me and the moon is in her eyes. She smiles. She smiles so much that she laughs and laughs with the pain in it.

She kisses me.

Acknowledgments

My heartfelt gratitude to Lois Wallace for her persistence, humor, and counsel. Thanks also to Sarah Knight and Cressida Connolly for their dedication and hard work.

Many thanks to the wonderful people at Counterpoint Press, especially Dawn Seferian and Trish Hoard, whose wit and charm were invaluable.

To my friends and family who believed in me, read, reread, and never lost faith.

Finally, to Daniel Gorczyca, whose love and support never faltered.